THE MISCHIEF THIEF

ROSE & THORNE #1

JOHNNIE ALEXANDER

MISTY WILLOW BOOKS

The Mischief Thief ~ Rose & Thorne Series #1

Copyright © 2020 by Johnnie Alexander

ISBN: 978-1-7347223-0-7 <> ASIN: B084TRYFTQ

All rights reserved.

No part of this book may be reproduced in any form or by any electronic or mechanical means, including information storage and retrieval systems, without written permission from the author, except for the use of brief quotations in a book review.

Scripture from KJV (public domain) or Tree of Life (TLV) Translation of the Bible. Copyright © 2015 by The Messianic Jewish Family Bible Society.

Cover by Roseanna White Designs

This story is a work of fiction. Names, characters, businesses, places, events, locales, and incidents are either the products of the author's imagination or used in a fictitious manner. Any resemblance to actual persons, living or dead, or actual events is purely coincidental.

Johnnie Alexander is represented by Tamela Hancock Murray of The Steve Laube Agency.

WELCOME TO THE MOSAIC COLLECTION

We are sisters, a beautiful mosaic united by the love of God through the blood of Christ.

Each month The Mosaic Collection releases one faith-based novel exploring our theme, Family by His Design, and sharing stories that feature diverse, God-designed families. All are contemporary stories ranging from mystery and women's fiction to comedic and literary fiction. We hope you'll join our Mosaic family as we explore together what truly defines a family.

If you're like us, loneliness and suffering have touched your life in ways you never imagined, but Dear One, while you may feel alone in your suffering—whatever it is—you are never alone!

Subscribe to Grace & Glory, the official newsletter of The Mosaic Collection, to receive monthly encouragement from

Mosaic authors, as well as timely updates about events, new releases, and giveaways.

Learn more about The Mosaic Collection at MosaicCollectionBooks.com

Join our Facebook Reader Community, too!

BOOKS IN THE MOSAIC COLLECTION

When Mountains Sing by Stacy Monson

Unbound by Eleanor Bertin

The Red Journal by Deb Elkink

A Beautiful Mess by Brenda S. Anderson

Hope Is Born: A Mosaic Christmas Anthology

More Than Enough by Lorna Seilstad

The Road to Happenstance by Janice L. Dick

This Side of Yesterday by Angela D. Meyer

Lost Down Deep by Sara Davison

The Mischief Thief by Johnnie Alexander

COMING SOON

- Our Summer Anthology
- Novels by Eleanor Bertin and Regina Rudd Merrick

*For the Kindred Heart Writers,
my cherished friends.*

*Clella Camp
Karen Evans
Laura Groves
Jeanie Wise*

*God brought us together
And distance didn't keep us apart.*

You keep in perfect peace one whose mind is stayed on You, because he trusts in You.

— ISAIAH 26:3 TLV (TREE OF LIFE VERSION)

PART I

CHAPTER 1

uesday Afternoon
The shadow, in the squat outline of a broad-shouldered man with a slight paunch, slid across the wrought iron table where Chaney Rose read a thick, well-worn paperback.

"Fancy finding you here," the shadow said. "You don't mind if I join you, do you?"

Chaney minded very much. But before she could respond, the shadow shifted as Special Agent Benjamin Grant settled into the seat next to her. He leaned back, propped his ankle on his knee, and stared at her from behind tinted sunglasses that hid his eyes. He wore khakis and a sports jacket over a pale blue shirt sporting the Florida Department of Law Enforcement's logo above his heart.

Except he had no heart. Only a stone where his heart should be.

His easy smile, no doubt meant to be charming, didn't fool her. Chaney slid her sunglasses down to hide her own eyes and closed her book.

"What are you reading?" He bent his neck to read the spine.

"*Grimm's Fairy Tales*. Seems like an odd choice for a young woman. Which one's your favorite?"

She inwardly scoffed at his vain attempt to make a personal connection. Before he could paw through her beloved book, she slipped it into the small backpack hanging by its strap on her chair. The very thought of him touching something that belonged to her made her want to gag.

"Why are you bothering me?" she asked.

He flung out his arms in an expansive gesture, palms open and fingers spread apart. All innocence. Yeah, right.

"The Dogwood Diner here is one of my favorite places to get a cold drink on an especially fine February day like today. Great to be outside, isn't it?"

As if she'd been summoned by him to appear at that exact moment, a waitress stopped at the table. A multitude of rings sparkled on her tanned fingers. "Why, howdy, Agent Grant. What'll you have? The usual?"

His expression, half smirk and half grin, clearly said, *I told you*. His gaze shifted from Chaney to the waitress. "That'd do me just fine, Gail. How are the boys?"

"Growing like weeds."

"Boys'll do that." He pointed at Chaney's to-go cup. "Want a refill? Something to go along with your drink? My treat."

He surely couldn't believe she'd ever take as much as a pressed penny from him. But despite how much she wanted to throw her drink at him, toss the table, and run away, her grandfather's lessons on the art of hiding in plain sight glued her to the chair. Only amateurs caused a scene. Unless there was an ulterior motive for causing a scene.

Chaney had purposely dressed in denim capris and a plain beige tee so she wouldn't stand out to the other diners. Though who wouldn't have noticed Grant parking himself at her table? The sports jacket didn't hide the holstered gun on his belt when he loomed over her. At least he hadn't slapped his handcuffs around her wrists.

Yet.

She darted a smile at the waitress. "I'm fine, thank you."

"I'll bring you a refresh anyway." Gail's rings sparkled in the sunlight. "The ice melts fast out here and no one likes watered-down soda. Let's see, you had a Pepsi with lemon slices, right?"

"That's right." Now please, go away.

"I'll be back in a jiffy with those drinks." Gail's broad smile covered both of them.

When the waitress left, Chaney glanced at Special Agent Grant, sensing his gaze. His amused expression made her feel as small as a mouse trapped by a cat. She wasn't fooling him with her outward poise and disinterested air. He'd been highly trained, too, and it would be a mistake to underestimate him. Though his training had taken place at an academy and during years patrolling the streets of Orlando, the City Beautiful. Hers had begun before she'd taken her first steps, a cute and happy pawn in her grandfather's arms.

She leaned forward and, with her elbows on the table, rested her chin on her clasped hands. "Don't you have anything better to do than follow me around? No drug deals going down? No jaywalkers to ticket?"

"I don't bother with jaywalkers." He flicked a spot of dust from his pants leg then stared at the businesses across the street. "Interesting view you've chosen."

She followed his gaze and consciously relaxed her shoulders while mentally preparing for his interrogation.

"Let me guess." His tone was as off-handed as if they were discussing the latest movies or the warm February weather. But she wouldn't be tripped up by his easy-going manner. "Giaquinto's Jewelry. I can practically see all those diamonds and precious gemstones glistening from here. An in-and-out snatch-and-grab for someone who knows what she's doing."

"You're right. Jewels are easy to steal." Chaney copied his offhanded tone. "But hard to fence. That is, unless you don't mind someone else knowing your business."

He nodded, that slow annoying nod of his, which seemed so patronizing. As if he understood when he couldn't understand. She'd done her homework on Benjamin Grant. Decorated officer. Married with three young children. When had he ever gone hungry? Or been left on his own to survive?

He turned his attention back to the other side of the street. "Surely not the bank? That kind of heist wouldn't be easy for a gal on her own. And you are on your own now that your cousin is behind bars."

He couldn't have cut her any deeper if he'd used a knife. Her guilt was already eating her up inside. She casually swept the bangs hanging over her eyes.

"Not impossible, though," she said, her tone easy. "And banks provide ready cash. As long as the bills are unmarked."

"But?"

"Too many variables. Besides, I don't have time to plan a bank heist."

"What's the rush?"

"As if you didn't know." Chaney peered past the detective's shoulder at two middle-aged women, one a few years older than the other, who were taking their time adjusting their chairs at a table adorned with an umbrella. Neither of them could sit completely in the shade given the angle of the sun, so they were maneuvering to share it.

A slender, sharp-nosed dude, probably in his early twenties and wearing a long thin coat, approached them. He said something and one of the women laughed.

"Let's see then," Grant continued. "That leaves the bookstore, the insurance agency, the dry cleaners, and the shoe store." He turned to her, his smile and tone confident. "And the hotel. Plenty of marks inside those walls."

The luxury four-story hotel with its restaurants, banquet rooms, and meeting spaces, anchored the city block. It catered primarily to a convention crowd. No doubt that's where the two women, who had finally settled in their seats, were staying. They wore lanyards around their necks, giving away their names and new-to-town status. Perfect marks.

"Most tourists carry debit and credit cards," Chaney said dismissively. "Those don't help me much."

"And yet that's why you're sitting here, isn't it?" Grant leaned closer, as if to see past the dark lenses they both wore to hide their eyes—those windows to the soul—and peer inside hers. "You're paying attention to who's coming and going. Sizing them up. Waiting for the perfect opportunity."

The sharp-nosed guy laughed, bent over one of the women, then walked toward Chaney's table.

"The perfect opportunity appears to be now." She stood and took the lid off her drink. "Watch my bag, will you?"

Before Grant could answer, she strode toward the guy and lightly bumped into him. Soda and ice spilled onto his coat as the cup fell to the ground. As if to keep herself from falling, she grabbed hold of his arm. "I'm so sorry," she said apologetically then laughed. "I am such a klutz. No harm done, is there? Except to your coat. You must let me have it cleaned for you."

She spouted an ongoing patter of apologies and offers to help while he tried to extricate himself. When she stepped back, he hurried on his way. After he turned the corner, she faced the agent and held up a necklace in one hand and a cell phone in the other.

Grant frowned and started to rise.

"Stay there," she ordered.

Much to her surprise, he did as she said. She strode to where the women were looking at their menus.

"Are these yours?" She placed the necklace and the phone on the table.

The women stared at the items then both started talking at once. Uncomfortable with the attention, Chaney held up her hands. "Just be careful who you talk to. And keep an eye on your stuff."

She glanced at their lanyards and stifled a giggle. "After all, you're not in Kansas anymore."

"How did you know we're from Kansas?" the older woman asked.

"Just a lucky guess." Chaney grinned and pointed at the lanyard. "Enjoy the rest of your stay."

She returned to her seat, picking up the fallen cup along the way, and removed her sunglasses. No more hiding.

Grant eyed her for a moment then removed his own. "Impressive. But if you'd given me a head's up, I could have arrested the guy. Gotten him off the streets."

"I would have loved recording a video of you chasing that loser." Her lips curled into a mischievous grin. "I'd have sent copies to all the news stations, to your boss, to the mayor. Even put it on the city's Facebook page."

"So you think you did me a favor by letting him go? Is that it?"

Chaney slid a wallet across to him. "This should help you find him."

Grant opened the wallet and held up the side showing the punk's driver's license. "What do you know? Home address right here." He checked the bills. "About thirty dollars. If I weren't an honest man, I'd give the cash to you as a thank you."

"If I had wanted it, I'd have taken it before giving you the wallet."

"Touché." Grant pulled out his phone and placed a call.

As he was reciting the pickpocket's name, address, and description, Gail arrived with their drinks. "A Pepsi with lemon for you," she whispered. "An Arnold Palmer for our friend."

Grant glanced at the bill she put on the table, gave her cash from his pocket, and mouthed a thank you.

After he finished the call, Chaney handed him a phone. "I got this, too."

"His?"

"His."

"How did you …?" Grant shook his head. "I was watching, closely watching, and I didn't see you take a thing from him."

Pride surged through her despite her grandfather's admonition sounding in her head. *Never take anything from a cop. Not even a compliment.*

"I'm good at my job."

"Except it's not a job, Chaney." Grant leaned forward, his expression intense. "You're intelligent and, okay, I'm just going to say it, you're also easy on the eyes. You could do something else with your life besides break the law."

"When did I break the law?"

"Are you denying it?"

She pressed her lips together. Special Agent Grant wasn't some small-town yokel who could be easily manipulated. Better not to talk at all than to say something she'd regret.

He glanced behind him at the women.

"You didn't have to retrieve their valuables." He shifted in his seat, stared at nothing as he worked his jaw. She'd rattled him. *Good.*

"Doesn't that violate some 'honor among thieves' kind of code?" he asked.

"If he'd stolen the necklace from the older woman, I might have let it go."

He studied her expression, but she refused to be intimidated by his stare. She leaned back and crossed her arms.

Finally, he shrugged. "Care to elaborate on that?"

"Look at the way they're dressed."

He turned in his seat, gave them a look-over. "Business clothes. Appear expensive."

"They are expensive. And expensive clothes are usually tailored. You might not have noticed, but the brunette's sleeves are a little too long and the shoulders don't sit right. Either she's borrowed that outfit or gotten it from a thrift store."

"Nothing wrong with that."

"I didn't say there was. It's just …" She pressed her lips together again. She was saying too much. And yet she wanted to make him understand that she had her own code. But could he step outside of his black-and-white world to enter the gray area where she operated? Even for a minute?

"Look at her shoes."

"Her shoes? What about them?"

"The heels are worn down. She's obviously had them a long time."

"Let me see if I've got this straight. You recovered her stolen necklace because she doesn't have new clothes and new shoes."

"She's wanting to look her best. That necklace *is* her best. Maybe it's the only jewelry of any real value that she has. Besides, it was a locket. It probably has sentimental value." Chaney looked the agent square in his eyes. "No one should take that away from her. No one."

Grant didn't flinch from her direct gaze but seemed to be sizing her up. Then he leaned toward her and gripped his cup. "Taking someone else's property is always wrong. Even if they have a lot of it or it doesn't have sentimental value. This isn't Sherwood Forest and neither you nor your cousin are Robin Hood."

"I never claimed to be."

"I guess not. At least Robin Hood gave his stolen bounty to the needy."

When she didn't respond, he stood. "I'm going to get statements from those women. Wouldn't mind having an official one from you, too."

"You want me to go to the police station? No, thanks." She stared at the luxury hotel. Despite what she'd said earlier, the guests who stayed there *were* pigeons waiting to be plucked.

But instead of sitting at the bar inside that hotel and sizing up enough marks to get the money she needed, she'd sat, lost for the umpteenth time in a fairy-tale world, at this sidewalk table. And as much as she'd like to think otherwise, it wasn't because she had a sense that Special Agent Grant was somewhere nearby watching her. She'd been able to hide her surprise at seeing him, but the truth was, she'd been shocked when he sat at her table.

She had slipped up and allowed her worry over Marshall to dull her observational skills. Something she couldn't afford to do when she was desperate for money. Five thousand dollars should be enough. A measly five thousand dollars.

"Stay out of the hotel, Chaney," Grant said. "All the hotels."

"Are you going to keep following me to make sure I do?"

"I wouldn't have to stay on your tail if your cousin wasn't so loyal." Grant smiled, but the expression in his eyes remained serious. "Usually I admire loyalty, but in this case? Let's just say, I wouldn't have to follow you if you were in a cell next to Marshall."

"You've got nothing on me."

He stood and loomed over her, his shadow again blocking the sun. "Not yet," he said with a smile as he put on his sunglasses. "Give me time."

CHAPTER 2

***T**uesday Afternoon*

Adam Thorne stared out the window of the Dogwood Diner, vainly wishing he hadn't agreed to this meeting. At least now he understood why Pete Davis, one of the board members at Gateway Community Church, insisted on meeting somewhere besides Adam's office at the church.

"You know none of us wanted it to end this way." Pete spread his hands on the table and smiled. "We're giving you a solid severance package. I insisted on that though it took some convincing to bring a few of the others around. We wouldn't want it to get around town that we didn't take good care of our ministers. Even when we have to let one go."

Adam had a sudden urge to punch the pompous—he refused to even think the next likely word—in the nose. Beneath the table, he flexed his fists then clasped his hands.

A godly minister didn't hit members of the board. Not even when the board met without his knowledge and blindsided him with their decision.

Adam focused on the diners sitting at the outside tables on the other side of the window while Pete talked about health insurance, housing allowances, and final payments. He should be paying attention, but Pete's voice faded as the scene outside the glass captured Adam's attention.

A young woman with cropped blonde hair and dark glasses sat with her arms crossed at one of the sidewalk tables. The big man sitting next to her wore a sports jacket that seemed stretched thin across his broad shoulders. He leaned forward, his hand pressing against the tabletop.

A dad lecturing his daughter? Or maybe she was getting fired, too.

Suddenly, she stood, walked straight into a skinny twenty-something with spiked hair, and spilled her drink on him. She appeared apologetic, brushing his long black coat with both hands. Yet Adam would bet his last hundred dollars, if he were a betting man, that she had bumped Skinny on purpose.

What was going on?

"Adam?"

He jerked his attention to Pete who forced a smile. But his narrowed eyes betrayed his annoyance.

"I asked if the severance package was acceptable. I promised the board we'd get this settled as soon as possible. It's best for you and best for the church to part ways as amicably as we can under the circumstances. You agree with that, don't you?"

Adam sighed, wondering if he'd missed anything important while he'd been distracted by what was happening outside. But he didn't care enough to ask Pete to repeat what he'd said. He wanted this meeting to end so he could drown his sorrows. Though how did a non-drinking man do that? With Oreos and a glass of milk? He'd asked himself the same questions last month when Piper broke his heart. God hadn't given him an answer then and He wasn't giving him an answer now.

"Do I have a choice?" Adam asked, not expecting an answer. "I guess the sins of the fathers can fall upon the heads of the children after all."

Pete seemed momentarily stunned then he smiled again. That fake salesman smile that had irritated Adam since the first time they'd met over a year ago. Back then he'd been bright-eyed and bushy-tailed, certain that his brilliant sermons would change hearts and transform lives. He'd quickly learned that even though the Sunday sermons mattered, they didn't matter as much as what he did or didn't do the rest of the week.

A few notable members who attended Gateway Community Church weren't pleased with Adam's efforts to feed the hungry and clothe the needy. With his oily charm, Pete had fought every single initiative Adam brought to the board that would have made a practical difference to those outside the church. Sometimes Adam prevailed. Sometimes Pete did.

Now their war was over, and Pete stood victorious. All he needed was Adam's signature on the resignation papers.

"No one believes you did anything wrong, Adam. Don't look at it like that." Pete's soothing tone made Adam's skin crawl. "We're all sorry about your father's troubles, but we can't close our eyes to them. They affect you. Therefore, they affect us."

"We don't even know if he was involved."

"The appearance of evil." Pete shook his head and bent his shoulders as if they carried the weight of the world. "It's a shame. But our reputation is at stake. None of us can stand idly by while our church is involved in even the hint of a scandal."

Talking about appearances, did Pete actually believe Adam was fooled by his fake sincerity? Never.

Adam gazed out the window again. The girl placed a wallet on the table. The man in the sports jacket appeared surprised as he opened it. A moment later he made a phone call.

Had the woman stolen Skinny's wallet?

Adam sat forward and stared out the window. Should he call 911? Tell the owner of the diner?

"Everything we talked about is outlined in here." Pete slid a folder across the table. "Look it over. If you have any questions, call me anytime, day or night."

He stood and gestured toward the waitress. "I'll get the check. After all, it's to everyone's benefit that we part on the best possible terms."

Don't do me any favors.

That was what Adam wanted to say. Instead he took Pete's extended hand. "Thank you."

Thanks for what, he couldn't say.

"As soon as this is signed," Pete tapped the folder, "we can all move forward. I'm sure you want that as much as we do."

"Absolutely," Adam said without enthusiasm. He had no other words. The writing on the church wall was as clear to him as when the mysterious hand appeared at Belshazzar's feast. That mysterious message—*mənē mənē təqēl ūp̄arsīn*—foretold the downfall of the Babylonian Empire. So said the prophet Daniel.

"Numbered, numbered, weighed, divided," Adam muttered to himself, translating the Aramaic words as Pete handed the waitress a twenty and refused any change. The tip was three times the cost of their beverages, but that was Pete. Generous to a fault with his money. Just not with his grace.

"You're staying here?" Pete asked when Adam remained in his seat.

Adam's attention was focused on the blonde and the man in the sports jacket. Both had taken off their sunglasses but neither seemed happy with the other.

He shifted his gaze to the folder and then to Pete. "I want to look through this." As if to make the words true, he opened the folder.

"That's fine, Adam. Just fine. But don't brood on what's happened. The good Lord doesn't like brooders."

Where's that verse in the Bible? Somehow, I missed it at seminary.

"Don't worry about me." *God works out everything for His own purposes and all that.* Adam might not be too pleased with

God's current plan, but he wanted to trust in that promise. Even when his current circumstances made doubt so easy.

"I'm sure you'll be fine, a smart young man like you." Pete opened his mouth again, closed it, then laughed. "I started to say I'd see you at church. Out of habit, you know. But I guess that won't be the case. You'll find another place to worship soon enough. Maybe even another ministry."

"Maybe."

"Just to be clear, this is effective immediately. I've already got someone lined up to take over your Bible study class tomorrow night. All you need to do is clean out your office. Maybe after the staff leaves today."

Adam forced a smile, but his stomach clenched at this latest blow. It was bad enough Pete had invited him to the diner under false pretenses then sucker-punched him with the board's decision. Now he wasn't even giving Adam the chance to say goodbye to his congregation or the staff, to facilitate the discussion of the third chapter of James at Wednesday night's Bible study, or give the sermon he'd been preparing on casting the first stone. Maybe he should email that one to Pete.

If Adam had been caught embezzling church funds or fooling around with the church secretary—something that would never happen even if she wasn't old enough to be his grandmother—he could understand the board's decision. But he had done nothing to deserve this kind of treatment.

Pete, still chuckling at his "out of habit" *faux pas*, left the diner. Adam tracked Pete through the window then turned his attention to the blonde. The man with her stood, a light breeze tugging at the hem of his jacket. Adam leaned closer to the window. A holstered gun rested against the man's hip. He was a cop?

As if to answer Adam's question, a patrol car pulled to the curb, lights flashing, and an officer got out. The man said something to the girl then he and the officer approached two women sitting at a nearby table. The girl rose from her chair and slung a black backpack over her shoulder. As if she sensed she was being watched, she faced the window and stared at Adam.

They held each other's gaze for a brief moment. Then she casually slipped on her sunglasses, waved her fingers at him, and walked away.

CHAPTER 3

Tuesday Afternoon

Fletcher Wilkes shifted in his seat and did his best to stifle the cough rising in his throat. He needn't bother asking Mickey Nolan to snuff out his fat cigar. He'd made that mistake once before, only to have Mickey accidentally-on-purpose burn a hole in the sleeve of Fletcher's favorite Brooks Brothers suit jacket.

Mickey had laughed at the incident, clapping Fletcher on the back in his good ole boy manner. But the coldness in Mickey's eyes had let Fletcher know he was being punished for stepping over a line.

If it had been anyone but Mickey, Fletcher would have fired him as a client. But no one fired Mickey Nolan. Not if they wanted to live to tell about it.

"Sandy-Lynne didn't just disappear," Mickey drawled for the umpteenth time. "No one can move a horse without someone somewhere seeing something. You find me that someone so we can take care of this business. That's your job, Wilkes. Why aren't you doing it?"

"Our inside man at police headquarters set an alert on her

credit cards." Fletcher kept his tone even despite the rapid beating of his pulse. Mickey always had to blame his troubles on someone else, and Fletcher, as his attorney, was a common target. "But there have been no hits."

"She probably sold that diamond necklace I got her on our last anniversary." Mickey puffed on the cigar then flicked the ash into the huge red and black ashtray on his desk. "That's theft, Wilkes. I paid a heap load of good money for that necklace. Sandy-Lynne had no right to sell it."

Fletcher didn't bother to point out the flaw in Mickey's thinking. The necklace, a gift, belonged to his wife. She could sell it if she wished. Perhaps she had, but not to any of the local fences Fletcher contacted. They were too smart to cross Mickey Nolan.

The horse, Sudden Mischief Ensues, had been a gift, too, though in that case, the ownership wasn't quite as clear-cut.

Mickey had given the thoroughbred to his wife, making a big show of the presentation in front of over a hundred guests at her last birthday party. But only Mickey's name appeared on the paperwork. He'd promised to sign the horse over to Sandy-Lynne more than once. Finally, Sandy-Lynne asked Fletcher for help. When he broached the subject with Mickey, his client made it clear that anyone who interfered in a private matter between him and his young wife must have a death wish. The next time Sandy-Lynne approached him, Fletcher refused to get involved.

"What about that veterinarian?" Mickey pronounced it vetra-naryan. "We got an alert on his credit cards, too?"

"Yes. But there's been no activity."

Mickey smashed the half-smoked cigar into the ashtray. "Are you telling me that quack can take off with my racehorse and my wife and just ... poof ... disappear?" He blew out air and gestured with his meaty hands, pressing his fingers together then spreading them apart. "Someone knows something, Wilkes. And that someone better be talking soon."

"We'll find them, Mickey." Fletcher's tone hit that fine line between confidence and subservience. Sometimes talking to his client was like talking to a two-year-old. You got better results by being persuasive yet firm. But even as he tried to assure Mickey, his own gut wrenched.

Sandy-Lynne must have carefully planned the theft of the horse—if it could be called a theft—or else they'd have discovered her whereabouts by now. They couldn't even be sure that the veterinarian, Tucker Thorne, was with her though he had disappeared at about the same time.

"Marshall Jacobsen poked around at the vet clinic," Fletcher said. "Pretended to be a dog food salesman or something like that. The receptionist told him that Dr. Thorne was at a conference in Atlanta but wouldn't provide any specifics."

"Don't tell me. There ain't no conference in Atlanta."

"Not that Jacobsen could find."

"Did he talk to Thorne's son?" Mickey lit another cigar. "The preacher?" He spat the word as if it left a bad taste in his mouth then blew smoke in Fletcher's face. The attorney turned away, swallowing a cough that nearly choked him.

"Jacobsen didn't get the chance—"

"Why isn't he here?" Mickey slammed his fist on the desk. "He should be the one telling me all about this, not you."

Fletcher looked at him in surprise. Did Mickey really not know?

"He's in jail."

"What for?"

"Breaking and entering. Theft." Fletcher shrugged. "I'm not sure of all the charges."

"How about that?" Mickey leaned back and eyed the lit end of the cigar. "Never expected to hear about a cop smart enough to nab the elusive Marshall Jacobsen. What's his name?"

Fletcher knew the answer, but he opened the portfolio resting on his lap and skimmed his notes. More than anything, he wanted to get out of Mickey's office and breathe fresh air. If he didn't answer too quickly, maybe Mickey would tire of his presence and dismiss him.

Fletcher ran his finger down his notes. "Special Agent Benjamin Grant. FDLE."

"Never heard of him."

Doesn't mean he doesn't exist.

"Must have been a lucky bust." Mickey chuckled.

Not for Jacobsen.

"Did this Grant get the girl, too?"

"The girl?" Fletcher didn't have to pretend this time. He honestly didn't know who Mickey was talking about. If Jacobsen had a girlfriend, Fletcher knew nothing about her. Jacobsen kept a low profile and his private life extremely private. Which was one reason he was so good at his job.

"If I remember right," Mickey said, "and of course I do, she's his cousin. She helps him out some, but he don't let anyone get to know her much. That's why you don't know nuthin' about her." Mickey chortled. "Not as smart as you think you are, are you, Mr. Wise Guy Attorney?"

"I suppose I'm not," Fletcher said, allowing a small smile because he knew Mickey expected him to appear chastised.

"I ain't never seen her myself. Maybe she's a ghost." Mickey rested the cigar on the lip of the huge ashtray and shuffled through the papers on his desk. "Did Jacobsen get paid?"

"He did." Men like Jacobsen didn't give out information for free.

"Sounds to me like he didn't finish the job before he got nabbed."

"I believe he might disagree with that assessment."

"He was supposed to *find* that horse doctor." Mickey punctuated his words by stabbing the desk with his thick finger. "Did he find that horse doctor?"

"No," Fletcher admitted. "He did not."

"Then he owes me. Either a location or a refund. Why hasn't he posted bail?"

"The prosecution requested Jacobsen be held without bail. Said he was a flight risk. The judge agreed."

"He must not have had a very good attorney."

"Some public defender." Fletcher checked his notes. "No one I've ever heard of."

"You'd think a guy as smart as Marshall Jacobsen would keep an attorney on retainer to handle these little legal problems. Like I do."

Fletcher pressed his lips together. Again, it was useless to point out the folly in Mickey's logic. Jacobsen's thefts and scams weren't lucrative enough to pay an ongoing retainer fee. Besides, Jacobsen rarely got caught. And when he did, he ran. The prosecutor and the judge had been right to consider him a flight risk.

Mickey took his time taking up the cigar, drawing in the smoke, and blowing a cloud toward Fletcher. "The girl will have to do it."

Had Fletcher heard him right? "You mean, his mystery cousin?"

"That's right. Jacobsen can tell you how to contact her."

"I doubt he will."

"If he don't, he might have an accident in that jail. You can tell him that." Mickey leaned back in his leather swivel chair, apparently comfortable in the knowledge that whatever he willed would be accomplished. Why wouldn't he be? Things always turned out the way he wanted.

Except when it came to Sandy-Lynne.

She'd stood up to him when he wanted to race her horse despite his lingering injury. Fletcher had admired her spunk, though he'd been afraid for her. Now he was afraid of what would happen when Mickey found her. And Mickey would find her. It was only a matter of time.

"Or maybe his cousin will have an accident," Mickey said. "Make sure he understands what can happen when a job don't get done."

"I'll go see him now."

When Mickey didn't object, Fletcher stood. "Maybe I could get him another hearing. Convince the judge to set a reasonable bail."

"He wasn't on a job for me when he got arrested, was he?"

"No, sir."

"Smart guy like Jacobsen can figure his own way out of his legal troubles." Mickey rocked back and forth in the chair, causing the springs to squeak, and chuckled. "We'll contract with the girl. See what she can do for us."

Fletcher easily read between the lines. Mickey schemed to use the cousin to control Jacobsen. Marshall would think twice about making any deals with the district attorney that could bring down the great Mickey Nolan if his cousin's welfare was at stake.

It's what Mickey did best. Control those around him and bend them to his will. If only Fletcher had been smart enough to figure that out before it was too late. But now he was in too deep. If Mickey ever went down for any of his crimes, Fletcher would end up in the cell next to him. The thought terrified him.

So he would do whatever Mickey asked him to do. Take the money that Mickey paid him for his smarts, his discretion, and his silence—money that supported the lavish lifestyle Mrs. Wilkes would never willingly give up. If it came to a choice between money and her husband, Fletcher had no doubts which one his loving wife would choose.

"I'll be in touch," Fletcher said as he walked toward the door of the office. Not too fast or Mickey would come up with an excuse to draw him back into a cigar-hazed conversation. Not too slow or Mickey would ask what was wrong and expect Fletcher to come up with an answer. He felt like Goldilocks in such moments—he had to pace his walk just right.

Control. That's what it was all about with Mickey Nolan. Control.

He was the puppet master and Fletcher was no more than a marionette with no way to cut the strings.

Once the office door closed behind him, Fletcher paused, took a deep breath, then put on his confident persona as if it were a suit of clothes and strode to the elevator. He gave the impression of a man in charge, but his gut still clenched, and his pulse still raced. It was all a façade, a charade. He'd give anything to get out from under Mickey Nolan's cigar-stained thumb.

CHAPTER 4

Tuesday Afternoon

Marshall Jacobsen sat in the hard metal chair, his hands cuffed to a ring in the table, and eyed his well-dressed visitor. Fletcher Wilkes obviously had influence since they were meeting in an interrogation room instead of the typical video-conferencing set-up. The well-fed attorney exuded calm and power. But the corners of his eyes were tight and small beads of sweat dampened his forehead. He stood by the table, his hands resting on his briefcase, and waited for the guard to leave them.

"Remember," Wilkes said when the guard reached the door. "This is a private consultation. No recordings."

"So you said already." The bored guard traipsed out of the room. The door closed behind him with a faint click.

A click Marshall loathed.

Wilkes waited a moment, as if he needed to brace himself, then he settled into the opposite chair. "Hello, Marshall. Are they treating you well?"

"Are you representing me?"

"That might be a conflict of interest."

The tiny ember of hope that Marshall had felt when Wilkes

walked into the room died. He didn't like the attorney, but he would be a welcome addition to Marshall's so-called legal team. The rookie from the public defender's office had let the prosecuting attorney run roughshod over him at the arraignment.

But Marshall refused to let Wilkes see his disappointment. No doubt the attorney had instructions to report everything about this conversation to his mobster-wannabe client. "A conflict of interest? How so?"

"I represent all of Mr. Michael Nolan's legal interests. You know that."

"I see." Marshall relaxed his shoulders as he slouched in his seat. Despite Wilkes' professional demeanor, he was nervous. Why? Was he afraid Marshall would shoot the messenger? With what? He didn't even have a straw to shoot a spit wad.

But Wilkes wouldn't be here unless Mickey Nolan had sent him. What could Nolan want with him now? There was little Marshall could do for the man behind these bars.

Unless Nolan wanted him to take care of someone who was also behind these bars. If that was the case, he'd have to find another chump to do his bidding. Marshall avoided violence as much as possible. Brains over brawn had been the family code for generations. He saw no need to change it now. Certainly not for the likes of Mickey Nolan.

Wilkes shifted in his seat, cleared his throat, and clutched at his tie while alternately smiling and frowning as if his face couldn't decide which expression better served his purpose. Marshall didn't say a word. His silence gave him control.

Eventually Wilkes stuck with the frown and clasped his hands on the table. "Mr. Nolan contracted you to recover a certain valuable piece of property. You did not fulfill your obligation."

"I was given a retainer to gather information. It's not my fault if the information isn't to Mr. Nolan's liking."

"Information? That Tucker Thorne was supposedly at a

convention that doesn't exist?" Wilkes huffed. "I could have found that out with a phone call."

"But you didn't."

"Because that was your job." Wilkes took a deep breath. "And you failed."

Marshall lifted his cuffed hands, jangling the metal links, a sound that jarred him even more than the click of the door. "Something else came up."

A flash of sympathy appeared in Wilkes's eyes then disappeared behind a hard gaze. "Mr. Nolan demands a refund or a fulfillment of the contract."

"Sorry, Fletchie." Marshall half-smiled, half-smirked. "The money paid the rent and I'm behind bars. Now if you want to do your attorney magic and get me out of this joint, I'd be glad to go back to work for Mr. Nolan."

Wilkes's eyes shifted. Again, with the nerves. But why? Marshall maintained his relaxed posture, but his gut braced … for what, he didn't know. He stared at Wilkes, endured the throat-clearing and tie-clutching, and waited.

"Mr. Nolan proposes an alternative arrangement." Wilkes paused, as if hoping Marshall would fill in the blanks.

His mind raced through possibilities, but he came up blank and said nothing.

Wilkes stared at the camera installed in a corner of the room then shifted his gaze to Marshall. "Mr. Nolan proposes your cousin—"

Chaney?

Marshall leapt to his feet, and his chair clattered to the floor. The upward jerk tilted the table causing the metal cuffs to cut into his hands. Wilkes tried—and failed—to catch his briefcase as it slid to the floor.

Marshall righted the table, his fingers clutching at the cuffs, and leaned forward. "Don't you dare go near her." His voice, low and guttural, cut through the air between the two men. "Don't you dare."

The door flew open and the guard rushed inside. Wilkes held up his hand in a reassuring gesture. "A mere accident." He smiled, showing off his large white teeth. "My briefcase tumbled to the floor."

The guard looked from Wilkes to Marshall, suspicion in his eyes. Marshall relaxed his facial muscles, lowered his shoulders, and took a deep breath.

"Our business is finished," he said, hating that he failed to control the trembling anger in his voice.

"I'm afraid it isn't." Wilkes gestured with both hands this time as if trying to placate Marshall and the guard. "This matter needs a resolution."

Marshall glared at the attorney. "None that involve my cousin."

"Mr. Jacobsen, you must know that you're in no position to refuse …" Wilkes paused and darted a glance at the guard. "This is the best solution."

"Get me out of here." Marshall spoke to the guard without taking his eyes off Wilkes.

As the guard escorted him back to his cell, Marshall sorted out his tangled thoughts. Neither Wilkes nor Nolan should have even known he had a cousin. Did that mean they also knew how to find her?

He needed to warn her to stay away from both men. Not an easy thing to do when he was caged like a rabid dog.

If only she'd stayed away from Calvin Brady and his crew, then Marshall wouldn't be in this mess. But she hadn't listened and now he was stuck here with no way to contact her.

As they neared his cell, he shook his head to chase away the *woulda-shoulda-coulda*'s and focus on the immediate problem.

"Don't suppose I could make a phone call?" he asked, his tone as off-handed as he could make it considering the adrenaline surging through his bloodstream. He couldn't fight his way out of this mess, but his body didn't seem to know that.

"Want to call a different attorney?" Now that the excitement was over, the guard's boredom had returned.

"How about you make a phone call for me?"

"Against the rules."

"You always play by the rules?" A hint of a challenge colored the words, but the guard's fatigued expression didn't change. Marshall hid an inward sigh. "You've been doing this job too long, my friend."

"Long enough to have heard it all, seen it all, smelled it all." The guard unlocked the cell door and opened it. "I know your type. All charm on the outside and nothing but poison on the inside, *my friend*."

Marshall entered the cell in the vain hope that his easygoing cooperation would make an impression. "It's important. Otherwise I wouldn't be asking."

"Everything's always important when you're a miscreant." The guard clanged the door shut and motioned for Marshall to put his hands through the slot so he could remove the cuffs.

"Miscreant?" What was up with that five-dollar word coming from the mouth of a two-bit brute. "That's a smart move, expanding your vocabulary. But despite his fancy suit, that lawyer is a miscreant, too. He's up to no good."

"I could have told you that. Maybe you'll learn a lesson about swimming with the sharks. Not a great idea for a little fish like you." Amused by his own wit, the guard chuckled and started to walk away.

"Hold on a minute." Marshall gripped the bars and willed his body to relax. His mind to think. Only one plan came to mind. Definitely not a good one. But when you didn't have a friend to count on, sometimes you had to count on an enemy.

"What is it?" The guard stared at him with that vacant look in his eyes. "I don't have all day to hang around here."

Because you have so many other exciting things to do?

"I want to talk to the FDLE agent who arrested me. Benjamin Grant. Today."

"Are you going to confess?"

"Just get him down here." Marshall hesitated a moment, licked his lips. He didn't need to fake his desperation. He had to get a message to Chaney before Wilkes found her. "Please."

Interest sparked in the guard's eyes. "Okay. I'll see what I can do." As he walked away, he raised his voice. "Confession's good for the soul, you know. Best thing for everybody."

Marshall stretched out on the hard cot and placed his forearm over his eyes. Wasn't it enough he'd purposely bungled the theft so that he was in this cell instead of Chaney?

His cousin was smart. Savvy. Fearless.

Except when it came to enclosed spaces and locked doors. He'd helped her, supported her, stood by her so that now she could ride in an elevator without freaking out. But Marshall feared that if she spent even one night in a jail cell, she'd spiral into such a deep hole that he'd never be able to pull her out again.

Special Agent Grant would come, Marshall was sure of that. While he waited, he needed to come up with a script that would persuade the agent to give Chaney a message.

And not get her arrested.

PART II

CHAPTER 5

Three Weeks Earlier

Sandy-Lynne Nolan tucked her hair into the stocking cap and slipped on her black denim jacket. She'd been planning this moment for several days, ever since she realized that no pleading, begging, or crying on her part would change Mickey's mind. He was determined that Mischief would run in the Golden Citrus Race, one of a handful of races that awarded points for horses bound for the Florida Derby.

Sandy-Lynne was just as determined that Mischief would not.

The thoroughbred had placed third in his last race, despite the tendon injuries in his legs that hadn't healed from the race before that. Tucker Thorne, their veterinarian, had recommended a rest, but Mickey laughed at the notion. To him, a horse was a horse was a horse. A commodity without a heart.

When Tucker refused to give Mischief a drug cocktail that would mask the pain during that race, Mickey fired him. The new vet, a regular at the track, had no such scruples. He wanted his clients' horses to win—no matter the cost to their health or well-being.

Though Mischief survived his race, another horse with the same injuries did not. He stumbled on the track and had to be put down.

That's when Sandy-Lynne and Tucker decided to take radical measures.

Sandy-Lynne took a deep breath then drove her BMW convertible to the racing stables. She stopped before turning on the graveled road leading to the back gate, gripping the steering wheel and gathering her courage. The sun would rise in a couple of hours, and she wanted to be as far away from here as possible before then.

"I belong here," she reminded herself. "And Mischief belongs to me."

Which wasn't true in a legal sense, even though Mickey had made a huge exhibition of presenting her the thoroughbred as her very own a few months ago at her birthday party. She'd had no idea then that he never intended to transfer full ownership to her. Or that he planned to race Mischief until his legs gave out then trade him in for a younger model.

Though why should she be surprised? He'd done the very same thing to Wife Number One and Wife Number Two. For all she knew, he'd already chosen a replacement for her. She didn't care. All that mattered was Mischief.

She picked up the burner phone and sent Tucker the text that would let him know her current location.

Point A. Check.

His reply sped back.

Proceed.

"I belong here," Sandy-Lynne said out loud. "I belong here."

She drove slowly both out of caution and habit. She didn't want the gravel to fly up and ding her Beemer's paint job. When she reached the gate, she entered the security code. The squeaking of the huge gate as it rolled opened on the runner seemed louder than she'd ever heard them before. As soon as there was room for the convertible to slip through, she gently pressed the accelerator.

No one seemed to be around, but she'd learned from one of the daytime security staff that at least three guards patrolled the stable grounds during the night. After she'd made a big fuss about her concern for Mischief's well-being and safety, the flattered day guard had gushed out all the information Sandy-Lynne needed. Even so, she and Tucker had methodically noted and memorized the location of all the cameras.

But she didn't need to hide from them.

"I belong here."

She parked the BMW in the lot assigned to the track's employees. At this time of night, only a few other vehicles were there. Hands in her pockets and her head slightly bent, she jogged toward the stables. Still no sign of any of the night guards. Hopefully, they were crammed in an empty stall playing a game of five-stud poker. The day guard had let it slip they did that sometimes.

"Only a few hands, though," he'd said hurriedly to make up for the gaffe. According to him, they never missed the hourly patrol. And what harm was there in taking a little break? They could keep as good an eye on the horses if they were inside the stables with them—even better!—than when they were walking the grounds. Besides, there was never any real threat. Who would try to steal a horse in the middle of the night?

She'd refrained from answering his question out loud.

Me.

Except she wasn't *stealing*. Only protecting what was rightfully, morally hers. It didn't matter whose name was on the ownership papers. According to their pre-nup, any gifts that Mickey gave to Sandy-Lynne during their marriage were considered non-marital property. She'd signed away her rights to his estate but insisted on that concession. And Mischief, from her perspective, had been as much a gift as the jewelry

Mickey showered on her in the early months of their marriage.

Sandy-Lynne entered the stables through a side door, unlocking it in less than fifteen seconds with a lock-picking tool from the kit that Tucker had given her. Her record was three seconds. A couple of mornings last week, when no one else was around, Tucker had stood look-out while she practiced on this very lock. But it had seemed a game then. She'd been exuberant at how easy it was once she got the knack of it. Now the situation was very real, and her hands shook as she turned the knob.

If someone asks, she reminded herself, *the door was unlocked and she'd simply walked in to check on her beloved horse.*

The door opened to a short corridor with closed doors on both sides before intersecting with the two long aisles housing the stalls. The interior was dimly lit with regularly spaced light fixtures set close to the ceiling. All was quiet, the air scented with the unmistakable odor of well-groomed horses, clean straw, and processed feed.

Sandy-Lynne halted at the first intersection, peering around the corner in both directions. Except for the occasional scuffling sound from one of the horses, all was quiet, as if she were the only person in the huge building. She turned right and walked with as much confidence as she could muster to Mischief's stall.

The dark bay nickered a greeting as she unlatched his door and slipped inside.

"Shh, boy." She rubbed the white blaze on his nose and pulled a peppermint-flavored horse treat from her pocket. His warm lips nuzzled her hand as he mouthed the nugget. "Good boy. That's my good, beautiful boy. I'm getting you out of here."

He stood perfectly still while she cinched a blanket beneath his belly. Bandages already wrapped all four of his slender legs, another cause of disagreement between Tucker and the new vet.

Tucker's philosophy was to use bandages or boots only when needed. Mickey's chosen vet said they were always needed. Sandy-Lynne wasn't sure who was right, but she knew who she trusted.

She snapped a lead rope onto Mischief's halter, and he nudged her shoulder as she opened the door. "No time for playing, Mischief. We need to go."

The aisle was still empty, and the other horses didn't seem to be disturbed by her presence. But then they were used to people being in the stables.

Mischief's hooves echoed on the textured concrete. Sandy-Lynne took long, slow breaths so he wouldn't sense her nervousness. When they got outside, she closed the side door and left it unlocked.

As she kept an eye out for the security guards, she led Mischief along the dirt path to the unloading area where her truck and trailer were parked. Though her hands still shook and her palms were sweaty, she managed to get him inside the trailer without any difficulty.

"You're a good boy," she told him again and again, as much for her sake as his. Once she had him settled inside, she closed and locked the trailer. All she needed to do now was rendezvous with Tucker.

"Who's out there?" a voice called from the shadows of the stables. The glow of a lit cigarette appeared then someone stepped forward, a darker shadow against the darkness of the building. The man wore the gray uniform of a security guard. A gun rested in a holster attached to his belt, and he carried a walkie-talkie in his left hand.

I belong here.

"Hello?" she said, adding a lilt to her voice. She approached the guard, wanting to keep as much distance between him and the trailer as possible. "Are you talking to me?"

"Hello, ma'am." He looked her up and down, and a slow

appreciative smile spread from one ear to the next. "What are you doing out here this time of night? This is no place for visitors."

Sandy-Lynne folded her arms and hardened her gaze. "Don't you recognize me?"

"Should I, ma'am?"

"Incompetence." She gave an exaggerated sigh and shook her head.

"Excuse me?" He took a long, deliberate puff of the cigarette then flicked the ashes on the ground.

"Smoking is so dangerous in a stable. I'm sure it's not allowed."

"That's why I came outside for my smoke break."

"My husband will want to know about this," she said, as if he hadn't spoken. "We trust our horses are in the best possible care while they're housed here. But I was so worried, I couldn't sleep. And then I find . . ." she gestured toward him, palm open, "you. Smoking instead of doing your job."

"Hey, now. There's no need to take that tone." He smashed the cigarette tip against the back of the walkie-talkie, started to toss the butt onto the ground, then apparently realized that wasn't a good idea. Instead, he gripped it between his index finger and thumb. "All's quiet here. You can see that."

She purposely let a couple seconds of silence slip by then softened her features. "You're right. My husband always says I put the woe into worry." She feigned a laugh and playfully tapped the guard's arm. "I'll leave you alone now." She waggled her finger at him. "But no more smoking. That could cause a lot of trouble."

"You can count on me, ma'am."

She tossed him another smile then returned to the truck. She should have texted Tucker again by now, but first she needed to get away before the guard realized anything was amiss. She'd managed to unsettle him by putting him on the defensive, and he'd been distracted by her looks—men so often were—but he might not be as stupid as he acted.

Sandy-Lynne drove carefully out of the loading area and onto the graveled drive, past the lot where she'd parked her BMW, and back to the main road. She couldn't resist glancing in the rearview mirror again and again, but no one seemed to be following her. No alarms sounded.

Hopefully the guard, fearful of being reported for smoking, wouldn't say anything to his buddies about her being there. That was the best-case scenario. And the best she could hope for at the moment.

When she reached the stop sign at the main road, she grabbed the burner phone and sent Tucker a second text.

Coming home.

His response was the thumbs up emoji.

She wasn't going home, though. Instead, she turned on the main road and headed for their rendezvous point.

* * *

SANDY-LYNNE HAD DRIVEN the truck before but never while pulling the trailer. The worry of hauling Mischief behind her added to the strain on her nerves. But the stress was slightly offset by the euphoria from getting him out of the stables without Mickey's knowledge.

She'd added a little something extra to her husband's nightcap to be sure he wouldn't awaken when her alarm went off at 2:30. Not that she needed the alarm. She wasn't sure she had slept a wink.

The meandering drive took her to Narcoossee Road where she turned south into Osceola County. If she'd been driving her BMW, she'd have already reached her destination. But she was too afraid of losing control of the truck and its precious cargo to risk going her normal speed.

With both a sigh of relief and a quickening of her pulse, she turned off her headlights and pulled into the entrance of the old Winn-Dixie parking lot. She maneuvered behind the grocery store to the far back corner where stands of trees and a brush-filled ditch separated the building from the neighboring businesses on the rural highway. Her headlights reflected off Tucker's pickup, parked nose-out as if ready for a quick getaway, and she stopped a few feet from his bumper.

After she turned off the ignition, she rested her head on the steering wheel. Her shoulders ached with the tension of gripping the wheel as she drove, but she'd done what she had set out to do. A sense of satisfaction flowed through her even though they weren't yet safe from Mickey's long reach.

Tucker tugged on the door handle and she unfastened her seat belt.

"You okay?" he asked. His expression was hard to read by the faint interior light. But she sensed his relief that she'd made it. Even so, it was too soon for congratulations.

"Fine." She slid out of the truck and her feet landed harder than she intended on the asphalt. She stumbled slightly and Tucker grabbed her arms to steady her.

"Whoa, there. Are you sure you're okay?"

"No. But I will be. As soon as Mischief is safe."

"It won't be long now." Tucker rounded the back of the trailer. "You got the key?"

She fished it out of her pocket and handed it to him. He unlocked the trailer's padlock then stood aside for her to enter. As she spoke to Mischief, her voice calm and soothing, she detached the guide ropes from the hooks inside the trailer then led him to Tucker's trailer.

If you could call the hunk of junk behind his pickup a trailer. Tucker had scrounged up the rusted scrap from a Craigslist ad. Cheap and disposable. Best of all, untraceable.

Unlike Mickey's newer, shinier model.

Both the truck and the trailer would be abandoned soon, but eventually they'd be found and traced to Mickey. All Sandy-Lynne and Tucker could do was buy themselves some time and not leave the truck/trailer combo anywhere that suggested where they planned to hide Mischief.

The solution had been genius in its simplicity. Tucker's trailer looked like a wreck from the outside, but he had put a thick layer of straw on the floor. Mischief would be fine. Sandy-Lynne got him inside, closed the door, and rested her hand against the metal exterior as Tucker added the padlock.

Step two, trailer exchange, done. Only one more task to complete, and they'd be on their way.

"You had no trouble then?" Tucker asked, wiping nervous sweat from his forehead and adjusting the old beret he often wore over his receding hairline. "No one saw you?"

"One of the guards. But I don't think he'll tell anyone. At least not anyone that matters."

"Oh?" The weight of that *oh* sounded heavy in Sandy-Lynne's ears, heavy with all the unspoken words it held.

"I caught him smoking."

Tucker hmphed. "Who hires these thugs?"

"They're friends of friends. You know how that kind of thing works. An opening comes up. It needs filled ASAP. Bruno's cousin needs a job and so does Bruno's cousin's nephew and the nephew's best friend. They all get hired and care more about each other than the horses. They don't tell tales."

"You're probably right." He walked with her to her truck. "You know what to do?"

"I do."

"Then let's go."

She climbed into the cab, maneuvered a tight U-turn, then headed back up Narcoossee Road toward the airport. She took Boggy Creek instead of the toll road to avoid any record of the vehicle going through a toll plaza, any photos of her driving the truck. Tucker, as arranged, followed her, far enough behind that no one would suspect they were caravanning. After driving several miles, she turned onto the access road leading to Orlando International Airport while he made a loop around the airport toward the cluster of hotels on the northern side.

After Sandy-Lynne parked in OIA's long-term garage, she slid the truck's key above the visor and left the door unlocked. It was doubtful the vehicle would be stolen, but she'd make it easy for anyone who tried. Another way to possibly cover her tracks.

Rolling her medium-sized suitcase behind her, she entered an elevator that took her to an underground passageway. The wide corridor ran under the traffic lanes to escalators and another bank of elevators.

Sandy-Lynne stepped on the escalator leading to baggage claim. From there, she exited the terminal and took the shuttle for the nearest Embassy Suites. She'd have preferred for Tucker to pick her up in the Arriving Passengers lane. But he was afraid the dilapidated trailer would stand out too much, that someone would remember it. He wouldn't take that chance.

For his part, he tried to convince her to take a cab to the hotel. But she didn't want to risk being recognized by an overly observant taxi driver. Of course, there was the same danger with the shuttle driver. But at least she wasn't the only one getting on and off the van. Hopefully, her face would blur with all the other faces the driver had seen during his shift.

At the hotel, Sandy-Lynne wandered into the vestibule. The sole desk clerk was checking in a family of five while two other couples waited their turn. She nonchalantly walked toward the atrium then took a side corridor to another exit. Tucker waited for her at the far end of the hotel's parking lot.

She wanted to run across the asphalt, to the safety of his truck. The closer she got, the more frightened she became, as if someone or something would snatch her away before she could climb inside the cab. Unable to keep up the pretense of a hotel guest heading to her vehicle any longer, she ran the last fifty feet, dragging the suitcase behind her.

Tucker climbed out and came toward her. She practically fell into his arms. He took her by the elbow and grabbed the handle of the suitcase. "Just get in," he said, his voice gruff.

Nerves. They were both a bundle of nerves.

She hoisted herself into the passenger seat while he put her suitcase in the rear seat. By the time he climbed behind the wheel, she had fastened her seatbelt and was leaning against the headrest, eyes closed, breath ragged.

"This is the home stretch," he said as he started the engine. "Mickey is never going to find us."

"He won't," she said with more confidence than she felt. After all, wasn't there a saying that every criminal makes at least one mistake? What had been theirs?

They'd tossed their cellphones. Avoided tolls. Had left no records for anyone to find or trace. Tucker had even disabled the GPS navigation system on his truck.

They had cash and wouldn't be using credit cards. They'd told no one of their plans, though Tucker had left a brief note for his son saying he'd gone out of town for a few days and not to worry. Nothing more than that. He'd thought it best if Adam could honestly say he didn't know where his father had gone. In case the wrong people asked.

But Sandy-Lynne knew it grated on him—the knowledge that Adam would worry anyway. That he wouldn't understand why his father had mysteriously disappeared. Tucker had his own reasons, besides protecting his son from the likes of Mickey Nolan for helping Sandy-Lynne.

She felt sorry for him because of that. Tucker was a good man. But he'd lost his way after his wife's death a few years ago. In a strange twist of fate, Tucker believed that helping her rescue Mischief would revive the good man inside of himself again. He didn't seem to realize the "good man" was still there. She'd known that from the first time they met.

But whatever Tucker's motives, she was grateful for his help. Grateful that Mischief wouldn't be racing in the Golden Citrus Race. Grateful Tucker had found a place to hide him from her husband.

PART III

CHAPTER 6

Tuesday Afternoon

After leaving the Dogwood Diner, Chaney aimlessly wandered Orlando's downtown streets. The fuel gauge on her vehicle, an unclaimed and ancient Ford Focus that Marshall had hustled from an impound lot, was close to empty. Since she was low on cash, she'd opted to leave the mustard yellow car, nicknamed The Sting, at home. With its black racing stripes, the Focus resembled a bumblebee, but the nickname was also inspired by the Paul Newman/Robert Redford movie she and Marshall had seen a zillion times growing up.

Besides, she never minded walking. Sometimes she ran into someone who needed a reminder to watch his wallet. She still needed to find such a person, but Special Agent Grant's appearance at the diner had her hightailing it away from the upscale hotel she'd been eying.

She wasn't surprised when she ended up at Lake Eola. The park, a sparkling oasis in the heart of downtown Orlando, was one of her favorite places. She and Marshall had discovered the lake shortly before Christmas a year ago. Despite temperatures that day that hovered around forty degrees, she'd persuaded him to rent one of the swan-shaped paddle boats. The air felt even colder on the lake, but Chaney hadn't minded. She loved being out on the water. Later, they had sat near the lake's edge, reminiscing about childhood Christmases—only the happy ones—while a pair of black-necked swans swam nearby.

She'd come here often since then, sometimes with Marshall and sometimes alone. She liked the park best when it was quiet, like today, with hardly anyone around. But she found it more profitable to come when multiple activities were going on—plays, musical performances, 5K races, non-profit events, art shows.

People enjoying a day at the park could be amazingly careless with their cash.

Chaney sat on a bench and stared at the multi-million-dollar fountain shooting a geyser high into the air. The encounter with Benjamin Grant had bothered her more than she wanted to admit. The agent's assumption was correct. Marshall sat in jail because of her.

Despite the warmth of the sun, she shivered. Marshall had sacrificed his freedom to protect her from her own demons. They'd always stood up for each other, even before their families' unconventional lives finally failed them. But the cost had never been this high.

Cousins who shared the same birthday, like twins, she and Marshall had napped together, played together, and learned the tricks of the grifting trade together. According to family lore, they'd even had their own toddler language that no one else could understand.

Their growing up years had been a hopscotch of living with various relatives and in foster homes. They were usually together in their younger years, but more often apart as they grew older. It didn't matter. They always managed to stay in touch. To be each other's best friend.

When Special Agent Grant had her in his sights, Marshall took the fall. Now she needed to help him. If only the judge had granted bail. Then, as soon as she found the cash to post it, they could have disappeared. But that's exactly why bail wasn't set. Everyone knew Marshall Jacobsen was a flight risk. The public defender was an incompetent idiot, but there was little he could have done to persuade the judge any different.

She'd been to the Thirty-Third Street Jail to visit her cousin on two occasions, both times disguised as a brunette and with a false identity, but he had refused to see her. That stung, and she couldn't understand his refusal.

How could she apologize if he didn't give her the chance? How could she know what to do without knowing his plan?

Because the one thing she could count on in this mess was that Marshall had a plan. He *always* had a plan.

She couldn't give up. Not yet. She had to reassure him that she would find a way to hire a good lawyer, one who could either get him out on bail or properly defend him during the trial. In case that didn't work, she needed to find a way to get him out. The Orange County jail wasn't a maximum-security prison. Sure, there were guards and security procedures, but she'd figure out something.

No time like the present.

Her mind made up, she entered the nearby public restroom as a blonde wearing a beige tee over capris and emerged a few minutes later as a brunette wearing a fitted jacket over a tank top. Only her shoes, a pair of stylish Sketchers, were the same.

Marshall often joked that her backpack was as magical as Mary Poppins' carpet bag or Hermione Granger's beaded bag, the one with the Undetectable Extension Charm. More than once he'd asked Chaney to pull the Sword of Gryffindor from it. Though right now, she'd prefer Harry Potter's Invisibility Cloak. That would get her past all the guards to Marshall's cell and the two of them back out again.

Then they could leave Orlando behind and go someplace new. Make a fresh start.

Again.

CHAPTER 7

***T**uesday Afternoon*
Adam stayed in his seat at the Dogwood Diner after Pete left him. Gail brought him a fresh glass of iced tea, flashed her rings, and asked if he needed anything.

Yeah, a new heart. A new purpose. A new everything.

Since he couldn't give her an honest answer, he told her he was fine. Then he started to read the cover letter explaining the board's sudden decision. But he couldn't finish it. The words blurred together as an unexpected tingling burned his eyes.

Get a grip, Thorne.

He'd fielded the questions surrounding his father's mysterious disappearance as if Dad's sudden absence was normal when it was the most inexplicable thing the man had ever done. Neither had Adam shed a tear—though he'd come close—when Piper returned her extravagant engagement ring.

So why would he snivel like a baby over getting fired?

Maybe because the supposed reason didn't make any sense. But then neither did his dad's cryptic note telling him not to worry or his fiancée's—make that ex-fiancée's—tearful good-bye.

He closed the folder and, seeking a ray of hope, gazed heavenward. At the diner's dingy, faded, aqua-painted ceiling. Hardly the view for someone desperate for God's understanding of the crazy turn of events his life had taken over the past couple of weeks.

Even though Pete had paid the bill and then some, Adam took a last sip of his tea then placed a couple of ones on the table. After he reached his car, a sporty Dodge Charger with a sunroof, parked about half a block from the diner, he sat inside, frozen, the key in the ignition, ready to crank the engine.

Where was he supposed to go? His office?

He needed to pack his books, his ordination certificate, his personal items. But Pete had practically forbidden him to go there until the workday ended. Just as well. The ministry staff would ask questions he didn't know how to answer, and his grandmotherly secretary might dissolve in a puddle of tears. She always did when something unexpected happened.

He wasn't ready to face their compassion. Or their pity.

Should he go home? Not yet.

He'd allowed Piper to add too many of her own personal touches to the place. Cutesy decorative pillows on the leather sofa. Colorful towels in the kitchen and bathroom. A few knickknacks here and there. All in preparation for her moving in after the wedding.

More packing up he needed to do.

Sweat pooled beneath his collar. He turned the key and leaned toward the vents as the a/c gusted cold air into the stuffy interior.

Without giving it much thought, he drove to Lake Eola. Two or three times a month, he and Piper came here after church for the Sunday Farmer's Market. Sometimes they ate lunch at one of the nearby restaurants or at one of the food trucks before exploring what the vendors had to offer. For him, it had been a relaxing way to unwind after a stressful week and all the activities involved with a Sunday morning church service.

No matter what month it was, the weather always seemed gorgeous on Sundays, as if God especially blessed His day of rest. Sure, it might be chilly enough to wear a jacket in January and so hot in July he changed from his suit into shorts before leaving the church, but he and Piper always enjoyed being outside, taking their time at the various stalls and even getting to know a few of the regulars.

He hadn't been to the lake since she dumped him.

But when a man wanted to brood, wanted to feel the cuts that had slashed his soul, didn't it make sense to go someplace meaningful? To crash through the memories and use the broken shards to cut out his heart?

He left his Charger and wandered to the sidewalk surrounding the lake. Jacob Summerlin, a cattle rancher known as the King of the Cracker Cow Hunters, had donated the land to the city over a century ago. The park was named for Summerlin's girlfriend who died before they could marry.

Another reason Lake Eola was the perfect place to wallow in self-pity.

When Adam got to the Walt Disney amphitheater, he plopped into one of the seats. Usually some kind of performance occurred here on the weekends. But not so often in the middle of the day in the middle of the week. Now the park was blessedly quiet with only a few people around.

Adam needed a plan, but his mind resisted coming up with one. If only he'd known the board's decision a month ago, he might not have moved from his condo. But all the circumstances, all the usual obstacles to transferring property, had fallen into place as if God was behind the scenes orchestrating all the necessary details to provide him and Piper the perfect home.

His condo had sold for more than he anticipated within days

of being listed. That was the most significant detail. But other things had happened, too, leading him to believe that, yes, this was God's plan for them. They'd be married in a few months. He'd be preaching at the church for years to come. And life would be perfect.

Piper had been so delighted the day he moved into the bungalow, and he'd been delighted by her delight. They'd hung a calendar on the kitchen wall so they could count off the days until she moved in, too.

He still hadn't taken it down though the crossed-off days pained him every time he looked at them.

A movement caught his attention—someone strolling along the sidewalk. He narrowed his eyes behind his dark sunglasses. The woman's back was to him, but he could swear she was the same girl who had waggled her fingers at him through the window at the Dogwood Diner. Same short hair. Same clothing. Same easygoing walk as if she wasn't in a hurry. Yet there was purpose in her stride.

If she noticed him, would she think he had followed her?

Great! Just what he needed. Some crazy stalker accusation.

He tracked her movements as she entered the public restroom. This would be a good time for him to leave, before she came out again. But he didn't seem to have the willpower to move. He leaned forward, legs apart and hands clasped, head bent. Someone seeing him might think he was praying. And maybe he was.

He couldn't figure out how he had been so wrong about the two most important areas of his life—his upcoming marriage and his career. How could everything that had seemed so perfect turn out to be so ... not?

And then there was Dad. Adam found it hard to admit his father, a respected veterinarian, had anything to do with the missing racehorse. But the timing was too coincidental for Adam not to wonder about his dad's possible involvement.

Though Tucker's clinic specialized in household pets, he'd also worked for a few owners at the racetrack for two or three years now. What started as a part-time gig seemed to take much of his father's time. The clinic no longer accepted new patients nor replaced staff members who quit.

"Where are you, Dad?" Adam sighed heavily as he gazed at the swan boats on the lake. He couldn't begin to count the number of times he and Piper had rented one of those boats. Their tradition. He picked up a loose stone at his feet and flung it, though he was too far from the shore to hit the water. He shook his head, preferring to think of his dad than his lost love.

A girl came out of the restroom. A brunette wearing a jacket. But with the same walk as the blonde, the same backpack slung over her shoulder as the girl from the Dogwood Diner.

How strange.

Stranger still if she caught him spying on her. He clasped his hands behind his head and lowered his head between his knees. If she noticed him, perhaps she wouldn't recognize him as the man who'd stared through the diner window at her. He slowly counted to a hundred while musing over his conversation with the women who had been robbed.

Adam had stopped at their table on the way to his car. The younger woman was almost in tears as she showed him the photo inside the locket. Her grandparents, she told him. Both gone now.

When Adam reached one hundred, he lifted his eyes. The girl had disappeared.

Time for him to leave, too. As he returned to his Charger, he reviewed his options. They weren't much different than before he drove to the lake. He still needed to pack his office. Still needed to sign the board's paperwork.

As he drove along Robinson Street, he noticed a sign for an attorney who advertised heavily on the local television and radio stations. Maybe he should have a lawyer look over the papers Pete had given him. They'd been drawn up by a lawyer representing the church. Who knew what kind of fancy language had been included that Adam wouldn't understand?

Adam hated the idea of seeking legal counsel for what should be a private matter between him and the board. But the board had taken action without giving him the slightest hint of their intentions. Only a month ago, they'd all praised him for the work he was doing with the teen mentoring program and the homeless shelter. A few short weeks later, they were ready to vilify him and not allowing him the opportunity to say goodbye. As if he were a thief or something worse. That was what got him the most.

He wouldn't go to the attorney whose face was plastered on billboards, but it seemed prudent to know exactly what he was agreeing to before he signed the papers. He turned at the next block then made his way to the interstate. Hopefully he'd catch Isaac Kinsley, his dad's long-ago college roommate and now a law professor at Rollins College, during office hours. At least the drive gave him something to do. Somewhere to go since he couldn't go back to his office.

CHAPTER 8

Tuesday Afternoon

Because of the distance, Chaney had no choice but to take a bus to the Thirty-Third Street Jail. When she arrived, she took a seat on an outside bench and stared at the imposing Orange County Corrections building. Marshall was somewhere inside there, locked in a cage with no way to escape. Her chest constricted at the thought, and she took deep breaths to stave off her rising panic. And to gather her courage to go inside. She'd gone through the same mental preparations the other two times she'd been here. First, she needed to walk through the large double doors.

One step at a time.

Her feet didn't move.

The sliding doors to the entrance opened and a well-dressed man carrying a briefcase exited. The same man who had hired Marshall to dig up information about that veterinarian suspected of stealing Mickey Nolan's horse. Chaney hadn't met him—Marshall didn't want her involved with the mobster. But she hadn't liked the idea of Marshall being involved with Nolan either. She had followed him to the meet. Even taken photos.

Maybe Nolan had sent his attorney—Fletcher Wilkes was his name—to help Marshall. If so, then he could convince the judge to reverse his decision about setting bail.

As the attorney neared her, she stood. "Excuse me. Haven't we met before?"

The question appeared to catch him off-guard. He avoided eye contact and frowned. "I don't believe so. Now, if you'll excuse me."

She brushed her hand against his jacket sleeve. "Are you sure, Mr. Wilkes? Were you perhaps visiting a friend of mine? In there?" She tilted her head toward the jail entrance.

That caught his attention. The frown softened as he met her gaze. "What is your friend's name?"

She hesitated to answer in case she was wrong. But she had helped Marshall with a background search on Fletcher Wilkes, Esquire. Mickey Nolan wasn't his only client, but he only represented those associated with his client. Like Marshall.

"His initials are M.J."

Wilkes's expression transformed into a cautious smile. "By any chance, are you Marshall Jacobsen's cousin?"

Relief washed through her. Marshall must have told him about her. "Did you see him? How is he? Is he doing okay, does he need anything?"

"He's doing as well as can be expected in such circumstances." Wilkes's eyes narrowed. "Haven't you seen him?"

"I'm going in there now." She didn't want to admit that Marshall refused to see her. "It's complicated."

"Have you talked to him?"

"Not since his arraignment."

"I see." His smile widened and his shoulders relaxed. "I must say I'm glad you stopped me, Ms....?"

"I'm Chaney. Chaney Rose." She wanted to shake his hand. Maybe even hug him. Instead she squeezed her fingers while bouncing on her toes.

"I'm extremely pleased to meet you in person." Wilkes gestured toward the bench and they both sat down. "I have an important matter to discuss with you. About a racehorse."

"Marshall told me about him."

"Mr. Jacobsen did not complete his contract." Sympathy softened his expression but not his unflinching tone.

The weight of the accusation pressed against Chaney's shoulders. "He couldn't," she stammered. "He got arrested."

"The problem is, Ms. Rose," Wilkes continued, "he was paid to do something that he didn't do."

He paused, as if waiting for her to fill in the obvious blanks. She could imagine him in a courtroom, his forceful words commanding a jury's attention.

"Do you want a refund?" As if that was happening. Any money she scrounged up was for Marshall's defense, not to pay back a lowlife like Mickey Nolan.

Wilkes's eyes flashed with amusement, but his voice remained resolute. "We want to find the horse."

"I see." Though she didn't. Marshall hadn't found any indication that the veterinarian he'd been told to investigate was involved with the horse's disappearance. Only the timing made him a suspect.

Wilkes smiled again. The polite smile of a salesman about to make a pitch. "I spoke to Mr. Jacobsen about asking you to fulfill the contract. Are you interested in such a proposition?"

Chaney studied his expression, the creases around his eyes and his mouth. The man's insincerity hung between them, a dense and palpable haze. She cloaked herself in a persona of innocence. "What did Marshall say?"

"What do you think he said?"

"Mr. Wilkes, why do I get the feeling you're being evasive?" She playfully tapped his arm. "I think he said no."

Wilkes chuckled as if embarrassed she'd called him out on

his deceit. "Perhaps Marshall doesn't believe you can do what he couldn't."

"Perhaps he doesn't want me involved with your client."

"He might have mentioned that, too."

Chaney focused on the doors to the complex, her thoughts whirling with the ramifications of Wilkes's proposal and his admission of Marshall's objection. If she hadn't been here—hadn't run into Wilkes—she might never have known of this opportunity. Surely their accidental meeting was a sign that she was meant to finish the job. But only on her terms.

"Will you represent Marshall?" she asked. "He needs a good lawyer."

"Of course," he said, as if that was a given. "That is, as long as this other matter can be satisfactorily resolved."

Relief mingled with excitement as her shoulders relaxed, finally freed from the heaviest of her worries. "I'll do it."

Wilkes arched an eyebrow. "You don't need time to think it over? Perhaps talk to your cousin and get his advice?"

What was there to think about? This was her chance—her best chance—to help Marshall. He might not like it, but she couldn't stand by and do nothing while he sat in that jail cell. Especially not when she could have been there instead.

Fear, as cold as death, threatened to paralyze her at the thought of imprisonment. She wrapped her arms around herself. "I'm more than capable of making my own decisions," she said, pushing away the fear. "And I can find Mr. Nolan's horse."

"Very good, very good."

Chaney listened carefully while Wilkes told her what he knew about the veterinarian. It wasn't much. Nolan had fired Tucker Thorne when he refused to clear Mischief for a race. A couple weeks later, the horse had been slated to race in the Golden Citrus. But on the morning of the race, his stall was empty. Both Mrs. Nolan and the veterinarian had also disappeared. Wilkes told her what Marshall had discovered—what she already knew—that Dr. Thorne's clinic staff thought he was attending a conference that didn't exist.

Wilkes consulted a file from his briefcase and jotted a note on a piece of paper. "This is Dr. Thorne's home address. Perhaps you'll find something helpful there. And that's my cell number. Call me anytime with whatever information you have. I'll expect regular updates."

She read the note and also between the lines. If she didn't find the missing doctor, both she and Marshall would be in trouble with Wilkes. Worse, they'd be in trouble with Mickey Nolan.

"I understand."

"Good." He pulled a money clip from an inner pocket of his suit jacket and handed her several bills. "To ensure you understand you're in Mr. Nolan's employ."

She avoided the temptation to count the money in front of him. "Thank you, Mr. Wilkes."

"Thank you, Ms. Rose. I look forward to hearing from you very soon."

He left her sitting on the bench, her mind already involved in plotting a course of action. First, computer reconnaissance. Looking up the address online. Familiarizing herself with the lay of the land. Then a drive-by. She needed to see how security-conscious the vet was ... did he have an alarm? A dog?

Better the former than the latter. Though if he had a dog, would he have left it behind? Probably not.

She glanced in the direction Wilkes had gone. He was out of sight, so she discreetly counted the money. Three hundred dollars. Not a lot but enough to splurge on something besides a fast food dollar menu.

After tucking half the money in her pants pocket and the other half inside her backpack, she faced the entrance doors. Maybe this wasn't a good time to see Marshall. He'd only get mad when—if—she told him about her conversation with Wilkes. She'd wait till after she finished the job. Then it'd be too late for him to get angry. And Wilkes would either get bail set or he'd defend Marshall at the trial. Either way, eventually her cousin would be free.

Maybe then, she'd be free of the guilt she carried. She could only hope.

CHAPTER 9

Tuesday Afternoon

Special Agent Benjamin Grant popped the top of a soda can and set it before Marshall Jacobsen. "Heard you're partial to root beer. I'm a Dr. Pepper man myself." It wasn't true. He preferred his mother's sweet tea to just about anything else. No one made tea like his mama. That's why he usually ordered an Arnold Palmer—iced tea combined with lemonade—when he was eating out.

"Where did you hear that?" Marshall's face might have been set in stone considering his lack of expression. He eyed the soda but didn't touch it.

"Around." Benjamin lowered himself into the metal chair and clasped his hands on the table. "You wanted to see me."

The muscle in Marshall's jaw twitched. He was a cagey one. Benjamin had been surprised to get the call from the jail's administrative office asking him to stop by. He'd guessed that Chaney had visited her cousin, tattled on Benjamin for pestering her at the Dogwood Diner, and now Marshall planned to chew him out. Or maybe, if Benjamin was lucky, Marshall would give him more information about his attempted art heist in exchange for a promise to leave Chaney alone.

But Benjamin had checked the visitor call log when he arrived. Marshall's only visitor since his arraignment had been the public defender, no surprise there, and Fletcher Wilkes who'd been there only an hour before. That had been a surprise. If Wilkes had been here, that meant Marshall was somehow mixed up with Mickey Nolan.

Was Nolan behind the heist?

Benjamin wouldn't have thought so, but stranger things happened in the criminal world.

Tired of Marshall's silence, Benjamin rapped the table with his knuckles. "I hope you didn't bring me all the way down here to look into your baby blues."

Marshall glared at him then turned away. A spider crawling up the institutional green wall seemed to hold his undivided attention.

Benjamin folded his arms and rocked back on the chair's rear legs. He could wait as long as Marshall wanted, or until five o'clock, whichever came first. That's when he transformed into super-dad and took off to coach his daughter's soccer team.

Marshall grasped the soda can and took a long swallow. "Tastes good. Thanks."

"You're welcome."

"Do you know Fletcher Wilkes?"

"I've heard of him."

"He seems to think I owe him money." Marshall shrugged one shoulder. "Not him, but one of his clients."

"Wilkes only has one client. At least only one who matters."

"Okay. So he thinks I owe his only-client-who-matters money."

"Do you?"

Marshall glanced at the spider again then tapped his fingers on the side of the soda can. "He asked me to gather information for him. But there wasn't anything to find."

"Is this about Mickey Nolan's missing racehorse?" Benjamin leaned forward. As far as he knew, Nolan hadn't filed any criminal charges against his much younger wife for taking off with the animal. But news of the disappearance had made for interesting conversation around the proverbial water cooler.

Benjamin didn't care about Nolan's domestic troubles, but Marshall wouldn't have called him down here without a good reason. And Benjamin cared about that.

"He said I didn't finish the job." Marshall's eyes lost their deadpan expression. "Since I'm in here, he wants my cousin to do it."

Benjamin hid his surprise. At least he hoped he did. Marshall had a known talent for reading people. But this was a development Benjamin hadn't anticipated. He feigned disinterest. "You mean, the same cousin who also belongs in a cell?"

"You've got nothing on her."

Benjamin had heard variations of that protest countless times, often shouted, always defensive. But Marshall's tone was almost light-hearted. Definitely confident. Unfortunately for Benjamin, he was also right.

"Only because of your arrest." Benjamin stared at him, hoping to intimidate him into an admission of Chaney's guilt. But Marshall pressed his lips together. For reasons Benjamin couldn't imagine, Marshall planned to take the fall for his cousin's crime. Worse, she was going to let him.

Benjamin followed Marshall's gaze to the spider. It reached the top of the wall and veered toward the corner. Wispy strands of a disturbed web clung to the ceiling.

"Don't let her do it."

Marshall spoke so low Benjamin wasn't sure he'd heard him right. He tilted his head. "Say again."

"Don't let her get involved with Wilkes." Marshall focused on the spider, his fingers tapping the can. "With Nolan."

"How do you propose I stop her?"

Marshall jerked his attention to Benjamin. "Talk to her," he pleaded. "Tell her how dangerous Nolan is."

"Do you think they're more dangerous than that crew she's hanging with? The one leaving you in here like some kind of scapegoat?"

"It's not like that." Marshall sounded like a stubborn two-year-old. Irritation had replaced the hopeful pleading Benjamin had seen in his eyes only a moment before.

"It's exactly like that. And I'm not your go-between." Benjamin's patience had reached its limit. "You call me down here to do you a favor, but you don't have the courtesy, the respect, to be honest with me. That's not how things work around here."

"Just talk to her, man." Frustration now edged Marshall's tone. "That's all I'm asking you to do."

"I already talked to her." Benjamin stood then pressed his hands flat against the table as he leaned forward. "Even saw her in action."

Marshall's eyes grew wide, but he didn't say anything. Never any trash-talk from this one. Benjamin couldn't help but admire his self-control. "She turned the tables on a pickpocket. Returned the stolen goods to the victims and handed me the scumbag's wallet and cellphone. We've already picked him up and booked him."

Pride.

Benjamin could read people, too, and Marshall exuded, of all things, *pride*. Because Chaney had outsmarted the scumbag or because she'd done a good deed? What was it with these two?

Marshall sat back in his chair, shoulders relaxed, fingers no longer tapping the can. "Sounds like you owe her one."

"She doesn't like me." Benjamin flipped his hand in a *there's nothing I can do* gesture. "She won't listen to me."

Marshall smiled, a small one, but still a smile. "She doesn't always listen to me either."

Benjamin guessed if she had that Marshall wouldn't be in this mess.

For the first time since Benjamin had Marshall on his radar, the young man appeared vulnerable. He obviously cared about his cousin's welfare. But it was all kinds of wrong for him to take her punishment. Maybe it was part of their grifter's code. Or some pact the two of them had with one another.

"Why hasn't she come to see you?"

"She has."

Benjamin's suspicion antennae went on full alert. How could she have managed to sneak in? "According to the logs, no one's visited you. Other than the attorneys."

"I refused to see her."

The antennae receded. But only a little. At least he didn't need to request a full-on security check of the jail. "Why would you do that?"

Marshall seemed to shrink into himself then he lifted his cuffed hands as far as the short chain would let him and pulled at his orange jumpsuit. "You think I want her to see me wearing this? I don't think so."

"She's your family, Jacobsen. She doesn't care what you're wearing."

"I care."

Most men would have shouted the words, yanked at the chain, created a scene. Somehow Marshall's quiet declaration seemed to have more potency, more poignancy, than a loud outburst.

Benjamin glanced at his watch and returned to his seat. He had a few more minutes before heading to the soccer fields. "That's your ego talking."

"Maybe." Marshall met his gaze. "Right now, that's about all I've got."

His hopeless demeanor touched a soft spot in Benjamin's calloused heart. Who was he kidding? His heart had never turned to cynical stone despite all the worst-of-humanity that he witnessed. For one thing, his wife wouldn't allow it, and he'd do just about anything to keep her happy.

"What's Chaney's address?"

"Don't know."

"Come on, Jacobsen. If you want me to talk to her, I have to know how to find her." Despite what he'd indicated to Chaney, seeing her earlier today had been dumb luck. He didn't have the resources to tail her 24/7. Nor the legal authority.

"She'd have moved as soon as she heard I got arrested. That's protocol."

"Grifters have a protocol?" Benjamin shook his head. "Of course they do."

"There has to be a way for you to find her. Where did she pick the pickpocket's pocket?" Marshall grinned, apparently amused by the wordplay. Benjamin was too, but not enough to show it.

"Downtown at the Dogwood Diner." He could alliterate too. "She was reading a book. *Grimm's Fairy Tales*. Looked like it had been read a few times before."

Benjamin didn't know what kind of reaction he'd hoped to get from Marshall by telling him of Chaney's reading choice. Maybe to learn that it was her favorite book or perhaps even surprise that she wasn't reading something more contemporary. But Marshall's expression didn't change. The look in his eyes didn't soften. He didn't show any interest.

"Find her," he said, more as a demand than a request. As if he were in any position to demand anything. Then his tone shifted. "But don't arrest her, okay?"

"Come on, Jacobsen," Benjamin scoffed. "If I catch her in

possession of something that doesn't belong to her, I'm going to arrest her. If she spits on the sidewalk, I'm going to arrest her. If she's chewing gum, I'm going to pretend this is Singapore, and I'm going to arrest her."

For the first time, Marshall seemed to flinch. The careful persona of the person who didn't lose control of his emotions slipped. "You can't do that," he said, defiance in his voice.

"Watch me."

Marshall raised his eyes to the ceiling, and his Adam's apple bobbed in his throat. Benjamin glanced at the round clock hung high on the wall. Five more minutes and then he needed to go. The red second hand clicked from one tick mark to the next. To another. To another.

Marshall took a deep breath and stared at Benjamin. Again his expression was veiled. "I don't expect you to understand. But I hoped you would want to do the right thing." He stood without shifting his gaze then raised his voice to call the guard. "We're finished here."

I'm being dismissed. Benjamin wasn't sure whether to be put out or impressed. He pushed back his chair and rose to his feet.

"I need a starting place," he said. "Unless you want me to put out a BOLO on her." A request for other officers to be on the lookout.

"You sure you want to do that?" Marshall actually smiled, though if Benjamin had blinked, he would have missed it. "Only if you want to drive her further underground. Though maybe that would be a good idea."

"Is that what you want?"

Marshall bent his head and his shoulders sagged. "We have an apartment. But she won't stay there."

"Your intake paperwork said you were homeless."

"A little white lie."

The guard entered and paused in the doorway. Benjamin

glanced at him then turned back to Marshall. "I'll see what I can do," he said. "What's the address?"

Marshall told him the name of the complex and the apartment number. "We also have a car. A fifteen-year-old Ford Focus."

"Not according to the DMV." Benjamin held up his hand. "I get it. The vehicle is registered in someone else's name."

"Maybe."

"Stolen?"

"Borrowed."

Benjamin emitted a skeptical huff. "Right."

"I'm telling you the truth, man."

Benjamin almost believed him. After all, Marshall wouldn't take a chance on Chaney being arrested for driving a stolen vehicle. He wrote down the license plate number so he could ask the patrol units near the apartment complex to keep an eye out for it.

After his daughter's soccer practice, maybe he'd drive there himself and hang around for a while to see if Chaney showed up.

He slid his memo pad into his pocket.

"Thank you," Marshall said softly.

Surprised, Benjamin glanced at him, but Marshall had his head down. Benjamin waited a beat, but he didn't move. Benjamin signaled to the guard and stayed in the room until Marshall was gone. He wasn't sure what he had expected. Maybe a final word. But Marshall hadn't even looked at Benjamin again.

Benjamin bit the inside of his cheek and shook his head. The kid was a twenty-something scumbag who was right where he needed to be. He'd probably spend most of his life in and out of one merry-go-round jail after another. But somehow he inspired a strange kind of respect.

Which made it harder to write him off as a scumbag.

CHAPTER 10

Tuesday Evening

Chaney parked The Sting, now with a full tank of gas thanks to Wilkes's money, near the entrance to an urban park located across the street from the one-story bungalow with its wide front porch. The neighborhood, north of Orlando's downtown area, was an older one with tree-lined sidewalks and no two houses the same. Much different than the newer cookie-cutter subdivisions on the outskirts of the city where bulldozers cleared the land of almost every tree as if the developer got a bounty on each one chopped into mulch.

Maybe he did.

Chaney preferred these older neighborhoods to the newer subdivisions. She loved driving along their shady streets, and she loved walking through them, even when the roots of a tree buckled the sidewalk or a branch hung so low she had to duck to get past it.

Dr. Thorne's house was similar to the one in the magazine picture she'd held onto since she was twelve, the folded one she had hidden in a secret pocket of her billfold. She dreamed of living in a home like that someday, if she was ever lucky enough to have a house of her own.

Marshall teased her about the photo, but he had the same longing she did for a home. Something more permanent than a pay-by-the-week motel room or a squatter's corner in an abandoned building.

She'd come here from their current place, a cheap second-floor apartment in a seedier part of town. Though Marshall had paid this month's rent, Chaney was leery of staying there any longer. Especially after Grant surprised her at the diner. Everything she and Marshall owned, which wasn't much, was in The Sting's trunk.

While she waited for darkness to descend and the streetlamps to come on, a few of the neighbors had returned home. They parked in their driveways or on the street, yet no one seemed to notice her. She wasn't surprised. A small grocery store on the corner near the park and a few other shops around the next block meant the residents were probably used to strange cars parking here.

A light came on in the front room of the bungalow, but Chaney was confident that it was on a timer. There had been no activity inside or outside the house, no shadows appearing in windows, and no other lights.

She waited another twenty minutes then drove around to the other side of the park and pulled into the empty graveled lot she'd scoped out earlier. As she slid from The Sting, she pulled the hood of her dark sweatshirt over her hair. With her leather cross-body bag situated at her hip and her hands in her pockets, she sauntered along the winding path leading through the park from this entrance to the one across from Dr. Thorne's home.

The same light as before shone in the bungalow's window. She jaywalked toward a neighbor's house then slipped around to the side. Hidden in the shadows between the bungalow and its neighbor, she squatted against the stucco wall and paused to listen.

She'd been trained to heighten her senses in such circumstances, to listen to the softest sounds, to be aware of the direction of the slightest breeze. To pay attention to tingling nerves or sudden impulses because a person's body often realized danger before the mind comprehended it. That's why her grandfather had raised her—whenever she was in the family's custody—to hone her instincts and to trust them.

Nothing seemed out of the ordinary, so she stood and, with her back against the wall, sidestepped to the back corner. A chain link fence, bordered by a thick hedge, surrounded the yard, but the gate was unlocked. A screened deck enclosed a rectangular swimming pool and a squat pool house. The detached two-car garage stood outside the fence. Two huge trees, adorned with Spanish moss, spread their thick branches over the well-tended yard.

Chaney tested the door to the screened porch. Not surprisingly, it wasn't latched. They seldom were. She skirted inside, bent low as she passed beneath a window, then reached the sliding glass door. The vertical blinds were open, and she peered inside to the kitchen dining area.

After picking the lock, she took a deep breath, then inched open the door. The lamp in the living room window provided little light, but her eyes were accustomed to the dark. In the kitchen, light glowed over the stove and from a plug-in nightlight near the sink. She turned on her phone's flashlight to explore the rest of the house.

In the living room, a huge television, surrounded by built-in shelves, hung from a wall. Below the television sat an entertainment center that held various gaming consoles behind glass doors.

Odd for a veterinarian nearing sixty, but to each his own. She had researched Dr. Tucker Thorne on her phone before driving to the park. He had lived in Orlando all of his life, was widowed, had one adult son—a minister—but no grandchildren.

She picked up a framed photo from one of the shelves that showed a good-looking man, probably close to thirty and sporting a trendy goatee, with his arm around an attractive brunette. Her hand rested on the man's chest, allowing her to show off a gorgeous diamond ring.

Chaney let out a low whistle. The ring's quality was evident and must have cost a pretty penny or two.

So the vet's minister son was getting married. How nice.

She looked closer at the man. Something seemed familiar about him, but she didn't know why.

Another room near the front of the house, probably meant to be a dining room, was furnished as an office. A large desk sat near the center of the room with a credenza behind it. Wooden shutters hid the window, so Chaney switched on a nearby floor lamp.

Above the credenza were framed diplomas. Chaney smirked. The vet must be proud of his education. She shone her flashlight on the diploma issued by the University of Central Florida, but the name on the diploma wasn't what she expected. Instead of Tucker Thorne, it read: Adam Buchanan Thorne.

The son.

She moved her light to the second diploma. This one, from Corinth Theological Seminary, conferred upon the younger Thorne a Master of Theology degree.

She swept the narrow beam across the other walls, confused by what she'd found. Maybe the good doctor kept his degrees at his clinic. But why were Adam's degrees displayed here instead of at his own home or office?

It was puzzling, but she wasn't here to figure out the doctor's decorating choices. She sat at the desk and switched on a Tiffany-style lamp. The top of the desk was neat and orderly.

Another framed picture of the happily engaged couple sat beneath the lamp. A decorative penholder held a prominent place of honor.

She opened the laptop and typed "password" in the box. The screen remained locked. Oh, well—worth a try. She rifled through the drawers, but the items she found only added to her confusion. The checkbook belonged to Adam Thorne. The files belonged to Adam Thorne. The books on the desk, one a Biblical commentary and the other a well-worn copy of *The Adventures of Sherlock Holmes* by Sir Arthur Conan Doyle, had Adam Thorne's name on the flyleaf.

Nothing in the desk gave her any clues to where the veterinarian had gone, whether he owned property that wasn't recorded with the property appraiser or the state, or anything else about him that would help her locate him.

Chaney leaned back in the chair. Had Wilkes given her the son's address instead of the father's? Unlikely. Besides, according to the Orange County Property Appraiser's Office website, which she'd checked before coming here, this was Tucker Thorne's home. Apparently, his son lived here, too.

She picked up the photo and stared at the man smiling from it. Where had she seen him? Then it hit her. He was the man, though now clean-shaven, who had stared at her through the window at the Dogwood Diner. Though he wasn't exactly *staring*. At least not in a creepy way. No, his expression had been curious. As if he was trying to figure out what she was all about.

Maybe he had seen her with Special Agent Grant and wondered about their relationship. Hopefully he didn't think she was Grant's girlfriend. Gag!

Next, she explored the three bedrooms. One, the master, had its own private bath. The other two were separated by a bathroom that opened into the hallway. Typical layout for this type of home.

She went to the master bedroom first. But here again, she

ended up confused. Another photo of the couple was lying face-down on the dresser along with a few knick-knacks. In one dresser drawer, she found a pile of receipts and a jar almost full of change. The walk-in closet wasn't large but as tidy and neat as the rest of the house. She opened the door to a built-in cabinet and smiled. A safe sat on the floor.

The model was a familiar one and it didn't take long, using the tools she carried in her crossbody bag, to crack the combination.

Inside were stacks of papers and a couple of jewelry boxes. She opened the red box first and gasped. The engagement ring from the photograph glinted in the closet's overhead lighting.

Interesting. A broken engagement would explain why the photograph was lying on the dresser. But who had called off the wedding? Adam or the attractive brunette?

The temptation to pocket the ring was strong. If Adam's heart was broken, it could be a long time before he noticed it was missing. But then again, what if he took it out of the safe every night and wished to be reconciled to the love of his life?

Besides, what she told Special Agent Grant earlier was true. Stealing jewelry was easy but fencing it was another matter. A distinctive ring such as this one would be easily traced.

She returned it to the safe and opened the blue box. This wedding set wasn't as opulent or modern as the other one, but the diamonds on the engagement ring and matching band appeared to be good quality. Even so, it resembled thousands, if not tens of thousands, of other traditional sets. Since it wasn't engraved, ownership would be difficult to prove.

Chaney knew a pawnbroker or two who would pay a fair price without asking awkward questions. Her conscience stung as she tucked the box into her bag. Maybe because she was stealing from a minister. Was that a worse sin than robbing a regular person?

Though shouldn't a minister forgive and forget?

He might, but would God?

Even though Wilkes had promised to represent Marshall, Chaney still needed cash. She'd be a fool not to take *something*.

A third box held Pokémon cards and sports cards, each one in a protective sleeve. The son's adolescent collection or a treasure trove? She had no idea, but it wouldn't be hard to find out. The box went into her bag.

Behind the files at the back of the safe, she uncovered a money pouch containing over six hundred dollars in tens and twenties.

Jackpot!

She took the cash and returned the pouch to the safe.

The other bedrooms didn't help her at all. One, outfitted with a queen bed, a dresser, and a nightstand, had all the impersonal charm of a room in a moderately-priced hotel chain. The third looked like a storage unit.

Packed boxes. Suitcases. Odds and ends of furniture. A stationary bicycle and a treadmill.

Chaney retraced her steps, ensuring all the lights she'd turned on were off again. Back in the kitchen, she surveyed the room, hands on her hips and lips pressed together. Nothing indicated the dad lived here. Only the son. So what had happened? It wasn't that long ago that Dr. Thorne had disappeared. Had Adam already packed up his dad's stuff and moved in? Surely not.

Maybe the key to the veterinarian's disappearance was in one of the boxes in the back bedroom. But she didn't have time to go through them tonight. She'd already lingered too long.

She left the way she'd come in. As she rounded the side of the house, she paused in the shadows to assess her surroundings. The street was quiet, and lights shone in various houses. Families gathered together after a day of school and work. Eating supper. Watching television. Kids doing homework.

All the normal things that hadn't been part of her childhood.

How she had longed to have a family like some of those in the books she'd read, devouring them again and again. Like Anne Shirley who had been adopted by an old maid and her brother. Chaney wouldn't have minded living at Green Gables as long as Marilla and Matthew adopted Marshall, too.

Chaney wasn't so naïve as to believe that life was perfect within all those homes. But she hoped, even prayed as she stood there in the shadows, that they were near perfect for the children's sakes. It seemed one of the few prayers she felt comfortable saying.

After all, if she remembered right from her one stint at Sunday school, Jesus had a hissy fit when his followers turned away children. "Let them come to me," he had said, or something like that.

Ten years or more must have gone by since Chaney heard that story. What she remembered most was her sudden longing to have been one of those children who rushed into Jesus' open arms. But that was a childish wish she had long outgrown.

She stuck her hands into the pockets of her hoodie and crossed the street to the park entrance. Suddenly the whoop-whoop of a police siren spoiled the evening peace, and blinking lights cut through the darkness as two patrol cars turned onto the street.

Without hesitating a second, Chaney scurried into the park, sticking to the shadows of the trees instead of running along the path, to make her way to The Sting.

She was about halfway through the park when someone stepped from behind a thick red maple and grabbed her by the arm.

"Let me go," she said as she tried to get away.

"Not happening." Special Agent Grant pulled her into the glow of an overhead lamp lighting the path.

"You can't do this." Chaney gritted her teeth. She struggled to get away, but his grasp was too tight. She'd have bruises from his fingers, but that didn't matter as much as escaping her nemesis.

"What makes you think I can't?" Grant kept his tone even and casual as if holding a young woman captive was an everyday occurrence for him. Maybe it was, but why did she have to be the prey?

He slipped handcuffs on her wrists and did a brisk pat-down of her waist and ankles.

"I don't carry weapons."

"What do you have?" He pointed to the bag at her hip. "Mind if I look?"

"I'm not giving you permission to look through my personal belongings," she retorted. Her feisty demeanor didn't seem to faze him even the tiniest bit. Could he sense that she was quivering inside like an autumn leaf about to fall? Her heart raced and she swallowed back tears.

This was exactly what Marshall had warned her would happen if she wasn't careful. The reason he had wanted her to leave Orlando. But she couldn't leave while he was stuck in jail. Though she wasn't going to do him much good now that she'd be in a cell, too. An uncontrollable shiver raced through her body.

"Are you all right?" Grant asked with what sounded like genuine concern in his voice. But the concern had to be an act. A ploy to get her to trust him. No way would she fall for his con. He didn't care about her welfare. He only wanted another arrest to add to his resumé.

"I'm fine." She practically spat the word.

"Are you cold? I can get you a blanket."

"Don't do me any favors."

"I already am." He shifted away as he spoke, the words muttered beneath his breath, so she wasn't sure she had heard him right. Yet somehow she knew she had. "When did you talk to Fletcher Wilkes?" he asked.

The knot in her stomach turned to lead. How could he have known? She resorted to Defense Rule #1: *Deny, deny, deny.* "I don't know what you're talking about."

"Marshall wants you to stay away from him."

Grant had talked to Marshall? When? Why? The questions swirled together in an incoherent tangle. She opened her mouth, but no words came out.

Grant took her arm again but this time with a gentler hold. She had no choice but to follow along and push what he'd said about Marshall aside to think about later. For now, she needed to focus on what would happen to her when Grant searched her bag. He obviously thought he had legal grounds to do so. And—who was she kidding?—he did.

He escorted her across the street. Both patrol cars were parked near the drive and three uniformed officers roamed the property.

As Chaney and Grant neared the house, a sports car pulled into the driveway. The driver stepped out, seemingly dazed by the scene. Chaney couldn't make out his face until he walked into the pool of light cast from a nearby streetlamp.

Just her luck. The guy in the photos. The guy from the diner.

She was going to jail.

Her knees turned to water, and Grant reached to support her as she started to fall. A giant shudder swept through her as fear pressed against her chest.

"You're okay," Grant said quietly.

His voice was surprisingly gentle, not at all what she would expect from the bulldog detective. She wanted to believe him, but that was impossible. She couldn't trust anyone. Not her grandfather. Not her family. And definitely not anyone wearing a badge.

Only Marshall. And he was in no position to help her. Not this time.

Grant pulled her close to the trunk of the nearest patrol car and greeted the officers. The driver, glancing from them to his house and back again, seemed uncertain what to do, what to say. Grant motioned him over.

"What's going on?" His glance shifted to Chaney and his eyes grew wide. So he recognized her, too. "What are you doing here?"

"She's robbing you blind," Grant put in before Chaney could answer.

Not that she had anything to say. She could hardly tell him the true reason she'd been in the house which wasn't supposed to be his home.

Grant apparently caught a nuance he'd missed before. "You two know each other?"

"We've ... met." The man seemed unable to take his eyes from Chaney, and she grew uncomfortable beneath the weight of his gaze. Then he extended his hand to Grant. "I'm Adam Thorne. I live here."

"Special Agent Benjamin Grant. FDLE." He set Chaney's bag on the trunk lid and pulled out the contents. He separated a couple boxes and the cash from a wallet, cosmetic bag, and other personal items. "Do these belong to you?" he asked, pointing to the boxes and money.

Adam stared at the items, a stricken look on his face. Chaney closed her eyes and tried not to think about Grant shoving her into the rear seat of the patrol car. About getting her photo taken and her fingers printed and the rest of the humiliation so euphemistically called "process."

But she couldn't push those horrors from her mind, even though they were nothing compared to the horrors that came after—a windowless cell with iron bars that clanged shut and couldn't be opened. Once again, her knees failed her.

This time, both Grant and Adam reached out to support her.

CHAPTER 11

*T*uesday Evening

Adam spontaneously reached for the girl, a blonde again, at the same time as the detective. The man who'd been sitting with the girl at the Dogwood Diner.

Between them, they got her on her feet.

"Are you okay?" Adam asked. "Can I get you anything?"

"She's a thief," Grant said, obviously annoyed. "Not your guest."

Adam ignored Grant and focused on the girl. This close to her, he could see she wasn't really a girl but a young woman. Probably in her early twenties, maybe five or six years younger than him. Her shoulders hunched together, and she didn't want to meet his gaze. The confidence, the spark he'd seen in her earlier that day, was completely gone.

Something about seeing her now, handcuffed and frightened, panged Adam's spirit. She was like a rabbit trapped by a fox, afraid to move, unable to escape.

"Mr. Thorne." Grant regained Adam's attention.

He almost, as a reflex, corrected him. *Not mister. Pastor.* But he wasn't a pastor anymore.

"Could you please identify these items, sir?"

Adam opened the box holding his card collection. It was surreal, seeing the individual sleeves illuminated by the streetlamp when they should be tucked inside his safe. Almost as if they weren't really his but belonged to another Adam Thorne in a weird alternate universe. But that kind of thing only happened in the movies.

"Do these items belong to you, sir?" Grant asked with barely restrained patience.

Adam started to speak, but a sense of dread clogged his throat. He frowned and nodded instead.

A look of satisfaction crossed Grant's face. "Chaney Rose, you are under arrest for burglary and grand theft."

He began to recite the familiar words of the Miranda warning, but Adam held up his hand. "Wait a minute," he said, not sure himself why he felt compelled to interrupt the agent.

"What is it, sir?"

Grant was exceptionally polite, Adam had to give him that. His mind flashed to the scene he'd witnessed outside the diner, his conversation with the women from Kansas. The girl—Grant called her Chaney—had returned the locket stolen by Spike Hair. The agent had appreciated her help then. Somehow it didn't seem fair that now he wanted to arrest her.

"Even if these are mine that doesn't mean she stole them."

Grant stared but Adam refused to flinch. Somehow, that refusal to back down under the agent's menacing glare strengthened his resolve. He didn't know why he'd defended her, but he knew what he needed to do.

Somehow it seemed God had placed them in a modern-day scene from *Les Misérables*.

Adam smiled at Chaney. "I'm sorry I wasn't here when you arrived. I was at the church." No need to tell them he was cleaning out his office.

He picked up the blue jewelry box, one that had been in the

safe next to the red box holding Piper's engagement ring. He glanced over the other items scattered on the trunk, but the red box wasn't there. He glanced at Chaney, a question in his eyes. *Had she left that ring behind? Why?* It was the more valuable one.

Chaney's eyes held their own questions. *What are you doing? Why are you apologizing to me as if we're old friends?*

"This isn't the ring I meant for you to take," Adam said. "There was another. The red box. Didn't you see it?"

"Yes," Chaney kept her gaze on him, staring deep into his soul as if trying to ferret out his motives. As if wondering if he was laying a trap for her or if he meant to help. She seemed scared to trust him but even more scared not to.

"The red box. It's still in the ... in your closet."

They held the gaze a moment longer, silently sizing each other up.

This was wrong, being on the side of the thief instead of the side of the law. Yet deep inside Adam knew he was doing right by showing grace to someone in desperate need of it. "You can't arrest her. I gave her those things."

"You gave them to her?" Grant's tone was filled with disbelief. And intimidating scorn. "With all due respect, you're not the bishop from a Victor Hugo novel. And Chaney Rose isn't Jean Valjean."

Adam had been emotionally beaten up once today. He wouldn't back down again. "The cards and money are hers. But not this." He placed the blue box in his pocket. "There was another ring I meant for her to take instead."

"Mr. Thorne, this woman broke into your home."

"Only because I wasn't here. And for that, once again, I apologize. Now, please. Remove those handcuffs."

Grant released a heavy sigh then unlocked the cuffs. "Looks like this is your lucky day, Ms. Rose. You're free to go."

Chaney rubbed her wrists and tossed a grateful smile in

Adam's direction. She pushed her personal items into her bag and started across the street toward the park.

"Wait," Adam called after her. "You forgot these."

Chaney turned and stared at him. He held out the cash and box of collectible cards. "Come back tomorrow and I'll give you the other ring. Say around ten?"

Adam didn't know why those words came out of his mouth. What was he thinking, inviting this thief to his home? Promising to give her Piper's engagement ring so she could do what? Pawn it for less than half its value?

Yet his heart, which had been in a turmoil for days, was at peace.

"Please say you'll come."

"Okay," she said quietly as she put the items in her bag.

"I'll make brunch. You like pancakes?"

"I love them."

"So do I," Grant said with a snort. "You going to invite me to brunch, too?"

"Why not?" Adam said with a magnanimous smile as he looked around at the officers. "You're all invited."

When he turned to share his smile with Chaney, she was gone.

Grant followed his gaze and shook his head. "Why did you do that, Mr. Thorne?"

"Do what?"

"You and I both know what really happened here. And you're a fool if you think she'll be back in the morning."

"Maybe I am," Adam said, nodding thoughtfully. "It wouldn't be the first time and probably won't be the last."

"Let me give you a bit of advice," Grant said. "Don't be taken in by the oh-so-innocent act. Chaney Rose is a grifter who comes from a long line of grifters. She'll rob you blind and laugh while she's doing it."

And sometimes she'll give a stolen locket to the person it belongs to.

"You seem to know a lot about her." *At least you think you do.*

"I arrested her cousin a few nights ago for an attempted art theft." Grant leaned against the patrol car. "But she was the thief. Not him."

"Who's her cousin?"

"Why do you ask?"

"I'm a minister. I'd like to pray for him. For you, too, if you don't mind."

Grant straightened, put his hands on his hips, then laughed. "Well, if that don't beat all. Did you hear that, Larsen?" he said to one of the patrolmen. "Mr. Thorne here is a minister."

"Was," Adam inserted, his inherent honesty suddenly insistent on linguistical accuracy.

"What's that?" Grant asked.

"I *was* a minister. At Gateway Community Church." He gave an embarrassed shrug. "I was let go today."

"May I ask why?"

"Long story involving my dad."

"By any chance would that be Dr. Tucker Thorne, the vet?"

"The one and only."

"Do you know where he is?"

"No. Wish I did, though. I'd go get him and bring him home."

"So you get fired from your church today. And this evening you let a thief go free." Grant laughed again. "Why do I get the feeling I've been conned by a man of the cloth?"

"No con here," Adam said. Only extending the grace that he'd been denied. But he didn't feel comfortable telling that to the detective.

Surprisingly, he still felt no regret for his part in setting Chaney free. He left the detective and the other officers with their vehicles and climbed the steps to his house. Once inside, he flipped on the light and looked around. Nothing seemed out of place, nothing appeared to have been disturbed. And yet, the woman had been in here. Snooping around. Going through things that were none of her concern.

He should feel violated. Angry even. But every time he tried to envision her opening his drawers and sneaking around his house, all he saw was the comical sight of her spilling her drink on Spike Hair, of handing the locket to a very grateful woman, of giving Grant a wallet and a phone.

Who was the real Chaney Rose?

He didn't know. But he wouldn't mind finding out.

CHAPTER 12

Tuesday Evening

Chaney jogged across the park to The Sting, slid into its sanctuary, and drove away. She didn't want to take a chance on Adam Thorne changing his mind and accusing her of theft. Her shoulders still ached from her hands being in the cuffs.

She wound her way to Bumby Avenue and headed south with no solid destination in mind except to get out of Grant's jurisdiction. Though she supposed the whole state was the jurisdiction of the Florida Department of Law Enforcement. At least she could put a few miles between the two of them.

With the unexpected money she'd gotten from Wilkes and from Adam, she could splurge for a night at one of the cheaper motels along U.S. Highway 192, the long thoroughfare that ran from the Disney area through Kissimmee and St. Cloud then all the way to Melbourne and the Atlantic coast.

With that plan in mind, she hopped on the 528, also known as the Beachline, and took it to John Young Parkway. But before she got to Highway 192, she changed her mind without realizing she had changed her mind.

Adam had given her the money, but that didn't make it hers. Even if she kept it, she needed a whole lot more to help Marshall. Wilkes had paid her to find out where Dr. Thorne was hiding. She might not be able to do that without Adam's help. Or, better yet, maybe she could convince him that *he* needed *her* help. She might gain his trust by returning his money. And the other items.

She'd understood the references to Jean Valjean and the bishop. *Les Misérables* was a classic story which she'd read after seeing the highly acclaimed movie starring Hugh Jackman as the escaped convict. Valjean was imprisoned for stealing bread to feed his sister's starving children. After his escape, he stole silver candlesticks from a poor bishop. But when the *gendarmerie* marched Valjean back to the scene of the crime, the bishop said he'd given the candlesticks to the thief.

Valjean had never been the same again. Instead of a bitter convict on the run from the law, he became a man with a deep conscience who did as much good for others as he could. Even when it cost him everything.

Perhaps this Adam Thorne thought his generosity would change her. But he'd be wrong about that. She didn't need to change. All she needed was for Marshall to get out of jail. And she'd do whatever needed doing to make that happen.

With her thoughts still in a whirl over the day's events and her narrow escape from spending the night in a prison cell, she finally pulled into the crowded parking lot of a Best Western. She selected a space near the rear surrounded by other cars, several with out-of-state plates, others that were probably rentals.

She backed into the spot so she could easily drive away in a hurry if the need arose. Then she climbed into the back seat, grabbed the drive-through cheeseburger and fries she'd picked up along the way, and ate in the quiet of the night. Eventually she fell asleep, her dreams disturbed by her fears of being locked up in a dark hole with no way of escape.

CHAPTER 13

Wednesday Morning

Chaney parked in Adam's driveway but didn't immediately turn off the engine. This was a mistake. And yet something had compelled her to accept his invitation to breakfast. Maybe it was some kind of strange perverseness in her personality—he'd invited her, but he probably didn't expect her to show up. And so she would, if only to see how he handled the awkwardness, this Adam Thorne with his perfect house and his perfect life.

No, not so perfect.

The diamond ring in the red box in his safe shouted to the world that he had heart trouble. Though maybe he was the one who had called off the engagement. After all, he'd offered to give Chaney the ring if she showed up today. If he was still in love with his fiancée, would he do that?

But the photos of the engaged couple seemed to tell a different story. In Adam's eyes, Chaney had seen true love. The brunette had radiated happiness, too, but her expression suggested she was more pleased with herself than that she was deeply in love with the man whose arms were wrapped around her.

It wasn't fair to judge anyone's relationship from such meager evidence. Still, Chaney had a hard time shaking the impression.

The house seemed quiet. At peace. She should march up the steps to the front porch and ring the bell. She also should have gotten a motel room last night so she could have showered this morning before showing up at his door.

Too late for that now.

She turned off the ignition, gathered her bag and the half-dozen pastries she'd picked up from a nearby bakery, and got out of the car. This could be the biggest mistake of her life. Or she could be one step closer to the vital information she needed to give Fletcher Wilkes so he'd represent Marshall.

The door opened before she reached the bottom step of the porch. Adam Thorne, looking casually handsome in tan shorts and a hunter green pullover, came toward her.

"You're here. I wasn't sure you'd come, but I got the griddle out anyway. Can I help you with that?" He pointed to the pastry box.

"Sure." Chaney handed him the box. His overzealous chivalry amused her but also put her on guard. What was he all about anyway?

She followed him into the house, through the living room and into the kitchen, where he gestured toward a stool.

"I guess you already know your way around, so I won't offer to give you the house tour," he said.

She stared at him, trying to gauge the depth of his annoyance. Though he hadn't sounded annoyed. Only a little amused.

"That reminds me." She placed the box of collectible cards and a stack of bills on the counter. "Here's your stuff. The money is all there, too, except what I spent on supper last night and at the bakery this morning. But I have the receipts so it will all add up to the same." She set the receipts on top of the money then leaned back with a gleeful smile. Part of her knew she resembled a toddler pleased with herself for accomplishing something new. But she couldn't help herself. Giving back money was a first.

"I told you to keep it. I only cared about the ring. It belonged to my mother so I'm partial to it."

"More than to your fiancée's engagement ring?" As soon as the question came out of her mouth, she regretted asking it.

His eyes momentarily clouded over then he smiled. A sad smile, but still a smile.

"Guess so." He scooped pancake mix into a bowl and added milk. "Though I don't have a fiancée. Not anymore."

She spoke, a tremor of hesitation in her voice. "I sort of figured that out when I found her ring in your safe."

"You know," he said, waving a wooden spoon in her direction. "I was with my dad when he bought that safe. I distinctly remember the guy at the hardware store saying it was crackproof."

"Your dad bought a safe at the hardware store?"

"Local place. Dad is friends with the owner. I'm pretty sure it was a special order."

"You should get a refund. An amateur could open a safe like that. It's ancient."

"Obviously it's time for an upgrade." He dropped a dollop of the pancake mix on the griddle. "There's orange juice in the fridge. Why don't you make yourself useful and pour us both a glass?"

Chaney stared at him a moment, but apparently he wasn't kidding. She retrieved two glasses from the cupboard he pointed to and opened the refrigerator. It was disgustingly organized and tidy. Not at all like a couple of the foster homes she'd been in where the fridge had overflowed with an assortment of ingredients, leftovers, and all kinds of yummy goodness. That's the kind of refrigerator she'd have in her dream home—abundantly full.

"I thought we'd eat outside if that's okay with you."

"Sounds wonderful."

She carried the filled orange juice glasses to the screened porch that covered the pool and connected with the pool house. The table was already set with placemats, dishes, tableware, and cloth napkins. A festive bowl of oranges, apples, and bananas served as the centerpiece. She placed the glasses beside the plates and stood back, hands on her hips.

What was going on here?

If she wasn't so curious about him, and so motivated to find out if he knew where his father was hiding, she wasn't sure she'd hang around. This all seemed too weird.

She wandered to the edge of the pool and bent to test the temperature of the water. Too cold for swimming today, but it sure would be nice in the summer. It was hard not to feel envious of Adam Buchanan Thorne. But this wasn't the first time she'd dealt with the green-eyed monster. She had plenty of experience trying to understand why some people had so much while others lacked even the basics.

Adam came through the patio doors carrying a dish stacked with pancakes, the box of pastries, and a bottle of maple syrup. "Breakfast is ready. Not much healthy except the fruit, I'm afraid."

"Healthy can be over-rated." Chaney joined him at the table and unfolded the colorful napkin.

"Do you mind if I say grace?" Adam asked.

Grace? "You mean like a prayer?"

"To thank God for this meal."

"Uh, sure." What else could she say? She closed her eyes then opened one to see what he did. His head was bowed, hands folded. She mimicked him.

"Thank you, Father, for the gift of this food. And thank you that Chaney came today. I ask your blessings upon both of us and on her cousin. Amen."

He prayed for her? For Marshall?

Grant must have told Adam about her, about her family. The big mouth.

She opened her eyes and found him smiling at her. "Dig in," he said. "I hope you're hungry."

"Starving." She'd resisted the temptation to eat one of the pastries on the way to his house. "It all looks great."

"I like to cook," he said. "Though there's not much to whipping up pancakes or putting fruit in a bowl."

"Why?"

"Why do I like to cook? I suppose because my mom did. I have fond memories of the two of us whipping up meals in the kitchen."

That wasn't the question she'd meant to ask. But she couldn't help noticing this was the second time Adam had referred to his mom in the past tense. She'd almost forgotten that his dad was a widower.

"How long since ... since your mom ...?"

"About three and a half years. She had a congenital heart condition. It finally got the best of her."

"I'm sorry, I shouldn't have asked."

"No, it's okay. She was a wonderful mom. A lovely woman. I never mind talking about her."

He might not, but suddenly Chaney did. Everything about this visit seemed surreal. She needed to stay focused on her main goal of gaining Adam's trust. But she refused to use the loss of his mom as the means to that end. To do so crossed a line. She'd use a different approach. One that would help her get to know him.

"What I actually meant to ask, before you talked about your mom, was why you invited me here this morning. Why did you fix me breakfast? How did you know I'd come?"

"I invited you because I wanted to talk to you again. I offered to fix breakfast to give you a reason to come. And then I hoped and prayed you would."

"You set the table."

"I expected God to answer my prayer."

"Whether or not I came was my decision. Not God's."

"True. You have free will. But like I said, I hoped. And I wanted to be ready in case you did." He handed her the syrup bottle. "Let's eat."

She drenched her pancakes and hoped there'd be no more talk of prayers or God or free will. There had to be more to him than religion.

"Tell me," he said as peeled a banana, "what do you do when you're not breaking into strangers' homes?"

"A little bit of this. A little bit of that," she said carelessly.

"You don't have a job?"

"What about you?" she countered. "I saw you at the diner yesterday."

"I saw you, too. And I talked to the woman with the locket." He cut half the banana into slices which he layered between two pancakes. "What you did for her was amazing."

Though she'd never seen anything like it, she refused to be distracted by his banana-pancake sandwich. Or his compliment. "Is that why you lied to Special Agent Grant? Or are you trying for sainthood?"

"Nothing of the kind," he said, chuckling. "It's hard to explain the reason. At first, I thought I was being noble. But I realized later I had an ulterior motive."

"Oh?" Chaney's guard went up. "What was that?"

"First, tell me why you broke in here. Why my house?"

"I'm not sure I can answer that." What would he think if she told him the truth? On the other hand, why did she care what he thought?

"Try," he urged.

She studied him, expecting to see a charming smile plastered on his face, a smile he relied on to persuade people to do as he asked and to get his own way. But he wasn't smiling at all. He seemed to genuinely want to know.

"No one was home," she said.

"I'm not buying that."

"How about this?" She ticked off the reasons on her fingers. "No alarm system. No dog. No one at home. Easy peasy."

He sat back in his chair and the smile came. But not an "I'm charming so do what I want" smile but an amused smile. As if he knew she wasn't telling him the truth, but instead of being mad, he considered her answer funny.

"I thought someone else lived here," she admitted.

"Who?"

"Your father."

"That's what I hoped you would say."

"Excuse me?"

"You're looking for my father, aren't you?"

"Do you know where he is?"

Adam bowed his head. Was he praying again? Or just thinking? Finally he met her gaze. "Not a clue. But I want to find him, too. To make sure he's okay."

"Do you think something happened to him?"

"I don't know what to think."

"Tell me about him." Maybe, by talking about his dad, Adam would inadvertently give her a clue. Besides, she was interested in the dynamic between the father and the son.

"He's a good man," Adam said. Then he ran his hands down his face, pulling his cheeks and jaw downward, distorting his features. "But I think he got involved with the wrong people."

If he meant Mickey Nolan, Adam was absolutely right. But Chaney hesitated to mention any names. She wanted to know as much as Adam would tell her before revealing the little she knew.

"What happened?"

"He's a veterinarian. The practice has been in decline since Mom died, but he's been unwilling to close the doors. I've been encouraging him to retire, to take it easy. However, some of his patients have been coming to him for years, and he didn't want to leave them." Adam picked up his orange juice glass but didn't take a drink.

"He'd cut back his hours," he continued. "At least I thought he had. Next thing I know, he's working out at the stables for a couple of the racehorse owners."

Including Mickey Nolan? Chaney took a large bite of her pancake, giving him space to tell her more about his dad.

"I grew up in this house. Dad gave me a bargain price then moved into a small apartment. Less upkeep, he said. This house was going to be our home. Mine and Piper's."

The move must have been recent, since Tucker Thorne still had this address listed as his own. Or maybe he'd moved into the apartment to hide from Mickey. No, that didn't make sense. Still, she might find the clue she needed in the vet's new home. Assuming Tucker actually had anything to do with the horse's disappearance.

"Maybe there's something at the apartment that would lead you to him." As long as she could follow Adam, learn everything he did, she might be able to find his dad.

Adam didn't reply. He seemed intent on swiping a bite of pancake through a pool of syrup.

What was the last thing he'd said? *Our home. Mine and Piper's.*

Her heart went out to him—she couldn't help it. He'd had dreams for this house. She sensed them, as if they were her own. Maybe because they were. She looked around the airy porch, imagined what it would be like to come home to a place like this every day. To be part of a family.

But his dream had ended. He was still trying to come to

grips with that truth. And added to that burden was the mystery of not knowing where his dad had gone.

"Are you all right?" she asked softly.

"Yeah."

She finished her breakfast, keenly aware that she didn't know much more than she had when she arrived. Only that Tucker had moved out and Adam had moved in. That explained the boxes in the small bedroom. Though who did they belong to? Were the boxes filled with stuff Tucker didn't have room for in his new place? Or stuff Adam hadn't yet unpacked?

She didn't want to go through them on the off chance she'd find a clue hidden among the packed possessions. There had to be an easier way to find Tucker. All she needed to do was find it.

CHAPTER 14

Wednesday Morning

Adam peered through the kitchen window above the sink as Chaney knelt by the pool, dipped her fingers into the water, and lifted them. Droplets fell from her fingertips. Then she slipped off her skimmers, rolled up her pant legs, and hesitantly stuck her toes into the pool. From her reaction, the water must have chilled her. But she didn't seem to mind it much.

Strange girl, this Chaney Rose whose cousin was in jail. Stealing from a pickpocket and returning the stolen goods. Stealing from his safe and, once again, returning the stolen goods.

When Adam got up that morning, he'd had his doubts she'd show up. He'd been even more surprised when she returned the trading cards and the cash. He picked up the receipts she'd placed on the stack of money. One from a fast food restaurant, the other from the donut shop.

Something more than curiosity must have brought her back to the scene of the crime. At least, he hoped that was true.

She hadn't admitted flat out she was looking for his father. Only that she thought his father lived here. Seemed like the next best thing to an admission to him. If she was looking for Tucker, then she might be his best hope for finding his father. But first, Adam needed to gain her trust. And, truth be told, Chaney needed to gain his.

He joined her at the pool, kicked off his flip-flops, and sat beside her. "Do you swim?"

"I know how, if that's what you're asking. But I don't get much of a chance."

"You can swim here if you want. Though it might be a little cold today."

"That's very kind of you. Maybe I will."

He chuckled, understanding the meaning behind the testing lilt in her tone. *Keep being nice to me*, she seemed to be saying. *We'll see if you really mean it when I show up in June with a swimsuit and inflatable raft.*

"Why are you looking for my dad?" he asked.

"What was your ulterior motive for inviting me for breakfast?"

"To find out why you're looking for my dad."

"I thought maybe it was a test."

"Maybe it was. Or maybe you're testing me. Stringing me along because you need something more than my money or my mother's rings."

She peered at him under her thick lashes as if assessing him. Sizing him up. "I'm not testing you," she finally said. "But I do need to find your father."

"So do I."

"Then maybe we can work together."

It was what he wanted, for her to make the suggestion instead of him, even though he knew in his gut that he needed her help more than she needed his.

"Where do we start?" he asked.

She seemed to look beyond the screen surrounding the pool and the fence on the other side. But he sensed she didn't see the chain links or the thick hedge that formed a boundary between the fence and the lawn's always-spreading St. Augustine grass. Nor the jasmine vines climbing the trellis by the garage or the gardenias and camellias his mother had lovingly tended. He waited, allowing her time to decide on an answer.

She pulled her purple-painted toes from the water and hugged her knees. "Why wouldn't your dad tell you where he was going? Or how to reach him?"

"I wish I knew." Adam had asked himself the same questions again and again. But Tucker had disappeared once before, shortly after Mom died. A couple of weeks later, he came back. No apology. No explanation. As if his grief excused him from seeing beyond his own pain to that of his only son's.

Adam's body stiffened as the memory rekindled the anger he'd felt at the time. He tamped down his resentment, choosing once again to forgive Tucker's lapse. Though it seemed he'd never forget the heartache of that abandonment.

"Dad left a note." At least Tucker had done that much this time. "Said he'd be in touch and not to worry."

"When did you first realize something was wrong?" Chaney asked.

"I didn't know anything was wrong until he was gone."

Chaney's lips curved into a slender smile. "You knew before then," she said. "There would have been little signs, things you dismissed as not important. But they were there. Think, Adam. When did you first sense something wasn't quite right with your dad?"

Adam dangled his feet in the cool water as he mulled over the past few weeks. Nothing stood out except for Tucker's suggestion that Adam move into the bungalow. His dad said he wanted a smaller place and both Adam and Piper were thrilled with the proposal. Especially given the low purchase price.

But the plan was supposed to occur after the wedding. Then all of a sudden, Dad changed his mind.

"When he insisted I move in here. I wasn't sure I was ready, and I didn't think he was either. I mean, he and Mom built this house before I was born. Suddenly, he's wanting to move? It didn't make sense."

"But you obviously went along with him."

"Because I thought he'd move in there." Adam pointed to the pool house. "It'd be like when I was in seminary. Except I was the one living in the pool house then."

Chaney tilted her head. "You mean that's like a real house?"

"More like a one-bedroom apartment. Which was perfect for me. Dad and I both had our own spaces, but we could still spend time together. The only rent I had to pay was to mow the grass and clean the pool."

"Sounds idyllic."

"That's why I thought Dad meant to live there. Instead he rented an apartment." Adam had pressed him for an explanation, but Tucker avoided giving him one. Once the wedding was called off, Adam offered to move so Tucker could return to the bungalow. But he'd refused.

"I saw your diplomas." Chaney's abrupt change of subject lured Adam away from trying to connect Tucker's change of address to his recent moodiness. "Are you a priest? A father?"

"I'm a pastor. A minister. At least I was until yesterday."

"What happened?"

"The board thought this situation with my dad reflected badly on the church." He shrugged as if this latest blow meant nothing. Though that was so far from the truth. "They let me go."

"They fired you?" Her indignant tone made Adam chuckle. She barely knew him but seemed ready to rally to his defense.

"To put it bluntly, yes."

"Can they do that?"

"Apparently. That's why I was at the Dogwood Diner. One of the board members gave me the bad news." And was very happy to do so. Too happy.

"I haven't signed the termination papers yet," Adam continued. "I kind of got distracted when I came home and found someone had broken into my house."

"You didn't have a very good day yesterday, did you?" The compassion in her voice lightened the weight of her words.

"No, I really didn't," he agreed.

"Then why were you so kind to me last night?"

Adam scrunched his eyebrows. "What does the one thing have to do with the other?"

"If I'd been fired and came home to find police everywhere, I don't think I would have reacted the way you did. As if it wasn't that big of a deal."

"Believe me, it was a big deal. Do you have any idea how late I stayed up talking to the neighbors? They didn't see you breaking into my house, but they were all kinds of interested when the police showed up. It almost became a block party."

Chaney's eyes twinkled. "Sounds fun."

Adam stared at her then realized she was right. "You know, in a strange way, it was. Mostly empty nesters live around here, folks about my dad's age. Their kids have grown up and moved away."

He narrowed his eyes and spoke in the voice he usually reserved for the youth group when they got too rowdy at the wrong time. "Don't you dare think of them as easy targets. Most have strong feelings about the Second Amendment and protecting their castles."

"I wouldn't." Chaney held up her hands. "Besides, I'm not really a burglar."

"Could have fooled me."

When she didn't answer, Adam glanced her way. She rested her chin on her knees, gazing straight ahead. She might have been made of stone. Had he hurt her feelings with his offhanded comment?

"Special Agent Grant called you a grifter," Adam said. "That's the same as a con artist, isn't it?"

"I suppose."

The stone speaks!

"Why are you a grifter?"

"You're a minister. You wouldn't understand."

"Maybe not. But I understand this. The woman at the diner yesterday sure was glad you returned her locket."

"Why did you talk to her?"

"Just being nosey, I guess. She told me the locket belonged to her grandmother. The photos inside were taken right before her grandfather went to fight in WWII. He gave the locket to his new bride to remember him by until he returned home. It's a precious family heirloom that means more to her than any amount of money."

"Perhaps she should be more careful with it then."

"Yesterday you were her hero."

"I get it now. You were 'paying it forward' by being nice to me." She actually used air quotes.

"It goes 'deeper' than that." He made air quotes of his own.

"Right, your ulterior motive. You want me to help you find your dad."

"Absolutely I do. But I also thought you needed grace."

"Grace? I don't know what you mean."

"It means you didn't go to jail. You're still a free woman. And you're the best chance I have of finding my dad."

They didn't talk for several minutes, then Chaney abruptly stood. "Maybe there's a clue at your dad's apartment. We should go there."

"I don't have a key." Adam got to his feet. The skin around

his tanned toes was puckered from the water. "He never gave me one."

Chaney glared at him, her unspoken message coming through loud and clear: *You've got to be kidding me.*

"Right." He pressed his lips into a grim smile. "You don't need a key."

CHAPTER 15

Wednesday Morning

For the life of her, Chaney couldn't imagine why anyone would give up a comfortable home in a reputable neighborhood for a place like this. The one-bedroom apartment, located in a tired building, held only the basics—a rickety table with two mismatched chairs in the eating area, a sheet-covered sofa, a mattress on a bed frame, and a nightstand in the bedroom. No television. No bookshelves. Nothing personal except for the clothes in the closet.

"I had no idea," Adam said for at least the third time. He seemed absolutely stunned, as if he couldn't believe what he was seeing. "No wonder he didn't want me to come here."

"Where did this furniture come from?" The side of the road? Goodwill offered nicer options. Prior experience had taught her that.

Adam shrugged. "He could have taken furniture from the house. I offered to help him move. But he said he wanted to start fresh." He waved his hand around the sparsely furnished living room. "This is 'fresh'?"

They had opened all the drawers, searched through the mostly empty cupboards. At least there were no signs of bugs or mice though they found roach traps under the kitchen and bathroom sinks.

"You'd think there'd at least be mail," Chaney said. "A utility bill. Something."

"I don't think he changed his address. His mail still comes to the house."

Chaney walked through the sparse rooms again. Had Tucker been distancing himself from his son? Maybe he didn't plan to return and didn't want to burden Adam with the chore of moving his belongings back to the bungalow. Disposing of this junk wouldn't take much time or trouble.

But if that was the case, it seemed unlikely his disappearance had anything to do with Mickey Nolan's horse. Perhaps it was only a coincidence that Tucker was missing, too.

Fletcher Wilkes didn't seem to think so. Neither did Marshall, though his efforts to find a link were cut short when he was arrested. Right now, Adam was Chaney's best lead.

"There's nothing here," she said, stating the obvious. "We might as well go."

She waited till they were in Adam's car to question him. She needed to know what he knew without giving away anything that Wilkes had told her. Even though Adam had guessed she was looking for his dad, he hadn't asked her why. Maybe he was afraid if he pushed for an answer, she wouldn't help him. Just as Adam was her best lead, she was his.

When they were on their way back to the bungalow, she decided to take the direct approach. "Tell me what you know about Mickey Nolan."

"I've never met him, but Dad has mentioned him once or twice."

"He worked for him?"

"Used to. Dad started working at the racetrack with a couple of the other owners. Nolan liked the way he handled horses and took him on." Adam checked his rearview mirror then slid into the turning lane. "His wife has disappeared too. Along with one of their horses."

"Do you think your dad had anything to do with that?"

"I don't know why he would."

"Maybe he was influenced by Mrs. Nolan." Chaney stressed *influenced* and hoped Adam understood the question behind her comment. She didn't want to accuse his dad of fooling around with another man's wife. But if they were together, then that might explain Dr. Thorne's strange behavior.

"You think my dad is romantically involved with Mrs. Nolan?" Adam's fingers gripped the steering wheel and his jaw muscle clenched.

"I don't know." She noted the shift in his breathing. The suggestion angered him, but his anger wasn't directed at her. Maybe he was mad at himself because he'd wondered the same thing.

"I saw a picture of her and her husband in the paper once," Adam said. "She's much younger than Dad. Besides, I don't think he ever got over losing Mom."

Who was Adam trying to convince—Chaney or himself? Dr. Thorne might still be grieving, but that didn't mean he wasn't lonely. Still, it wouldn't do any good to say that to Adam. She couldn't blame him for wanting to believe in his father's faithfulness to his mom's memory.

They drove the rest of the way to Adam's bungalow in silence. After climbing out of the car, Adam headed for the porch, but Chaney stopped on the sidewalk. He turned to face her.

"Thanks for breakfast," she said. "It was a nice way to start the morning."

"Aren't you coming in?" he asked.

"I've imposed enough on your hospitality." She dug through her bag for her car key and headed for The Sting.

Adam joined her. "You're not imposing. I need your help." He glanced inside her vehicle, did a double-take, then stared at Chaney. "Are you sleeping in your car?"

"No."

"You're lying."

"It's a temporary situation."

Adam's eyes bored into hers as if searching out every lie she'd ever told. She hadn't realized how gray they were until now.

"Why don't you stay here?" he said. "I've got a guestroom. I'd offer the pool house, but it turned into a storage unit after I sold my condo."

The pool house would have been tempting, she had to admit. But after last night's *Les Mis* moment, she was already in his debt. Not a place she ever liked to be.

"It's kind of you to offer," she said. "But I can't."

"Where are you going to go? What about finding my dad?"

"Someone has to know something," she assured him. "No one can drive off with a horse trailer and turn invisible."

"You're not giving up?"

"Not yet." Not ever when Marshall's freedom depended on her finding the horse for Nolan.

She rounded The Sting and opened the driver's door.

"Wait a minute." Adam stood on the other side, staring at her across the roof. "You left the money on the kitchen counter."

On purpose.

Did he think her conscience was that jaded? Sure, she needed cash. But she'd find another way to get it. "That's your money. Not mine."

"Okay then. I'm hiring you to find my dad."

Chaney tilted her head, listening for voices from her past. Two men wanted to hire her for the same job? Her grandfather would definitely approve.

She closed the door, hit the lock button on her remote, and strolled beside Adam into the bungalow.

CHAPTER 16

Wednesday After Chaney once again refused Adam's offer to stay in his guest room, he offered to reserve a room for her at one of the hundreds of hotels in Florida's tourist mecca. She'd almost said yes but ended up turning him down again. She could almost feel her grandfather's earlier pride, even though imagined, turning to scorn. In her place, he'd have taken Adam's generosity as his due and been vindictive when the largesse stopped.

But she wasn't the chip off the old block her grandfather expected her to be—only a splinter who soaked up his lessons but somewhere along the way discovered a different moral compass.

She also declined Adam's invitation to stay for lunch. Instead, she ate a salad at a nearby bistro then drove to the Central Library. The rest of the day flew by as she read each internet link she could find that mentioned Mickey and Sandy-Lynne Nolan, his third red-headed wife, and on Dr. Tucker Thorne who had won a few accolades over the years from the local animal welfare organizations and a couple of civic groups.

None of the three had a large online presence, but Chaney followed a few rabbit trails into the mysterious world of horse-racing, the so-called sport of kings. She read the horrific story of Tommy "The Sandman" Burns who, in the 1980s, electrocuted show horses for a cut of the insurance money, justifying his crimes as providing a painless death for the animals.

A Wikipedia article called "Horse Murders" named other individuals involved in similar cruelties. That article led to searches on Helen Brach, the candy heiress who may have been murdered because she had information about such criminal activities. The investigation into her 1977 disappearance resulted in one man serving a life sentence for his probable involvement in her death. But her body was never recovered.

From there, Chaney read about doping scandals where horses were given drug cocktails to mask the pain from their injuries. Sickened by what she'd read, and unable to find any information that might lead to Dr. Thorne's whereabouts, she entered a new internet search: *best places to live in the U.S.*

Browsing the lists of the different locations was much more fun than reading about the crimes of the equine world. She took several of the quizzes, but the answers were a mixed bag—everything from Austin to Seattle to Chicago.

Time slipped by while she mused all the options she and Marshall could explore once he was out of jail. The dream of her own home seemed too far away to grasp. But she couldn't give up hope. Maybe it would look like the magazine photo in her wallet. Or maybe it would look like Adam's bungalow. As long as it was a place of safety, of comfort, of stability—that's what she wanted most.

In the morning, she'd go to the Thirty-Third Street Jail again. Marshall could refuse to see her, but he couldn't keep her from showing up. He'd give in before she gave up.

The sun was low enough in the western sky for the streetlamps to shine their spotlights on the sidewalk in front of the library. Chaney crossed the street to the parking garage and climbed the steps to the third floor. She fished her key out of her crossbody bag before opening the steel door leading from the stairwell.

As she neared The Sting, she clicked the unlock button on her remote. Someone appeared beside the vehicle and opened the door. She halted then stepped back.

"Thanks, Chaney." Calvin Brady, six feet of tanned handsomeness, waved to her. "I was beginning to think you planned to stay out all night."

"Get away from my car, Calvin."

"Be glad to. As soon as you bring me what you owe me."

"The Barrington Blade?" She hmphed. Unfortunately, Marshall had been caught with the medieval dagger that she was helping Calvin steal from a local art museum. Her cousin didn't want her involved with Calvin's crew, so he interfered in the heist. "You know very well it's locked up in an evidence room somewhere."

Calvin smacked the roof, startling Chaney so she jumped. She tried to calm her breathing, to appear confident and in control. But her knees had turned to jelly, and her heart pounded against her chest.

"That's because your cousin mucked up the plan. What was he even doing there?"

"I know you're mad," she said, trying to placate him. "He got to the blade before we did." Then allowed himself to get caught when the police swooped in, giving her a chance to run. Like a sniveling coward, she'd taken off, leaving him to take the blame. She braced herself against the guilt flooding over her and took a deep breath.

"There's nothing we can do about that now," she continued.

"You owe me, Chaney Rose."

"I have nothing to give you, Calvin Brady."

"That's why I'm taking this." He smacked the car roof again

though not as hard this time. "We'll call it collateral. Just need you to give me the key." He rounded the trunk and held out his hand.

"I don't think so." She started for the stairwell but was grabbed by huge hands reaching out from the shadows. She twisted and squirmed, but the man's thick arms surrounded her chest and squeezed. Nero, Calvin's muscle and right-hand man.

Chaney's breath caught as the pain increased, and she fought the panic rising within her. She rammed the end of the key into Nero's thigh, hitting again and again until he loosened his hold and gripped her wrist. The key fell to the ground.

"Let her go, Nero." Calvin came nearer. "We don't want any bruises on that lovely body."

Nero chuckled but released her, then picked up the key and tossed it to Calvin. Chaney stepped away, glaring at both of them as she took slow, painful breaths.

Calvin waved the key. "This doesn't nearly repay me."

"Take it," she said. "Just let me get a few things out of the backseat."

"Sorry, babe."

"My clothes are in there." *My laptop. My backpack. My copy of Grimm's. Most of the cash from Adam and Wilkes—hidden where you'll never find it.*

"Doesn't matter." Calvin stepped closer, backing her up until she was against the door. He trapped her face between his cheek and the palm of his hand. His thumb caressed her skin. "You owe me," he whispered, his breath warming her ear. His fingers moved to grip her jaw as he shifted to look into her eyes. "One way or another, I expect payment."

She couldn't speak, could barely breathe. Her jaw ached from the pressure of his fingers. Suddenly, he laughed and released her. "See you around, Chaney Rose."

He tossed her key back to Nero. "You know where to take it," he said as he sauntered toward a nearby SUV.

Chaney shrank against the door as both vehicles exited the garage, the drivers honking the horns at one another as if they were adolescent joyriders. Her chin and her chest ached, but at least she could breathe. At least they hadn't taken her with them.

But only because they were grifters. Despite Calvin's veiled threats, he wasn't a rapist or a murderer. He wanted payment for what she had cost him. In their world, he was justified to demand it.

Grandpa's imagined scorn pushed Chaney to the cement floor where she fought against tears and vainly wished for a different kind of life.

CHAPTER 17

Thursday Morning

Chaney awoke, stiff and cold from sleeping on the cushioned glider. It took her a moment to remember where she was, then a sinking feeling filled her stomach as she remembered why. She lightly touched her chin, still tender from the pressure of Calvin's fingers. If there was a bruise, she couldn't go to the jail. Just her luck, this would be the day Marshall would agree to see her. The incident would only upset him and give him something else to brood about.

She sat up, grimacing as a sharp pain gripped her ribs, then slowly stretched her toes to find her shoes.

"Looking for these?" Adam stood near the patio door, her skimmers dangling from his fingers.

Great. She'd hoped to leave before he realized she'd camped inside his screened porch. Why hadn't she set her alarm so she could have slipped away before he got up? She rubbed her eyes then rested her chin in her hands, grimacing at the touch. "What are you doing with those?"

"What are you doing out here?" The compassion in his voice almost did her in.

She bent her head, determined not to fall apart like she had last night in the parking garage. Why hadn't she stood up to Calvin? He respected strength, and she had let him bully her. Though, in her defense, he'd had an unfair advantage.

"Why didn't you come inside?" Adam said, his tone lighthearted. "We both know you don't need a key."

"It was late when I got here. I didn't want to wake you." *Or talk to you or see you. Or let you see me.*

He pulled up a chair and sat so his knees practically touched hers. But there didn't seem to be anything intimate about the gesture. No more than if Marshall had done the same thing.

"Your car isn't out front." He placed the shoes at her feet.

"No. It's not."

"How did you get here?"

"What is this, twenty questions?" She shoved her feet into her shoes and gasped as the sudden movement tugged at her ribs.

"What's wrong?" His voice deepened with concern.

She gave him a weak smile. "Guess I slept wrong."

He tilted his head, studying her. "Is that a bruise on your chin?"

Heat warmed her cheeks as embarrassment covered her like a fiery cloak. If only it made her invisible so she could walk away with her dignity intact. Without letting him see her pain.

But invisibility wasn't going to happen.

"Okay, don't tell me." He stood and returned his chair to its spot. "I'm fixing scrambled eggs and toast for breakfast. Why don't you come inside?"

She wanted to refuse. But her stomach chose that moment to grumble as if the mere mention of food had caused a Pavlovian reaction.

Adam chuckled. "After that, I'm not taking no for an answer. You can shower first if you want."

"Is that your polite way of telling me I *need* a shower?" She tried to sound indignant, but a hot shower sounded so luxurious, she couldn't muster enough resentment to be insulted.

"I'd like that," she added before he could answer.

"Great." He stepped aside so she could precede him into the house. "You'll find towels in the linen closet. Give me a second, and I think I can even scrounge up a change of clothes. Be right back."

She stood near the kitchen table, her hands gripping the back of one of the chairs. Perhaps she should leave and never return. But her feet refused to move. The truth was, she was tired of running. Tired of suspicion. Tired of struggling so hard for the basics of life that so many people took for granted.

Adam returned and handed her a UCF Knights sweatshirt that would hang to her knees and a pair of black yoga pants.

"These yours?" She pointed to the pants.

"Only the sweatshirt. Piper kept a few things here when we were engaged. She missed packing those."

"She might not like another woman wearing them."

"I don't imagine she'll ever know." He pulled a muffin mix from the pantry. "Don't rush. I'll wait till you're done to put these in the oven and scramble the eggs."

Chaney merely nodded and headed for the bathroom, the clothes in her arms. Few people but Marshall had ever shown her so much unnecessary kindness. Maybe that's why she'd been compelled to come back here. A safe place. A comfortable place.

The kind of place she had so often dreamed about.

When she got to the bathroom, she took a deep breath and examined her face in the mirror. The bruising wasn't bad, but it was definitely noticeable. Hopefully Adam wouldn't ask her about the injury again.

She took a huge fluffy towel from the linen closet, placed it on the nearest towel rack, and ran the water. The stream was hot before she'd completely undressed. She stepped under the invigorating spray and let the water wash away the stench of the last two days as tears flowed for all she wanted out of life and for the little she had received.

CHAPTER 18

***T*hursday Morning**

Adam had been astonished to see Chaney curled up in the glider when he'd gone out to the porch with his morning cup of coffee. He hadn't wanted to wake her, even though she didn't look at all comfortable. Neither did he want her taking off without talking to him. So he had picked up her shoes and was carrying them into the house when she awakened.

He stirred the wildberry muffin mix with a half-cup of milk as he pondered what had brought her back to his house. How and when had she arrived? Where was her car?

And most importantly, what had caused the bruise on her chin? Or, more accurately, who?

She'd tried not to let him see it, resting her chin in her hands and turning away. Though faint, it was still noticeable. The sight of it caused a primal anger to rage within him. An anger unlike anything he had felt in a long time.

He'd been able to hide the outrage, to press it down and close the lid on it, as he did with any emotion that seemed too out-of-control, too huge for him to handle.

He spooned the mix into the cups of a miniature muffin tin then gathered the other ingredients he needed. He chopped leftover bacon, diced onions, and grated cheddar cheese. When everything was ready, he warmed his coffee in the microwave.

With nothing left to do but wait for Chaney to emerge from the bathroom, he sat at the table with the massive study Bible he kept nearby. He didn't open it, though. He wanted to pray—for himself, for his dad, for Chaney. But his thoughts scattered from one thing to the other, bouncing around like an out-of-control pinball machine.

Until about six weeks ago, his life had followed a more or less orderly progression. The only trauma he'd ever experienced was the death of his mom, a devastating tragedy that had upended his world. But, as cliché as it might sound, his faith—the faith Mom had bestowed upon him—saw him through the worst of those days and helped him to cope with his heartache. He didn't use his grief as an excuse for lashing out, for harming himself, for turning his back on God.

Instead, he found comfort in knowing Mom was in heaven. That she was among that "great cloud of witnesses" mentioned by the writer of Hebrews. All he ever wanted to do was to make her proud.

He finished seminary with a solid 3.8 grade point average. He accepted what he considered at the time to be an amazing job offer. He met the perfect woman and made plans for their future. He bought a ring, got down on one knee, and asked her to be his wife.

He moved into his boyhood home, excited that this was where they'd raise their children. Where they'd add to the happy memories already lived within these walls. The future looked bright.

Who was he kidding? The future *was* bright.

And then all the dreams and hopes came crashing down. The

broken engagement that tore his heart in two. The disappearance of his dad. The firing.

And then this imp of a girl had waved at him through the Dogwood Diner window. Less than forty-eight hours later, she was taking a shower in his bathroom.

God works in mysterious ways, all right. Still, this was crazy! Chaney had asked him yesterday when he first noticed something was different about his dad. He'd given her an answer, but was it the right one? Her question had stayed with him, but he hadn't come up with anything different. Not yet.

Down the hall, the bathroom door opened. Adam rose from the table and slid the muffins into the pre-heated oven then pulled the egg carton from the refrigerator. He didn't want to stare at Chaney when she returned. Nor did he want the raging anger to rise within him again at the sight of her bruise. That wouldn't do either of them any good.

"How was the shower?" he asked when he sensed her presence in the dining nook. He snuck a quick glance, enough to see that the sweatshirt was way too large for her slender frame. It somehow suited her, though. Allowed her to hide within its folds.

"Luxurious," she said. Her voice sounded different than it had on the porch. Stronger, Happier. "It's amazing what a hot shower can do. You know, to make you feel better. Clean. Better. I said that already."

And also a little flustered. He chuckled. "I know exactly what you mean. Hungry?"

"Starving."

"Good. This will only take a few minutes." He whisked the eggs while heating the skillet. "Coffee? Juice?"

"Coffee sounds good. I can make it."

"You'll find pods beneath the Keurig." He pointed to the machine. "Take your pick. Mugs are in the cabinet above it."

"Anything I can help you do?"

"Just tell me what a great chef I am after you eat."

"I can do that."

The timer on the oven dinged as Adam plated the scrambled eggs. He placed the dishes on the counter separating the kitchen from the dining nook, then took the muffins out of the oven. Without him asking, Chaney had set the table. Once the muffins were in the breadbasket, Adam joined her.

"You don't mind—"

"If you say grace? No."

She bent her head, and Adam couldn't resist staring at her before closing his own eyes. Someone had hurt her, he was sure of it. He took a deep breath, squelching the bile that rose in the back of his throat, and tried to center his thoughts on giving thanks for the breakfast.

"Thank You for this food, Father. Thank You for my unexpected guest. Amen."

"That was short," Chaney said. "Is that all you need to say?"

"For now." Adam handed her the breadbasket, this time allowing his gaze to connect with hers. To his surprise, she didn't look away. Her jaw stiffened, though, whether in embarrassment or defensiveness, he wasn't sure. Then she blinked and focused on buttering her muffin.

Maybe the way to her heart was through her stomach. Not that he wanted her heart. Only her trust so she'd tell him what had happened between the time she left him yesterday and came back again sometime during the night. More importantly, why was she looking for his dad?

She'd deflected the question when he asked her yesterday with a question of her own. He didn't expect he'd get a straight answer from her now. But maybe, just maybe, if he could get her to see him as a friend instead of a means to an end, she'd tell him what he needed to know.

That was the prayer she hadn't heard him pray.

CHAPTER 19

Thursday Morning Chaney wasn't sure she could eat anything with her mind and stomach in such a turmoil. But the hot eggs and buttery mini-muffins were so delicious, she practically inhaled her food. Adam, apparently amused by her voracious appetite, scrambled more eggs.

When they finished breakfast, he started to clear the table. "Let me," she said. "You cooked."

He seemed about to protest then changed his mind. "Okay," he said. "If you don't mind, I'll be in my study."

After he left, Chaney gathered the dishes, rinsed them, and loaded them into the dishwasher. When the kitchen was tidy, she wandered into the living room and curled up on the couch with her feet tucked beneath her. The hot shower and the good food had made her sleepy. She tried to stay awake, but her eyes grew heavier and heavier until she gave in to the weariness.

When she awoke, she was stretched out on the couch with a cover thrown over her. She yawned, feeling groggy and lethargic.

"Hey, sleepyhead." Adam sat in a nearby chair. He closed the book he'd been reading. "Feel better?"

"What time is it?"

"A little after noon."

"I need to be going."

"Where?"

Good question. Where did she need to go? Somewhere besides here where peace and comfort softened the edges of who she was. Edges she needed to survive.

She twisted to sit up, and pain gripped her sides. She grimaced, both at the aching twinges and the remembrance of Nero's crushing hold. Of Calvin's theft.

"Who hurt you?"

Chaney refused to look at him, not wanting to see his pity or his misgivings. He must regret inviting her into his home. She refused to involve him in her personal problems.

"Thanks again for breakfast." She stood and folded the blanket with careful movements to keep the pain at a minimum. "I'm going to change into my clothes and be on my way."

"No need. Besides, your clothes are in the dryer. I don't think they're—"

"You washed my clothes?" She didn't know whether to be insulted or grateful or horrified. True, they needed to be laundered. But how presumptuous for him to touch them. She'd left them neatly folded on the bathroom vanity, not in a pile on the floor.

"Just straightening up a little and decided to do a load of laundry."

She glared at him. "How long before they're dry?"

He didn't seem at all uncomfortable by her glare or annoyance. "It'll be awhile. I put them in the dryer about ten minutes ago."

She plopped back onto the sofa. "I guess I have to wait then."

"While you're waiting, could you do me a favor?"

"Maybe." She rarely committed to anything without knowing the details. Another of her grandfather's rules to live by. Though she couldn't help feeling her reluctance seemed ungrateful after all he'd done for her.

If he thought so, too, he let it pass.

"Tell me what happened."

"What do you mean?"

"You know what I mean." Anger—not pity or regret—flashed in his eyes. But she sensed the anger wasn't toward her. "Who hurt you?"

"It doesn't matter."

"Yes. It does."

The flash of anger shifted to a tenderness she'd rarely seen. At least not directed at her. That tenderness countered her resolve to keep him out of her personal life. She bent her head, not wanting to look at him any longer.

Besides, when she came back here last night, had she honestly thought she could slip in and out without giving him an explanation? Or had she nurtured a tiny hope, one she trembled to acknowledge, that he'd insist she tell him? Not from curiosity but because he cared about her. Not like a boyfriend, ugh, no. But as a person. As, maybe, a friend.

Though of course, the man was a minister. He got a paycheck for caring about people. Or at least he did until a couple of days ago.

"What are you going to do now?" She shifted to peer at him.

He drew his eyebrows together as if confused by her change of topic, then his mouth quirked. "Sit here until you answer my question."

"I mean what are you going to do about a job? Don't you need a new church or a new parish or something?"

"I don't know what I'm going to do. Besides, it's too soon to think about any of that."

"It is?"

He leaned forward, hands clasped between his knees, and held her gaze. "Chaney?"

"Yes?"

"What happened?"

"A little misunderstanding," she said, her tone casual and dismissive. "That's all."

"Seems like more than that. Certainly looks like more than that."

Apparently, he wasn't going to give up. Agitation stirred within her. Perhaps it was time to see how Mr. Les Mis Bishop handled the problems of someone who hadn't grown up with his advantages.

"Someone stole The Sting."

"The what?"

"My car." The words came out hard and flat. "I tried to stop them, but I was outnumbered." Outmatched. Outsmarted.

"Did you call the police?"

She didn't bother to answer but hugged the folded blanket to her aching chest.

"That FDLE agent, Grant," Adam continued. "He might be able to find it."

"I don't need the police or Grant." She released a heavy sigh. "I can get it back on my own."

"How?"

"It's not worth anything except to me. Which means they probably sold it to a junkyard." If you had the right connections, stealing an old beater was one way to raise a few hundred dollars. Despite what he'd said about Chaney owing him, Calvin's motive wouldn't have been the money. Last night, he'd been more interested in humiliation.

"They sold it without a title?" Adam asked, his eyes widening.

Oh, how innocent he was. "It happens," she said lightly.

"Okay." Adam grew thoughtful then his face brightened.

"Then we call around, see who has it, and show them the proof it belongs to you."

"Or I find out where it is and quietly take it back."

"You can't just take it."

"Why not? It belongs to me. Besides, the buyer knew it was stolen. I'm simply reclaiming it without going through the paperwork."

"Is that legal?"

"It's my car."

They stared at each other, but Chaney refused to concede. The only hitch in her plan was locating The Sting.

Adam gave in first. "You've got a point. But I still think if we call the police—"

"Paperwork. Delays. Lies."

"I don't think Grant would lie."

"Forget about Grant. If the police show up at a junkyard and ask about a 2005 Ford Focus, the guy who bought it will say, 'there ain't no car like that here.' It's easier to look for it myself."

"Does, what did you call it? The Sting?"

She nodded.

"Does The Sting mean so much you'd risk breaking the law?"

She focused her gaze on the large picture window. The branches of the trees in the park across the street fluttered in a gentle breeze. Another lovely, perfect day in the Sunshine State.

"Everything I own is in it," she said softly. Not that anything she owned had much value except for her laptop and, of course, the cash. But a few things, the items she'd held onto since childhood, were priceless. At least to her.

"I see." Adam rubbed at his jaw. He clearly hadn't shaved in a day or two, as dark whiskers shadowed his skin. "What are you going to do? Wait till midnight and climb the fence?"

Typical rookie. The man had a lot to learn.

"What are you going to do about the dogs?" he asked.

"What dogs?"

"You know," he said. "Junkyard dogs. They roam around at night and bite anyone who trespasses."

"You've been watching too many movies."

"Then what's your plan?"

"The direct approach." Chaney plucked at the blanket. The soft fabric warmed her fingertips and the motion soothed her spirit. "All I have to do is find the right place and pretend I need a part. I have my cousin's key so, if at all possible, I can drive it out of the lot."

"Oh."

Was it her imagination, or did he seem disappointed?

"You wanted to actually break into the place, didn't you?"

"Of course not. That would be wrong."

She tilted her head and glared at him until his shocked expression faded into a sheepish grin. "I guess it sounded kind of exciting. You know, put on the camouflage paint. Hop a fence. Feed steak to the dogs to distract them."

"Like I said. Too many movies."

Adam pulled out his phone and tapped the screen. "So, the first step is to find the junkyard. Any ideas on how to narrow that list?"

"A few."

Together they came up with a list of ten possibilities, junkyard dealers known to turn a blind eye to legalities and not far from Calvin's base of operations. Though Chaney didn't tell Adam about that second criteria. She'd managed to avoid going into details about what had happened last night. Hopefully Adam wouldn't ask again.

And maybe she'd kiss a prince disguised as a frog.

CHAPTER 20

*T*hursday Afternoon

At the fourth junkyard, they hit pay dirt. And a metaphorical wall in the form of a literal fence. Adam shoved his fingers through the chain link separating the sections of the junkyard. The cars available for pull-and-pay salvage were on this side of the fence. Chaney's dented Ford was parked on the other side.

She hadn't wanted him to accompany her on the search. "If we're caught, you'll be an accessory," she'd said. He'd countered by pointing out her obvious need for transportation. "Unless you want to spend all day on a bus."

As soon as her clothes were dry and she'd changed, they'd headed for the first place on their list. They told the lot attendant they needed parts for a Ford Focus. He didn't want to hear the story they'd made up on the drive over. Totally disinterested, he'd waved them through the open gate.

The second place required an admission fee of two dollars each. Adam paid it while Chaney pretended to be engrossed in something on her phone so the attendant didn't get a good look at her.

When they struck out at the third place, her earlier high spirits faded. She shifted in her seat as if she couldn't get comfortable. Before they left the house, Adam had tried once more to find out what happened to her. But she'd deflected his questions.

This place, their fourth, charged a flat five-dollar-per-vehicle entrance fee. Adam had driven slowly between the rows of junked automobiles. When they reached the east side of the lot, he noticed several cars in a separate enclosed area. He parked and jogged to the fence. Chaney, moving more slowly, followed him.

Her Ford, a strange mustard-y shade with black stripes, was parked between a Volkswagen Bug and a pickup. He turned, grinning broadly. "Found it."

She joined him at the fence. "Maybe they haven't processed it yet."

Adam scrutinized the layout. The drive into the secured lot was close to the office building. "I don't see how you're going to drive it out of there without being seen."

"I can't." She studied the fence, shaking the links as if to test their strength.

"Why don't we talk to the attendant? Maybe if you can prove the car is yours, he'll let you take it."

"I can't prove that."

Adam's eyes widened. "Did you ... Is it stolen?"

"Of course not. But my name isn't on the title." She shook the fencing again. "I've got to get my stuff."

"Wouldn't whoever took the car have taken your belongings?"

"He probably took the laptop. But I doubt he took the time to go through everything."

He? Something about the way she said the word sounded personal. As if she knew who *he* was. Then why was she so reluctant to call the police? To press charges?

"I could probably climb this fence," she said.

"What if the attendant sees you?"

She turned her attention to the ground then walked along the fence line, her fingers trailing across the chain links. At the third section, she looked at him with a satisfied expression, bent down, and shimmied beneath the fencing.

Adam sprinted toward the spot as she crouched on the other side. The ground had been dug out around the pole, perhaps by a dog or maybe even a coyote.

"What are you doing?" he whispered. He didn't know why he'd lowered his voice. They were the only two out here.

"Stay there," she ordered.

He didn't have much choice. He pulled at the loosened links, but he didn't think he could squeeze through the small opening. Despite her slender frame, he was impressed Chaney had managed it.

After a nervous look toward the office building, he squatted near the hole. Though again, he wasn't sure what good that would do. Hopefully the attendant was too busy to pay attention to them.

Chaney scampered to her car, bending low and clutching at her side. She opened the rear door and returned with a backpack and a duffle bag. Adam pulled the backpack beneath the fence, but the duffle bag was too large.

"I'll be right back." She sprinted to the car, opened the trunk, and returned with a couple more bags and a pair of wire cutters.

"You just happened to have a pair of those?" Adam shook his head.

"Doesn't everybody?" she asked with a grin.

"Give them to me."

She hesitated a moment then handed them over. He cut enough links to pull the duffle bag through while she made two more trips. With each passing second, the unease in his stomach grew. As he carried the bags to his car, he rehearsed his defense in case a police officer materialized out of thin air and confronted them.

"This isn't theft—everything we took from the Ford belongs to my accomplice. I mean, to this young woman. Yes, I was the one who cut the fence. I'll gladly pay for the repair."

Would that be enough to save them from being arrested?

Chaney arrived with another load. "This is it," she said. "We better go."

"I'm past ready." He closed his trunk lid, then they both scrambled into his vehicle. As he put on his seatbelt, he glanced toward Chaney's car in the other lot. "Did you lock your doors?"

"Sure did. No one will know I was there."

"I hope you're right about that."

"We did nothing wrong."

"Except cut a fence. That's got to be vandalism." Or maybe something worse.

"I could have done it."

"Still vandalism." Somehow, he had to make this right. But how?

That wasn't his only problem. As he drove away from the junkyard, he puzzled over the conundrum named Chaney Rose. She couldn't spend another night sleeping on his porch. But would she finally agree to stay in his guest room?

"We should go to your dad's clinic," she said, interrupting his train of thought. "Maybe he left a clue there."

"We're not that far away. I've talked to the staff, though. No one knows anything."

"Are they there now?"

"Until six. Maybe a little later." He maneuvered to the left lane so he could turn at the next intersection.

"We should wait till they're gone," she said decisively.

"You want to break into my dad's clinic?"

"Don't you have a key?"

"Sure, but—"

"Then it's not a break-in, is it?" She shifted in her seat and looked out her window.

But he'd seen her grimace before she turned away, obviously still in pain. How could he help her if she didn't confide in him?

It wasn't a question, but a prayer. One of several he needed God to answer.

CHAPTER 21

Thursday Night

Chaney followed Adam into the clinic, standing by the door while he turned off the alarm. From somewhere inside the building a dog barked.

"Tell me again why we couldn't do this when the clinic was open," Adam said as he turned on the lights.

"Other people were here." Chaney glanced around the waiting room. A shelf-lined wall held merchandise, including candles to hide pet odors and a variety of pet foods. Framed posters and a bulletin board displaying photos of pets available for adoption decorated another wall. A long counter separated the administrative desk from rows of seating.

"You don't like people?" Adam asked.

"People ask questions."

"People also provide answers." He locked the door behind them. "Isn't that what we're after?"

"You told me that your dad's receptionist has worked here forever. If anyone knows where he is, she should. And yet, what did she say when you talked to her?"

"That he was at a conference in Atlanta."

The same thing she had told Marshall when he talked to her. "Do you think she was lying?"

"No." Adam scratched at his whiskered jaw. "Angela has been with my dad for a long time. If she said he was in Atlanta, then she believed he was in Atlanta."

"Where's your dad's office?"

"Back here." Adam led the way down a short hallway to two doors, one on each side. Both were labeled "Private." Adam tried the knob to the one facing the street.

"It's locked."

"Don't you have the key?" Chaney asked.

"Nope. I guess you'll have to do the honors."

"No need." She went to the front desk and searched through the center drawer. Returning to Adam, she held up a silver key.

"How did you find that?"

"You said Angela had been with your dad a long time. No surprise she'd have a key to his office."

"I picked a lock once." Adam chuckled at the memory. "We had this dog, a handsome blue merle collie named Griff. He'd go in the bathroom and push the door shut. One day, he locked himself in there."

"How did he do that?"

"The door had a push button lock and somehow he pressed it hard enough to lock the door. The key wasn't over the door jamb, so I straightened out a paper clip. It took some doing, but I finally got it open."

"Lock-picking is a good skill to have. All you need is a kit and practice." Chaney unlocked the office door and switched on the light.

"What are we looking for?" Adam asked.

"Anything that will give us a clue."

She studied the room to get a feel for the man who worked here while Adam rifled through the desk drawers. Bookshelves lined one wall of the small room. The books, mostly textbooks and manuals, didn't seem to be in any particular order. Stacks of paper were shoved here and there along with a variety of tchotchkes—dog and cat figurines, plastic jaws, a plush toy horse. His diplomas centered the brag wall. Other frames held certificates and photographs.

One photo showed a much younger Dr. Thorne—Chaney recognized him from the images she'd seen online—dressed in hunter's gear and holding a turkey by its feet.

"Your dad hunts?" she asked.

"He used to. Not so much anymore."

Chaney took a closer look at the photographs. The more recent ones showed Thorne receiving an award or with his staff at what looked like a party of some kind. Others showed him as a sportsman, sometimes alone with his gear or his trophies, sometimes with another pal or two.

"Who is this guy?" Chaney asked. She took a photo from its hook and held it out to Adam.

He looked up from a stack of files he'd pulled from a drawer. "That's Uncle Buddy. He's not my real uncle, though. Just a friend of Dad's."

"Close friends?"

"They were the best men at each other's weddings. But I think they had a falling out. I haven't seen Buddy since Mom's funeral."

"What was the argument about?"

"No idea. Dad doesn't talk about it."

Chaney hung the photo back on the wall and took a closer look at the others that showed Buddy. She couldn't be sure, but it looked like similar elements appeared in most of them.

A dirt road. The corner of a wooden house, the boards weathered to a light gray. A firepit and a lean-to.

A tingling sensation shot through Chaney's spine, a familiar feeling that told her she was on to something.

"Where were these photos taken?" she asked, keeping her voice casual.

Adam glanced at the pictures she indicated. "That's Uncle Buddy's hunting camp. Down in Osceola County."

"Have you been there?"

"A few times. When I was a kid." He closed one folder and opened another one. "These look like invoices, correspondence. Nothing important."

"I had an 'Uncle Buddy,' too." Chaney sat in the chair opposite the desk. "His real name was Horatio Wallace."

"No wonder he went by Buddy." Adam replaced the folder. "My Uncle Buddy's name is Duncan Birch. He lives in Sanford now."

Duncan Birch, Sanford. Thank you, Adam.

The important questions were whether Mr. Birch still owned the hunting camp and where it was located. Though perhaps it didn't matter if Birch still owned the property. Dr. Thorne would have taken the horse, if he was responsible for its disappearance, somewhere quiet and isolated. And familiar. Someplace he'd been before.

She didn't need Adam's help to find the location of the camp. She'd investigate Duncan Birch first. Then, once she knew something for certain, she'd tell Adam. If she asked him too many questions about the camp, he'd jump to his own conclusions and might insist on going there tonight. She couldn't let that happen. Not yet.

She picked up the old-fashioned page-a-day calendar from the desk. "Have you looked through this?"

"Yeah, I went back a couple of weeks. He likes to doodle."

Chaney pushed the pages over the metal arches to the beginning of the year then turned them one by one. Adam was right. The pages were sprinkled with primitive drawings and jotted notes. A dog's head. A side-view of a cat. Stars and flowers. A reminder to pay a bill, to fill a prescription. The profile of a horse drawn January 23rd, a few days before Dr. Thorne disappeared.

Chaney glanced at Adam, sitting in the chair behind the desk, flipping through the pages of another folder. She envisioned an older version of him—his dad—sitting in that same chair, talking on the phone, doodling a horse because that's what was on his mind.

Was he talking to Sandy-Lynne Nolan? Or was he talking to Duncan Birch? An old friend who, despite a falling out, could be trusted to keep a secret.

Chaney looked through the rest of the pages until she reached the date of Thorne's disappearance, the date the calendar had been opened to, and replaced it on the desk.

"Finding anything?" she asked.

"No." Adam sighed in frustration. "There's nothing here."

"He'll call, Adam."

"You think?"

"Eventually, yes. He's not going to want you to worry."

"It's a little too late for that." He rose from the chair. "Anything else you want to see while you're here?"

She was itching to get to a computer, but she also needed to be sure she wasn't overlooking anything. Plus, Adam needed a distraction. "Why don't you give me the tour?"

They closed up his dad's office and Chaney pointed to the door labeled "Private." "What's in there?"

Adam opened the door. Metal shelves held bags and cans of pet food, neatly folded blankets and towels, puppy pads, packs of toilet paper and paper towels, and assorted other supplies.

Chaney laughed. "Why is all this private?"

"Someone's idea of a joke, I suppose."

They poked their heads into the examining and surgery rooms, wandered through what Adam called the command center where meds were locked behind glass doors, a couple of microscopes rested on metal tables, and other equipment and supplies were stationed. Unlike Dr. Thorne's office, everything here was neat and tidy.

Adam pointed out the post-op area, a room with several crates of different sizes, then pushed through the door to the kennel. A soft light illuminated the room enough for them to see two dogs were spending the night. Chaney wanted to let them out to play, but Adam said absolutely not.

She contented herself with holding her fingers close enough for the dogs to sniff her hand, and to touch them as best she could.

On the way out, she returned the spare office key to Angela's desk, exactly where she'd found it. Maybe when this was all over, she'd give Adam his very own lock-picking kit. Just in case he ever got locked out of a bathroom again.

CHAPTER 22

***F*riday Morning**
Chaney, wearing her brunette persona, boarded the bus and took a seat near the back where she could keep an eye on the other passengers. She didn't plan to pickpocket any of them, but old habits were hard to break. *We don't got eyes in the backs of our heads,* her grandfather often said. *Folks will stab you in the back given half a chance.*

Not all folks.

Not Adam Buchanan Thorne.

He'd insisted Chaney spend the night in his guest room, and she hadn't refused. Without a vehicle of her own—or a place to go—what choice did she have? Besides, it was late when they returned from the clinic. She was tired, and her body still ached. The only thing she did before crawling into bed was an internet search for Duncan Birch's hunting camp. The Osceola County Property Appraiser's Office made the location easy to find.

After breakfast this morning, while Adam was busy in his study, she'd donned her brunette wig, left him a note, and hurried to the nearest bus stop. She didn't want him playing chauffeur again today. Or knowing her whereabouts.

When she reached the Thirty-Third Street Jail, she sat on the bench for a few moments, gathering her courage. Once inside the double doors, she hurried to the women's restroom to calm her shaking nerves and take a good look in the mirror.

She'd plastered on enough makeup that morning to cover the fading bruise on her jaw. Hopefully Marshall wouldn't notice any discoloration. If he even agreed to see her. If he'd really talked to Grant about Fletcher Wilkes, though, then perhaps he was counting on her to come. She hoped so.

Satisfied with her appearance, she checked in at the visitor's desk with her fake ID and took a seat. The minutes crawled by, the passing of each one increasing the tension in her stomach. Finally, the name of her brunette persona was called. Marshall had agreed to see her.

A guard escorted her to the visitation room and indicated her seat. A few moments later, Marshall appeared on the other side of the wired plexiglass. He smiled as he sat across from her, but the lines around his eyes and mouth had deepened, as if he'd aged a decade in only a few days.

They picked up their phones.

"How are you?" Chaney asked. "I've been worried."

"You shouldn't have come." Marshall glanced at the guard. "But I'm glad you did. Have you talked to Grant?"

"I've seen him."

"Did he give you my message?"

Chaney hesitated a moment, then nodded. Relief washed over Marshall's features as his shoulders relaxed and the tension eased around his eyes. A breath later, guilt pressed against her chest.

"That's great news." Marshall's easy grin added more pressure.

"He was too late," she blurted then lowered her voice, choosing her words carefully so that anyone who was listening wouldn't understand the conversation. "It's okay, though. I think I know where they are."

Marshall stared at her, his skin pale and his mouth grim. In his face, she read his concern, his unspoken plea for her not to get involved with Wilkes and Nolan.

"You'll have a new attorney," she said quietly, knowing he would understand the agreement she had made.

"Have you told him …?" Marshall asked, leaving the rest of the question unspoken: *him, meaning Nolan, where to find the horse?*

"Not yet. I want to be certain I'm right." She wished she could tell him about Adam, about the photographs she had seen in Dr. Thorne's office. About Duncan Birch and his hunting camp in rural Osceola County. But she didn't dare. Not with unseen ears listening, unseen eyes watching. Those invisible monitors didn't need to know of her involvement with Wilkes and his unsavory client.

"You can't tell him." Marshall's eyes softened. "I've been thinking about some of the stories Grandpa used to tell. He had a friend, involved in insurance, I think. Anyway, when they were young, they used to ride the rails. Like hobos. Got into all kinds of mischief. Sounds fun, doesn't it? But it could be dangerous. They never knew from one day to the next what might happen."

The nonsensical anecdote held a message. She'd picked up on the words he accompanied with a tap of his fingers on the table in front of him. *Insurance. Mischief. Dangerous.* The entire last sentence.

He was warning her that the horse, Mischief, was in danger. But why *insurance*? Unless … she willed herself not to react. Marshall leaned closer to the glass and pressed the side of his fist into his chest, as if pushing a knife into his heart. Then he rubbed his thumb against his fingers, the gesture small and hidden from the cameras. The universal gesture for money.

Insurance fraud. Nolan meant to kill Mischief.

Her breath caught.

"You're sure?" she mouthed.

He slowly blinked his eyes. *Yes.*

"I know you want to help me," he said, his tone normal. "But you should leave Orlando. We'll catch up again when I'm out of here."

"I can't leave you here. Not when—"

"Don't say it. You made a choice, and so did I."

Chaney blinked back sudden tears. She refused to cry, yet it was hard not to when Marshall had sacrificed his freedom for her sake. And, even worse, she was to blame.

"If only ..." she hesitated, knowing she couldn't mention the heist that had put Marshall behind bars. "We'd both be somewhere else right now. Two ordinary people."

"Us ordinary?" His voice sounded as sad as she felt. Almost hopeless. "The past is a heavy chain to drag around."

Someone, she couldn't remember who, had once told her the past was set in concrete. Both sayings were right. She and Marshall couldn't change the family they'd been born into, the lessons they'd learned, the petty crimes they'd committed in the name of survival.

But they still had a chance to do something about their future. Didn't they?

"I'll talk to the attorney about your bail," she said firmly. "And I'll let the doctor know about that other thing." That is, if she found Dr. Thorne at the hunting camp. Perhaps he'd know of a way to stop Nolan without betraying her involvement. Then Wilkes would still help Marshall and Mischief wouldn't be killed.

"You're walking a narrow plank," Marshall said. "With gators on one side and a sinkhole on the other."

"It's not the first time we've walked that plank."

"No." He gazed at her with an expression in his eyes she'd

never seen before. His affection for her was there, as always, and his respect. But also a sadness, as if things were changing between them. But that couldn't be.

"I'm not out there to have your back," he said. "What happens if you fall?"

"I won't." She placed her hand on the plexiglass. "Believe in me."

Marshall pressed his hand to the other side. "I do believe in you. I always will."

When Chaney walked out the doors of the compound, a sharp breeze scented with rain gusted the palm trees lining the street. Dark clouds swept across skies that had been clear and blue when she'd gone inside.

Typical Florida weather.

The darkness of the early afternoon matched her fallen spirits. No matter what Marshall said, she was responsible for the mess they were in. Not him. That's why she had to do whatever it took to get him out of that awful place.

Wilkes needed to know she might have a lead on Mischief's location. Dr. Thorne needed to be warned of Nolan's plan for the racehorse.

Only one question remained—how was she going to explain all this to Adam?

CHAPTER 23

Friday Afternoon

Adam hadn't been pleased to find Chaney's cryptic note, but what could he do about her sneaking out? Nothing. She was a grown woman, and he wasn't her guardian. So why did he feel responsible for her? At least she said she'd be back. She just didn't say when.

He unloaded the bags they'd left in his Charger last night and put them in the garage next to the boxes he'd brought home from the church office. She could decide what she needed to take into the house when she returned.

After lunch, Isaac Kinsley, his dad's lawyer friend, called to discuss the finer points of the severance package and make a few recommendations. Adam jotted notes, but he wasn't sure he wanted to get into a negotiating battle with the board. Maybe he should sign the document, dust off his feet and gird up his loins—metaphorically speaking—and pray for God to open a door. Open a window. Open a porthole. Open … something.

A couple of hours later Adam left a note for Chaney telling her where he was going in case she returned to the bungalow before he did. Then he drove in a downpour to the community center for the weekly GED preparation class he taught, arriving early so he could speak to Hector Reyes, the program administrator before the students arrived.

He found Hector in the cafeteria, a mug of coffee in one hand and a red velvet cupcake in the other.

"Care for a snack?" Hector gestured toward a variety of cupcakes, brownies, and granola bars arranged on the counter.

"No, thanks," Adam replied. "Do you have a minute? I need to talk to you."

"Sure." Hector led the way to an isolated table. "What can I do for you?"

Adam sat across from him. "I'm not sure where to begin."

"How about at the beginning? That always seems a good place to start."

"Okay." Adam pressed his lips together, buying himself an extra moment while he gathered his thoughts. This wasn't going to be easy. Admitting failure never was. "I met with Pete Davis a few days ago. The board asked for my resignation."

Hector stared at him, the cupcake halfway to his mouth. "What? Why? I don't understand."

"Neither do I. Not really." Adam took a deep breath. "Pete said this situation with my dad's disappearance made the church look bad."

Hector snorted. "That's ridiculous."

"You don't feel the same way?" At Hector's quizzical expression, Adam rushed to explain. "I thought maybe ... because of this thing with my dad and then me getting fired ... maybe I should step down. Appearances do matter, especially to a nonprofit dependent on donors."

"Character matters more. As long as you're willing to volunteer your time, you're welcome here." Hector bit into his cupcake. "Sure you don't want one of these?"

"Not now. I better get to class." Adam stood and extended his hand. "Thanks, Hector. I didn't want to walk away when we're so close to finishing the course."

"I'd never let you."

Adam started to leave but turned back when Hector called his name. "It may not seem like it right now, but God *does* have a plan for you."

Adam hoped Hector was right. He certainly didn't have one of his own.

* * *

WHEN THE CLASS ENDED, Adam stayed afterwards to talk to a couple of the older students. The men, who both worked in the hotel industry, were eager to get their GED certificates so they could begin earning their college degrees. Adam answered their questions about the class material then asked about their families. The men were more than students; over the past several weeks, they'd become friends.

Adam was walking through the lobby with them when a familiar voice called his name. Piper stood in the doorway to the room that served as the center's library. "I thought I'd find you here," she said. "Could we talk a moment?"

Adam managed to keep his surprise from showing on his face, though he wasn't sure how. Seeing her was the last thing he'd expected. And she was the last person he wanted to see.

"I don't have a lot of time." Which wasn't at all true. What did he have to do? Go home and feel sorry for himself? He might be feeling even sorrier after this conversation, though he couldn't imagine what they had to talk about. Unless she wanted her yoga pants back. That thought amused him, but it wouldn't amuse her.

"This won't take long," she said.

Adam said goodbye to his students then followed Piper into the library.

"My mom said you quit your job." She set her designer bag on a table. "I told her she must have been mistaken. But then I went to your office and your secretary said it was true. You didn't quit because of me, did you? I mean, because of us?"

Is that the story Pete was passing around? The reason he had insisted Adam stay away from the staff? From Bible study and from Sunday service? "I didn't quit. I was ... terminated."

"You mean you were fired?" Piper's face paled and her eyes widened. "Why?"

Adam paused before answering. He didn't want to talk to her about his dad's disappearance. Or about his meeting with Pete. He'd shared too much of his heart with her already, only to have it broken.

"Different philosophies," he finally said. That was true enough, given the many clashes he'd had with Pete over the past months.

"I am sorry." She rested her hand on his arm, her touch electrifying his skin. He wanted her to move away. He wanted her to never leave him.

"If you want someone to talk to," she continued, her voice soft and enticing, "you will call me, won't you? I want us to stay friends."

She sounded so hopeful, so sincere, and totally oblivious to what her presence was doing to his heart.

"We will," he said with as much warmth as he could muster, even though the words were a lie. He wasn't in the mood for her sympathy, her compassion. "It's been a rough few days, though. I'm sure you understand."

"I do," she gushed, giving him the gorgeous smile that turned his heart to mush.

He returned the smile, knowing she believed she understood, that she knew him so well that she could practically read his thoughts. But she could never understand. When had anyone ever broken her heart? Never.

But this was the second time she'd broken an engagement. Maybe he should have seen it coming.

Except they'd seemed so perfect for each other. Never an argument, rarely even a disagreement.

Apparently, that had been part of the problem. Piper had realized she was too willing to go along to get along rather than express her true opinions. Adam had disagreed, but she took that as proof she was right. It sounded like a circular argument to him, especially since she couldn't give examples of when he hadn't listened to her, hadn't supported her. After all, he wasn't a caveman who dictated everything they did or made all their plans. To his mind, they made decisions together. Plus, they had the same interests, the same values.

They were perfect for each other. Maybe, if it was possible, too perfect for each other. At least, she believed that so deeply she returned his ring.

And shattered his heart.

"I need to go," he said. "I'm sorry."

Tears formed in her eyes. He shifted away, not wanting to make the mistake of taking her in his arms. If he did, he'd never want to let her go again. But she was no longer his to hold onto.

"Hey, Adam." Chaney's voice came from the foyer. She caught his gaze and hurried to him. "We need to talk."

Despite her rain-dampened sweatshirt, she looked like a breath of fresh air as she bounced toward him, her eyes shining and bright, her short blonde hair tousled from the wind. His spirits lifted just looking at her, and so did his hopes that she had found something that would lead him to his dad.

But the timing couldn't have been worse.

Or maybe the timing was spot-on. He had nothing more to say to Piper, and he wasn't sure she could say anything else to him that mattered.

"What is it?" he asked as Chaney came nearer.

"I think I know where to find your dad." She beamed at him then energetically shook her head. "I mean, I could be wrong so don't get your hopes up. But it's a definite possibility."

"Where?"

Before Chaney could answer, Piper stepped to Adam's side and looped her arm through his. "You know where Tucker is?" she asked.

The light in Chaney's eyes dimmed as she looked from Adam to Piper and back again. "We should talk about this in private."

She'd obviously recognized Piper from the photos she'd seen at his house.

"I agree." He gestured in Chaney's direction with his free hand. "This is a friend of mine, Chaney Rose. Chaney, this is Piper Hadley."

"Chaney Rose?" Piper said. "Unusual name."

"Chaney is an unusual person," Adam said with a smile.

"I thought I knew all of your friends." Piper glanced at Adam then at Chaney. "How did you and Adam meet?"

A spark of mischief shone in Chaney's eyes. Adam could only imagine how she would answer if he gave her the chance. But Piper didn't need to know they'd met after Chaney had broken into his house. "At the Dogwood Diner," he said before Chaney could respond. "You know, that little place over by Giaquinto's Jewelry." Where he'd bought her ring.

"I know it." She smiled at Chaney, a plastic smile Adam had rarely seen. "Adam is a magnet for people in trouble. I don't know how many times I've told him to be careful of those who want to take advantage of him."

"How wonderful he has you around to advise him," Chaney said, nodding. "If not for your influence, he might do something really crazy. Like give an expensive diamond ring to a complete stranger."

"Excuse me?" Piper's eyes narrowed in confusion. "You can't be serious." She lowered her voice, practically hissing through her teeth. "You gave her my engagement ring."

"*Your* engagement ring?" Chaney surprised expression was clearly feigned. "I thought the ring belonged to Adam. Not that it matters. I didn't accept it."

Chaney grinned at Adam, amusement dancing in her eyes. "We really do need to talk. I'll wait in your car." She held out her hand and he tossed her his key.

At least he could be thankful for her quick thinking, if not for her sense of humor. Piper's grip on his arm had tightened and her jaw was set in stone. She was obviously not amused. Truth be told, neither was Adam. But at least Chaney had the grace to go away and give him a chance to do damage control.

"I'll be out in a couple of minutes," he said to Chaney.

"Great. Nice meeting you, Piper." After another quick smile, she turned on her heel and headed toward the exit doors. She pulled the hood of her sweatshirt over her head before running into the rain. With no umbrella. Why hadn't he noticed earlier? He could have given her his.

Once she left, Piper let go of his arm. "Please tell me you're not in a rebound relationship," she said. "Oh, Adam. You have to see that girl is not your type."

"My type? I didn't know I had a type."

"It's obvious that she and I have nothing in common. It's as if you purposely found someone who is the exact opposite of me."

"How can you know what she's like? You met her two minutes ago."

"I *know* people. What does she do? Has she even graduated from college?"

He had no idea how to respond to the first question, and he didn't know the answer to the second. What did it matter?

The light he'd used to view Piper shifted slightly to illuminate a facet of her personality he hadn't seen before. Or perhaps he had but chosen to ignore it until now.

None of that mattered now, but it didn't lessen the pain in his heart.

"We're not dating." He paused. "She isn't a rebound."

"I'm glad to hear it." Piper stepped close enough for her fragrance to swirl around him. "I meant what I said. If you need to talk, if you *want* to talk, then call me. It'll be like old times."

Like old times? Who was she trying to kid? Him or herself?

Maybe she was regretting the break-up. A small flame of hope flared then quickly died. A reconciliation was no longer possible. Too much had happened since they broke up. The disappearance of his dad and losing his job had blunted the pain with their own sharp jags, but it was still there. Especially when she was standing in front of him, her hand on his chest, her eyes gazing into his.

He covered her hand with his and squeezed her fingers.

"I have to go," he said, his voice hoarse.

The warmth in her eyes faded. "Yes. Your *friend* is waiting."

"Take care, Piper." He moved past her and didn't look back. In his rush to get away, he forgot to grab his umbrella. He stood on the porch under the awning and debated whether to go back for it. But he couldn't bring himself to turn around. Instead he ducked his head and started to run to the parking lot when a horn honked. His car, Chaney in the driver's seat, sat at the curb.

He wasn't sure whether he was glad she'd driven around to pick him up or annoyed that she'd presumed to drive his car.

It doesn't have a heart, he reminded himself as he jogged toward it. He'd heard the mantra at a church camp when he was twelve or thirteen years old. The speaker, an athletic missionary home on furlough, had the boys wanting to be him and the girls swooning over him. He loved his car, he'd told the boys. A restored Mustang, if Adam remembered right. But it didn't have a heart—people did—and material possessions belonged to God to be used for His purposes. Other lessons Adam had learned that summer were long forgotten, but that one had stayed with him and taught him to hold his possessions lightly.

Still.

He didn't like not being in the driver's seat.

CHAPTER 24

Friday Afternoon

When she had unlocked Adam's car, Chaney vowed not to say anything to him about the beautiful, gorgeous, mean-spirited Piper Hadley. How dare she be so dismissive of Chaney's name? What kind of name was Piper?

For a brief moment, Chaney considered returning to the community center and revealing more details to Piper about how she and Adam met. What would Ms. Piper Hadley think about that? She'd probably never broken into anyone's house in her life.

Chaney grinned at the thought. As if Piper's lack of thieving skills was a bad thing. If Chaney's own upbringing had been different, she wouldn't be breaking into houses either.

She started the engine and pulled around to the front of the community center. When Adam emerged from the building, she honked to get his attention. Fingers crossed he wouldn't be aggravated that she was driving.

He slid into the passenger seat and shook the raindrops from his head. "Forgot my umbrella," he said.

"You use an umbrella?"

"Don't you?" He held up a hand. "Never mind. I saw you leave without one."

"I don't like them," she said nonchalantly. "They're cumbersome. And they drip."

"When you don't use one, you drip," he retorted.

"Wow. Grumpy much?"

He avoided her gaze by fastening his seat belt. "It's been a challenging day," he said. "Sorry."

"Apology accepted." She drove toward the exit. "What's the best way to get to your house from here?"

Adam confirmed the route she thought was the right way. The windshield wipers swept away the rain with rhythmic thwacks as she followed the curve of the road. Adam was quiet, giving her time to think about her afternoon.

After she returned to the bungalow and read Adam's note, she'd removed the wig, tousled her short strands, taken several deep breaths, and called Fletcher Wilkes.

He'd sounded overjoyed to hear from her, but his enthusiasm faded when she presented her plan. Its simplicity was genius and ensured the attorney would keep his part of the bargain. He agreed to text her proof once he had filed a motion requesting another hearing for Marshall.

Meanwhile, Chaney would verify that Mischief was where she suspected before giving Wilkes the location. She didn't tell him that she intended to share Mickey Nolan's plan with his wife, Adam's dad, or whoever else might be with the horse. They'd have time to leave their hiding place before Mickey showed up.

But Chaney would have kept her side of the bargain, and she expected Wilkes to keep his.

She'd decided to tell Adam about the hunting camp, but he seemed too out-of-sorts. Had he planned to meet Piper at the community center, or had she surprised him? Chaney suspected the latter, given his troubled demeanor.

They drove in silence until the rush hour traffic made it impossible for Chaney to merge into the left turn lane at a major intersection.

"You can turn at the next light," Adam said. "Do you have plans for supper?"

"Only to eat," she teased.

He pulled out his phone and tapped the screen. "Why don't we get a pizza? We can pick it up on the way home."

"Sounds good." Even better than the pizza was the way he said *home*. As if she was welcome there, belonged there. Though that wasn't true. He'd said it out of habit, nothing more than that.

"What toppings do you like?" he asked.

They negotiated their choices—absolutely no black olives for Chaney and no green peppers for Adam—ending up with pepperoni, bacon, roma tomatoes, and onions. He directed her to the restaurant, a local place instead of a chain. Dodging raindrops, they raced inside and waited on a bench for their to-go order.

He held out his hand, palm up, and Chaney made a show of reluctantly returning his key. "Thanks," he said. "What did you do today?" He leaned closer, his shoulder pushing against hers, and whispered, "Pick any pockets? Break into any houses?"

He likely meant to tease, but the accusations still stung. She jutted out her chin. "Nothing of the sort. I went to see my cousin."

"I would have driven you." Adam's quiet voice held no hint of teasing, no pompous superiority.

"I needed to go by myself."

"Maybe another time then."

"Maybe." Though probably not.

"How is he? Does he need anything?"

"To get out."

"Afraid I can't help with that." His eyes rounded. "You're not planning to..."

Was he joking? His appalled expression indicated he wasn't.

"I don't have the know-how to orchestrate a break-out," she whispered. "I'm not really Jean Valjean, you know."

His shoulders sagged in relief, and Chaney giggled at how horrified he had sounded and his unjustifiably high opinion of her criminal abilities. Or would that be a *low* opinion? She giggled again, causing him to laugh. The other patrons shot amused glances their way.

"To go order for Thorne," the teen at the counter announced.

"That's us." Adam wiped his eyes before retrieving their pizza. Chaney managed to settle her giggles as she prepared to dash to the car. A car without dents that would transport them to a safe, cozy house where she could peacefully sleep in a warm, comfy bed.

She'd have to leave it all behind soon. But not tonight.

* * *

"I'VE BEEN THINKING," Adam said as he lifted a second slice of pizza from the box, "about this Sherlock Holmes story, 'The Adventure of Silver Blaze.' Do you know it?"

"I don't think so." Chaney popped a pepperoni into her mouth.

"It's the one with the line about the 'curious incident of the dog in the night-time.'"

"The dog that didn't bark," Chaney chimed in. "That I've heard about. But I don't know what happened in the story."

"Quick summary. A stolen racehorse turns out to be hiding in plain sight. His white markings were dyed so that even his owner didn't recognize him."

"You think Mischief has been dyed?"

"Probably not," Adam admitted. "It was an old trick, and

racehorses these days have lip tattoos and microchips. But maybe he's with other horses. In a pasture somewhere or maybe at a riding stable."

"I suppose it's possible." Chaney avoided eye contact as she placed the uneaten portion of her pizza on her plate. Despite only knowing her for a few days, he knew that expression.

Adam set down his own piece. "You know where Mischief is." His tone dared her to deny it.

"I have a hunch."

He sat back, stunned, as if her words had pushed him. "Where?"

"The hunting camp."

"Of course." He scratched his chin as he tried to order his muddled thoughts. Hidden in the woods, miles from the closest town, the remote camp was the ideal place to get off the grid. Why hadn't it occurred to him? "I should have known. It's perfect."

"It's only a hunch," Chaney cautioned. "I checked online, and Duncan Birch of Sanford owns acreage in southern Osceola County. But the online records also indicated that your dad still lived here. We both know how that turned out."

"'You see but you do not observe.' Me, not you," he clarified. "It's an Arthur Conan Doyle quote. From 'A Scandal in Bohemia.'"

"Sherlock Holmes again?"

"It was the photos at the clinic, wasn't it? You saw them and you knew." He was too flabbergasted to eat his pizza.

"I had a hunch."

"Why didn't you say anything last night? We could have driven down there today."

"I had things I needed to do today. And so did you."

"Nothing I couldn't have gotten out of." Frustration laced his words. If only she had said something last night, then he'd know by now if his dad was at the camp. Chaney didn't need to go with him if she needed to visit her cousin instead.

"You're mad at me," she said.

"Irritated." He gazed out a nearby window where the heavy downpour streamed along the glass and lightning split the darkness. How rain-proof was the cabin at the camp? The men used to take care of the upkeep, but as far as he knew, his father hadn't been there in several years.

"I'll go." Chaney carried her plate to the sink and tossed her paper napkin in the trashcan.

It took a moment for her words to sink in. She was in the hallway before he realized what she'd said. He shoved back his chair and followed her.

"Go where?"

She turned, shrugged. "Away."

"In this weather?"

"I've been in worse."

They stared at each other for a long moment.

"I'm going to the camp tomorrow," he finally said. "You can come along if you want."

A kind of veneer—obstinance? defiance?—seemed to slide from her shoulders as she visibly relaxed. "I'd like that."

She still hid something from him, of that he was certain. But he'd never find out what if he didn't keep her close. The long drive to the camp would give them plenty of time to talk. All he had to do was earn her trust.

The trust of a thief.

CHAPTER 25

*S*aturday

"I think this is it." Chaney glanced from the print-out of the map to the dirt road that headed to the west. The hunting camp didn't have an address, and Adam had told her he was about fourteen the last time he was there. The two of them had consulted a satellite mapping site last night to pinpoint the location. Adam suggested calling his Uncle Buddy to find out if his dad was there and to get directions. But Chaney had persuaded him not to do that.

She didn't want to take a chance on Birch warning Tucker. Even if he wasn't aware that they could be at his camp, he might interfere in some way. Adam didn't seem to know the reason for the falling-out between his dad and Birch. If it had been bad enough for the two men to avoid each other, with the exception of Mrs. Thorne's funeral, then who knew how Birch would react to the news that his estranged friend was hiding out on his property?

Adam turned right onto the dirt road, driving slowly to avoid the ruts. They were getting farther and farther from civilization. Florida might have an overpopulation problem, but not out here.

Their route had taken them south on John Young Parkway to Kissimmee then east on Highway 192 toward St. Cloud. The construction on the highway going into the town, nicknamed Soldier City, was torture, but Adam knew how to avoid the worst of it by detouring down Lakeshore Drive, a street running along the southern shore of East Lake Tohopekaliga.

Chaney had never been to the well-kept lakefront. Adam passed the time by filling her in on the town's history. It hadn't grown as quickly as Kissimmee, which was located closer to Disney World, but was definitely no longer the sleepy town that had invited Union soldiers to make their home there after the Civil War. The early founders welcomed their former enemies by naming the north/south streets after states such as Vermont, Pennsylvania, New York, and Michigan.

With anyone else, the history lesson might have been boring. But Adam's entertaining anecdotes held her interest. Maybe because he was one of those rare species, a native Floridian, and he cared about the state's rich, multicultural heritage and its fabled, though sometimes ridiculous, occurrences.

Chaney had never thought much about Florida's past beyond the basics. Pirates in Tampa. The five flags flown over St. Augustine. The manatees at Blue Springs. Beach-driving in Daytona. And the possibility of gators in every single body of water, no matter how shallow.

According to Adam, his grandfather had filled out the paperwork to receive the distinguished Florida Pioneer Family designation. He'd been able to prove a direct lineage to an ancestor who had settled in what was now Orange County before Florida became a state.

The little green-eyed monster popped up its ugly head again. Chaney knew her grandparents' names on her mother's side of the family but nothing beyond them and little on her father's side. Both families were wanderers, moving from place to place in the search of their promised land. Unlike the wandering Israelites, they'd never found it.

She and Marshall, the only ones left as far as they knew, were still looking.

If a "wandering gene" existed, it ran in their family. Perhaps she'd never have a stable home of her own. But she longed for one.

Someday, Marshall had often promised. But if it wasn't in their DNA to settle in one place, did they really have a choice? A chance at a different kind of life?

Adam hit a large bump, jarring Chaney from her thoughts. Long-horned cattle grazed in the pastures on both sides of the road. Slender white birds, perhaps a type of ibis or egret, perched on their backs.

"This is like driving into the past," Chaney said. "I can imagine a cowboy galloping along any moment to round up these longhorns and drive them to market."

"On some of the ranches around here, they still do," Adam said. "My dad and I went on a historic roundup after I graduated from high school. It was supposed to be one of those father-son bonding moments before I went to college."

"Supposed to be?" Chaney asked gently.

"Turned out it was," he said. "At first, I pretended like I wanted to be anywhere else, but deep inside I was so pumped. We rode horseback all day, slept under the stars at night." He laughed to himself as if reliving the experience. "I sure was saddle-sore, I can tell you that."

Chaney could relate. She'd never gone on a roundup, but her grandfather's list of life skills included riding horses, swimming, tennis, and self-defense. She rested her fingers on her tender ribs. Maybe she needed a refresher course on that last one.

"We'd been having a hard time," Adam continued. "Dad and

me. I was ready to spread my wings, and he wasn't quite willing to let me go."

As Adam shared a couple of stories from the trip, Chaney tried to imagine what it must be like to have a parent like that— one who was reluctant to push their child into adulthood.

"Sounds like it was a great experience," she said.

"Better than either of us expected." Adam slowed the car even more. "I think there's a turn up here somewhere. Keep an eye out."

"Is that it?" Chaney pointed to a wooden sign next to a lane even more rutted and muddy than the one they were on. It read *Birch Camp*. "Do you think they could have pulled a horse trailer back there?"

Adam slowed to a crawl. "If they were desperate enough. Desperate people do desperate things."

They sure do.

Adam made the turn and braked.

"Are you okay?" Chaney asked.

"Fine. I just need a moment."

He bowed his head.

He's praying? For what?

She'd gotten used to him praying before their meals, but why now? What would it change?

She straightened in her seat, watching him from her peripheral vision. After several seconds, his shoulders rose, as if a weight was being lifted, and the tension faded from his face.

He lifted his head, caught her gaze, and smiled. "Ready?"

A twinge of guilt squeezed at her gut. Maybe she should tell him about Wilkes and Nolan. But what if no one was at the camp? She'd still need his help to locate his dad.

"I'm ready."

Adam crept along, maneuvering the Charger around the ruts and mud puddles.

"Sure hope we don't get stuck," Chaney said.

"Wish I had Dad's truck," Adam replied.

The one-lane road curved between giant trees that had probably been planted more than a century ago. Spanish moss hung from the sweeping branches. Another turn and they reached a locked gate.

"I don't remember this being here," Adam said. "Guess maybe it was left open back in the day."

"I'll get it." Chaney eased out of the car, glad for the rubber boots they'd picked up at Tractor Supply since her feet sank into the mud. One stumbling step at a time, she made her way to the gate and swung it open.

When Adam drove through, she closed the gate and sloshed to the Charger. She opened the passenger door and peered inside. "Maybe we should walk the rest of the way. Catch them by surprise. Besides, my boots are a muddy mess."

"Good idea. The rest of the way might be even rougher after all that rain yesterday." Adam turned off the engine.

"Though we don't want to surprise them too much," Chaney said as he joined her. "Does your dad have a gun?"

"Probably. But he won't shoot without knowing what—or who—he's shooting at."

"I hope you're right. Though don't be surprised if I stay behind you."

"Is that the way it is?" Adam said with a teasing laugh. "No one's going to get shot."

Chaney's skin tingled, and she zipped her jacket against a sudden gust of wind. They'd probably find no one at the cabin, and Adam's high estimation of her deductive abilities would sink as deep as her boots were sinking in this mud.

As they rounded a bend, the wooden house she'd seen in Dr. Thorne's photos came into view. Several trees sheltered the lopsided wooden front porch. Log benches surrounded a fire pit in a nearby clearing. All seemed quiet, too quiet. Almost eerie.

"I don't see his truck." Adam stepped closer to the house and called out. "Dad? Hey, Dad, are you here?"

No one answered.

"His truck might be around back," Chaney said.

Adam started to answer, but a helicopter flying overhead drowned out his words. He waited for it to pass. "Let's check inside."

Together they climbed the porch steps. Adam knocked on the door, waited a moment, then tried the handle. It turned in his hand and he opened the door.

"Dad?" he called again. "Are you here?"

Chaney surveyed the grounds then scraped the worst of the mud from her boots before entering the house. She had such hopes that his dad would be here. For Marshall's sake most of all, but also for Adam.

She'd enjoyed hearing about Adam's adventures with his dad on their roundup. No matter what happened in the future, the memories of that trip would always be with him. She wanted, more than she had realized till this moment, to be part of their reunion.

The whirring of helicopter blades sounded again. Chaney hadn't paid much attention when the chopper flew over before, but now her gut constricted.

"Maybe we should get out of here," she said.

"I don't think so. Look at this."

She joined him in the galley kitchen. A small coffee maker stood on the counter beside a stack of paper plates and a roll of paper towels. He opened the refrigerator door. A gallon of milk, a carton of eggs, creamer, and a few other items sat inside.

"None of this stuff has expired," he said.

"Let's check out the bedrooms."

A short hallway led from the living room to two bedrooms and a bathroom. Towels hung on hooks that hung over the bathroom door. Sleeping bags, pillows, and blankets covered the beds.

Adam returned to the living room and held his hand above the ashes in the fireplace. "They're warm. Let's go around back."

They went out the kitchen door. A huge truck was parked between the house and a three-sided lean-to.

"That's Dad's truck." Adam sounded both relieved and anxious.

Chaney peered into the open side of the lean-to. Fresh straw covered the dirt floor and the smell of horse manure sharpened the air. "I think Mischief is here, too."

Adam cupped his hands around his mouth. "Dad!" he yelled. "Where are you?"

Still no answer.

Chaney studied the sky, straining to hear. The whirr of the blades was back. Adam took a breath to yell again and she grabbed his arm. "Don't," she whispered. He gave her a quizzical look.

She scanned the sky but couldn't see the helicopter. "Listen."

The sound came closer then faded.

"What is it?" Adam asked.

"I've heard that helicopter three times now. We need to get out of here."

"Because of a helicopter?" Adam shook his head. "I'm not leaving till I find my dad."

"Adam, please. Trust me." She almost choked on the words. How could she expect him to trust her when she hadn't told him that she was working for Mickey Nolan?

"Go back to the car if you want. I'm going to check the woods." Without waiting for a response, he strode away.

She followed him, desperate to find a way to convince him they needed to leave. As she rounded the lean-to, she almost bumped into him. A horse trailer, an old one, was parked there.

"Does that belong to your dad?"

"No." Adam's mouth quirked as he scrunched his eyebrows. "I've never seen it before."

Something rustled in the thick stand of trees behind them, startling them both.

"Adam? Is that you?" An older man carrying a rifle traipsed toward them. "What are you doing here?"

"Dad?" Adam approached his father. "I've been so worried about you."

"I told you not to do that." Tucker Thorne turned back toward the woods. "Come on out, Sandy-Lynne. My son is here."

An attractive woman with coppery curls emerged from the woods leading a dark bay thoroughbred.

Mischief.

"This is Sandy-Lynne Nolan," Tucker said. "My son, Adam."

The woman came closer, a wary look in her eyes. "I've heard a lot about you," she said, but her tone wasn't welcoming.

"I'm sorry I can't say the same," Adam replied.

"Who's your friend?" Tucker tilted his head toward Chaney. Adam made the introductions. "She's the one who figured out where you might be.

"That so." Tucker eyed her suspiciously. "How did you go about that?"

"I saw the photos of the camp in your office. It seemed like a good place for you to hide."

"You were in my office?"

"We both were," Adam said, obviously trying to soothe his father's ruffled feelings. "I asked Chaney to help me find you. How did you get mixed up in this?"

"Your father was helping me," Sandy-Lynne said. "He's a very brave man. If not for him, Mischief could have been seriously injured. We refused to let that happen."

"Why don't we go back in the cabin," Tucker suggested. "More comfortable to talk in there."

"I think we should leave," Chaney said.

"Not yet." Adam's firm tone sent shivers up Chaney's spine. "I've got questions and I'm not leaving until I get answers."

"It may not be safe to stay," Chaney insisted.

"What do you mean?" Sandy-Lynne stood close to her horse. "Were you followed?"

"No," Adam said. "Believe me, we were the only ones on those rural roads."

"We might have been," Chaney contradicted. "I've heard a helicopter three times since we arrived. Why would a helicopter be anywhere around here?"

"Do you really think a chopper followed us from Orlando?" Adam asked her, his tone dismissive. "We would have noticed."

"The Mormons have a helicopter," Tucker said.

"What Mormons?" Chaney asked.

"The Mormon Church owns hundreds of thousands of acres in the tri-county area," Tucker explained. "I've seen helicopters flying around here before. The pilot is probably wondering what you're doing here. Wants to make sure you don't trespass on their land."

"I don't know." Chaney bit her lip. Her instincts told her the helicopter was trouble, but there wasn't much she could do if Adam and Tucker refused to listen to her. If Tucker knew that she'd broken into his home—well, Adam's home, but she doubted Tucker would make that distinction—he'd never tell them anything. A thief was a thief, he probably thought. And not to be trusted.

Though his own hands weren't completely clean.

"You two go on inside," Tucker said. "We'll take care of Mischief and join you in a few minutes." When neither Adam nor Chaney moved, Tucker touched his son's elbow. "Go on now. We've got sodas in the fridge. Help yourself."

Adam still hesitated, but his father nudged him.

"Come on, Chaney." Adam grabbed her hand, giving her little choice but to follow him to the cabin.

Once they were inside, she pulled free. "We need to leave. All of us."

"And go where?" Adam opened the refrigerator door. "Root beer, ginger ale, or Coke?"

"Adam, listen to me—"

"I'm not leaving till I've talked to my dad. You heard what he said. And I know for a fact no one followed us out here."

He was right about that. But it was hard to ignore her instincts when they'd kept her out of trouble more times than she could count. Maybe if she told him about her deal with Wilkes ... but how could she explain why she'd placed his father in danger? Why she hadn't been honest with him?

Would he ever forgive her?

Would she ever forgive herself if anything happened to him? Or if she failed to help Marshall?

Her cousin needed to be her primary concern. But that didn't mean she could leave Adam, his dad, and Sandy-Lynne to face Nolan if he was in that chopper.

Adam stood beside the fridge, the door still open. "Chaney? Drink?"

"Root beer."

He handed her a 12-ounce bottle, grabbed a Coke for himself, and shut the refrigerator door. He leaned against the counter as he twisted the cap. "I wanted to find Dad, but I didn't really think he'd be here," he admitted. "I guess I didn't want to believe he'd let himself get roped into some married woman's drama."

His tone sounded disappointed, hurt even.

Chaney pulled one of the chairs from the table, its legs scraping the linoleum floor, and sat down. She hadn't considered what it would be like for Adam to find his father here with a woman who wasn't his mother. Though he must have noticed that both the bedrooms were being used. It didn't seem as though they were sleeping together.

Still, she guessed that didn't absolve his dad of guilt in Adam's eyes. Sandy-Lynne had needed help, and his dad had stepped up. He'd abandoned his practice, and, in a way, he'd abandoned Adam. For what? And why?

As she twisted the cap from her root beer, the foam hissed and expanded. She waited for the airy bubbles to settle before taking a long drink. The chilled beverage had that warm mellow taste she liked in a root beer. It was hard to enjoy anything, though, when all she wanted to do was run from the cabin, jump in Adam's Charger, and speed away. If she had the key, she'd probably do just that. Let him and his dad and Mickey's horse-thief of a wife face the consequences of not listening to her.

Except those consequences could be deadly. At least for Mischief. Hopefully Mickey wouldn't go so far as to harm his wife. Though what would he do to Tucker if he believed the veterinarian had betrayed him? Men like Mickey didn't take kindly to betrayal.

Adam's fingers gripped the soda bottle. He didn't move from his position by the counter as he waited for his dad and Sandy-Lynne to come to the cabin.

Chaney pulled her phone from her bag for no other reason than to have something to do with her hands. She rarely corresponded with anyone by email and stayed off social media except to stalk a mark. And she had no one to call or text. Just as well, since the phone showed only one bar. She opened a game app and played solitaire.

Losing again and again.

CHAPTER 26

*S*aturday

Sandy-Lynne patted Mischief's neck as she scanned the thin white clouds stretched across the light blue of the sky. The helicopter was nowhere to be seen.

"What if that girl is right?" Her voice trembled from the shock of seeing two strangers in their hidden sanctuary. Over the past several days, she'd allowed herself to be lulled into a false sense of security. To relax and even enjoy the solitude. But now their refuge had been invaded. When she'd first heard Adam call out for his dad, she'd reflexively reached for the snub-nosed revolver in her jacket pocket.

"We go to Plan B," Tucker replied.

"Which is?"

"I don't know yet." His nonchalant demeanor wasn't reassuring, not when worry clouded his eyes.

"Do you believe her story? About how she knew where to look for us?"

"No one but Duncan knew where we were. He promised not to tell Adam." Tucker scratched the back of his head, an unconscious habit that indicated uncertainty. "How else could she have guessed?"

After two weeks at the cabin, Sandy-Lynne knew Tucker's gestures and moods as well, maybe even better, than she did Mickey's. But even before they ran away with Mischief, she'd come to think of him as a surrogate father.

To her husband, Tucker had been nothing more than hired help, easily replaced by a veterinarian who cared more about money than Mischief's well-being.

Though he'd never admit it, Mickey also treated Sandy-Lynne as if she were little more than an employee with a very specific job description. She was the trophy he showed off to his buddies at their fancy gambling parties, at the racetrack, at the social events where Mickey hungered to be part of the inner circle. Whenever he needed arm candy, he counted on her to squeeze into a curve-hugging dress that flaunted her breast implants or her long, shapely legs. Preferably both.

During their brief courtship and the early days of their marriage, she'd reveled in the glitz and the glamor. The lavish dresses, the sparkling jewels, a thousand and one other luxuries. All hers because, with her at his side, Mickey had what other men wanted—a flirtatious plaything to indulge his appetites.

For a while, she'd happily played the role Mickey assigned her. But even though she still loved beautiful clothes and expensive jewelry, she'd wearied of their small-minded, gossipy circle and the lack of anything with authentic meaning in her life.

The change in her outlook occurred soon after Mickey surprised her with Mischief. Growing up, she'd spent summer vacations with relatives who operated a cattle ranch in Texas. She and her cousins often rode horses, and she'd always wanted one of her own.

Practically every day since her birthday, she'd opted to visit the stables instead of the shopping malls. Riding the spirited yet gentle horse transported her back in time to those glorious days at the ranch. Simpler times she now longed to recapture.

Then the new year came, and Sandy-Lynne learned that Mickey's gift came with strings. Mischief officially became a two-year-old on January 1st. He wasn't yet two, but in the world of racing, all horses shared the same birth date, no matter what month they were actually born. Mickey turned Mischief's care over to the trainer of his other two racehorses, and Sandy-Lynne was no longer permitted to ride him.

Nothing she said, not her tears, not her pleading, softened Mickey's heart. Mischief was a racehorse. He was going to race no matter the risk to his legs. Or, like the colt who had stumbled, his life.

"It never occurred to me that someone could look at those pictures and guess we were here," Tucker said, drawing Sandy-Lynne from her thoughts. "But I don't see any other way she could have known."

"She's apparently very astute." Which meant she was also dangerous. Or was that Sandy-Lynne's nerves talking? It was hard not to feel paranoid when you knew someone was after you.

"Let's go in and talk to them. See what they have to say," Tucker said. "After they leave, if it'll make you feel better, I'll hook the trailer up to the truck. Just in case."

"Just in case." Three little words, ominous with their weight.

Sandy-Lynne led Mischief inside the lean-to and closed the metal gate they'd installed. She unfastened the lead rope from his halter then brushed his coat while Tucker added fresh water to the trough. Mischief stood quietly, occasionally flicking his tail from one side to the other. The rhythmic movements alleviated the tension that had built up inside Sandy-Lynne since Adam and Chaney's arrival. The familiar bonding ritual with her beloved horse also strengthened her resolve to protect him. No matter the risk. No matter the cost.

CHAPTER 27

*S*aturday

Adam straightened when the door creaked open. He glanced at Chaney who alerted at the sound, her body stiff and tense, as if she were a pointing dog. Not a kind comparison, but that's exactly what she reminded him of as she focused on the door.

His dad and Sandy-Lynne entered and took seats at the wooden table. Adam joined them.

"It's not safe here," Chaney said.

Tucker stared at her. "Tell me again who you are."

"I told you, Dad. She's a friend." Adam silently prayed that Chaney wouldn't talk about the break-in. His dad wouldn't be amused.

"Hmph." Tucker shifted in his seat and scratched the back of his head. "Are you the reason Piper broke off the engagement?"

"Me?" Chaney shifted her glance from Tucker to Adam to Tucker again. "You think I ... that Adam and I—"

"Dad!" Adam jumped in. "You are way out of line. Chaney and I only met a few days ago."

"Seems you've gotten mighty chummy in those few days. Breaking into my office together. Coming here together."

"There are ... circumstances."

"What kind of circumstances?"

"We can talk about that later." Adam focused on calming the turmoil in his stomach. The initial relief he'd felt at finding his dad safe and unharmed had faded, leaving frustration and hurt in its place. "Why are you here? With Mickey Nolan's wife?"

Maybe he shouldn't have said that last part. But ever since Tucker had sent him into the cabin, which seemed the equivalent of sending him to his room, he'd been brooding over his dad's relationship with Sandy-Lynne. Sure, it appeared they were sleeping in separate rooms. But who knew what went on in this secluded cabin?

Dad had a lot of nerve questioning him about Chaney when he was hiding out with another woman. A married woman.

"I already told you," Sandy-Lynne said. "He's helping me. Protecting me."

"From your husband?" Adam bit the inside of his lip. He hadn't meant to sound condescending, but that's how the words spilled from his mouth.

Sandy-Lynne scratched at a stain on the Formica tabletop. "My husband isn't a very nice man. He sees Mischief as a means to an end. Not as a beautiful, sweet-tempered colt who needs to be cared for when he's injured."

"What's wrong with him?" Chaney asked.

"His tendons are swollen," Sandy-Lynne explained. "It's a common injury with racehorses. If he races, he could break his leg and then—" her voice caught, and she took a moment to compose herself.

"Mischief needs weeks to recover, but my husband was determined to drug him up and race him anyway." She paused and blinked a couple of times. "I couldn't let that happen."

Adam shifted his gaze to Chaney, who was contemplating

Sandy-Lynne with admiration. A shared understanding seemed to pass between the two women. Great! Now his only ally had gone over to the other side.

A childish reaction on his part, but he couldn't push the feeling aside. Nor could he tamp down his growing anger. He was grateful that his dad was okay. But he was also mad.

Mad at the way Tucker talked to Chaney as if she were some kind of interloper.

Mad at him for getting involved in this unhappy woman's marital issues.

But most of all, he was mad because Tucker hadn't confided in him. Hadn't trusted him.

"So you spirited him away. Good for you." Chaney's eyes brightened as if this was the most exciting news she'd ever heard.

What else could you expect from a thief? She and Sandy-Lynne were kindred spirits.

"We did." Sandy-Lynne directed her gaze at Adam. Her eyes were light blue and dark-rimmed, an unsettling and attractive combination. Perhaps they were the weapon she used to bewitch his dad into behaving so foolishly. "I couldn't have managed without your father's help."

Adam bit his lip in frustration. She'd make a great witness for the prosecution if Tucker ended up taking the fall for the horse's disappearance.

"You can't stay out here forever," Adam said.

"The last qualifying race for the Florida Derby takes place next week," Tucker responded, sounding exasperated. "We only have to hide Mischief until it's over."

"Then what happens?" Adam countered. "You drive him to the stables as if nothing happened?"

"You don't need to worry, son." Tucker's attempt at a comforting smile failed miserably. Apparently, he was more worried about the situation than he wanted anyone else at the table to know. "I'm a big boy. And I knew what I was getting myself into when I agreed to help Sandy-Lynne."

"At least you're admitting this was all her idea. Maybe that will help you stay out of jail if her husband decides to press charges."

"That's not going to happen," Sandy-Lynne said firmly. "I won't let that happen."

"You couldn't keep your husband from racing that horse." Adam pushed back from the table and paced the narrow space behind his chair and the wall. "How will you keep him from blaming all of this on my dad? Because that's what he'll do, you know. He won't drag his wife's name through the mud, but he won't care about Dad's reputation."

"Sit down, Adam," Tucker soothed. "You're getting worked up over nothing." He leaned back in his chair, suddenly jovial. "You know, in a way, I feel like Queen Esther."

Adam stopped pacing and stared at his dad. "Queen Esther? You?"

"Remember what her uncle told her? Something about 'such a time as this'?"

"I know the story." Not only had he heard it multiple times in Sunday school, as his dad surely knew, he'd written a research paper on the Biblical book for one of his seminary classes.

"Maybe the good Lord had me at those stables for 'such a time as this,'" Tucker continued. "So I could protect Mischief." He chuckled, a hearty laugh that Adam hadn't heard in way too long. "Not that I'm comparing that racehorse to all the Jews that Haman wanted to kill, mind you. But you know better than I do how God uses His people in mysterious ways."

Adam huffed and shot a look at the ceiling. How did he respond to something so ... so ...?

"Who's Queen Esther?" Chaney asked.

Adam's mouth dropped open.

His dad chuckled again. "Tell her the story, son. I'll grill us some burgers."

"We don't have time for stories or for burgers." Chaney shifted toward Adam. "We should go."

"What's your hurry?" Sandy-Lynne asked, a slight edge to her voice. Adam guessed the "understanding" he'd sensed earlier between the two women had been too fragile to last very long.

"We're not safe here," Chaney said.

"Only because the two of you showed up," Sandy-Lynne challenged her.

"No one knows we're here." Adam returned to his seat. "We weren't followed."

Chaney gazed at him, but her eyes were unreadable. "You're right," she said, a cheerful lilt in her voice.

Too cheerful.

Adam couldn't deny she had good instincts, but his dad wasn't concerned about the helicopter. Why was she?

Was it possible she knew something his dad didn't?

Not only possible, but probable.

If only she'd tell him what it was.

CHAPTER 28

Saturday

Chaney slipped out the back door while Adam helped his dad with meal prep in the narrow galley kitchen. They were talking about sports as if the emotional turmoil from the earlier conversation had never existed. Sandy-Lynne, announcing she had a headache, had gone to her room.

Leaning against the truck's fender, Chaney listened for the chopper but heard nothing. Maybe Tucker was right. She hoped so. But the knot in her stomach told her that he wasn't.

She wandered to the lean-to and reached over the gate. Mischief came to her and sniffed her fingers. "I don't have anything to give you." She caressed his white blaze. "Only a pat or two."

He nodded his head as if to give his permission. She chuckled at his playfulness then spied the curry brush in a wooden carry-all containing other grooming tools and riding gloves. Without hesitating a second, Chaney climbed over the metal gate and slipped her hand beneath the brush's leather handle.

"I can see you don't need me to do this," she said. His dark bay coat already gleamed. "But I need it." As she brushed his shoulder, he bent his neck toward her and blew warm air from his nostrils. He seemed to be smiling, and Chaney chuckled again.

"I should take you out of here myself," she murmured in a low voice. "All I have to do is hook the trailer to the truck, lead you into the trailer, hot-wire the truck. And not get caught. Easy-peasy."

Not.

"Or I could tell Adam about my deal with Fletcher Wilkes. Except he'd never understand." To him, she'd be a traitor, and traitors belonged to a specific circle of hell. She'd read about that once, though she couldn't remember where. "I bet Adam with all his fancy education knows who wrote it."

Mischief whickered softly.

"The thing is, I need Wilkes to help Marshall. He's family, and family always comes first." That truism had been instilled in her since she lifted her first wallet. Though the family rule could be confusing. The adults didn't always follow it, but the younger ones were never allowed to forget it.

Her grandfather had left her to get out of scrapes on her own a number of times—scrapes he'd gotten her into.

But Marshall was different. He'd feel the sting of her betrayal. Even if he forgave her, the threads holding them together would fray at the edges. She couldn't let that happen.

Mischief nudged her shoulder as she brushed his coat. He arched his neck, ears pointing forward, then whinnied and scampered to the back of the lean-to.

Chaney stepped to the gate and strained to hear what he heard. The whoop-whoop of the helicopter blades came closer. And closer.

As the helicopter came into view, an engine roared from the drive. She dropped the brush in the carry-all, slipped through the gate, and hurried to the far side of the front porch between the railing and a hedge. A black SUV sped around the bend, bouncing along the rutted lane like an out-of-control bronco, on the other side of the house. The helicopter hovered overhead.

The front door of the cabin flew open as Adam, Tucker, and Sandy-Lynne emerged onto the porch.

Adam held her gaze a moment then motioned for her to step back. She crept beside the house, her back pressed against the cabin's wooden boards. What should she do now? She'd tried to warn them, but they wouldn't listen to her. And now they were trapped.

She had no doubt Mickey Nolan was in that SUV. He'd come for Mischief, and he wouldn't have come alone. Despite her earlier determination, not even Sandy-Lynne could stop him from taking the racehorse.

Uncertain what to do, Chaney stayed against the wall. The SUV's brakes squealed as it came to a stop. Car doors opened and a voice boomed.

"Thought I'd never find you, didn't you?"

That had to be Nolan. Pompous and pleased with himself.

Chaney knelt and peeked through the porch railing. Adam's and Tucker's legs blocked her view, so she shifted her vantage point, moving slowly to avoid drawing attention to herself, until she could see Mickey. He stood beyond the porch, a few yards from the railing, a bantam rooster wearing a tailored suit and a felt hat. Could the man be more of a caricature of a 1940s gangster?

Behind him, two beefy men stood by the vehicle. Both had shoulder holsters beneath their jackets.

"Go home, Mickey," Sandy-Lynne's voice rang out. "Mischief isn't ready to run again. Not yet."

"But darlin', we got a race coming up. I already paid the entry fee and you know as sure as I'm standing here that fees are non-refundable."

"You're not taking him." Sandy-Lynne tried to sound firm, but an emotional tremor caused her voice to waver.

Mickey summoned someone with the flick of his index finger. Another man stepped from behind the SUV. He wore jeans over cowboy boots, a blue chambray shirt, and a Stetson. With the gait of a man who was more comfortable riding a horse than walking, he followed the lane toward the back of the house.

He'd find the lean-to, the trailer, the truck. He'd find Mischief.

Chaney wrapped her arms around her aching stomach and cowered beneath the hedge.

Why hadn't they listened to her? Why hadn't she insisted they leave?

CHAPTER 29

*S*aturday

Adam didn't know what prompted him to glance at the other end of the porch. From his peripheral vision, he had seen Chaney peering around the corner of the house and gestured for her to hide. He breathed a prayer of thanks that she'd slid from view. Then Mickey had flicked his finger and the cowboy sauntered toward the lean-to.

Modern-day cowboys weren't a rare sight in this rural county where students got a school holiday every February for Rodeo Day. Adam and Tucker had gotten acquainted with a few when they went on that roundup.

Still, there was something surreal with what was happening right before Adam's eyes. A squat but powerful man dressed like a mobster-wannabe from the last century and another man who belonged to the century before that had driven in and taken charge. The trio on the porch was outnumbered.

At least Chaney was out of sight. Adam wished he had paid more attention to her misgivings. But Tucker's off-handed explanation seemed so sensible that Adam had gone along with it.

Sandy-Lynne pushed past Tucker then pulled a snub-nosed revolver from her jacket pocket and pointed the barrel at Mickey's paunch.

"I told you no." Her voice trembled and her hands shook. "Leave now or I'll pull this trigger. I swear I will."

Adam's feet seemed glued to the wooden porch and his stomach lurched. The next few seconds passed by in a blur as if a movie projector had been placed on high speed. Sensations hit him, one pulsing moment after the other, but his brain couldn't process what was happening before his eyes.

His dad yelled.

The bodyguards pulled guns.

Shots rang out.

Adam threw himself at Tucker, tackling him and knocking him to the porch. Sandy-Lynne dropped her revolver as she fell to her knees beside them. Liquid warmth oozed beneath Adam's fingers.

His head cleared.

"Dad?" His voice was barely audible.

Tucker's eyes flickered then closed. Sandy-Lynne removed her jacket and pressed it against his shoulder.

"Dad?"

"He'll be okay. He has to be okay." The fear on Sandy-Lynne's face sent Adam into a tailspin. She folded the sleeves onto the jacket as she pushed the blood-soaked material into the wound.

Footsteps sounded on the porch and Mickey loomed over them.

"Sorry, doc," he said with an unperturbed air, an unlit cigar dangling from his fingers. "Tragedies happen when people stick their noses into my affairs."

Adam started to his feet, his hands balled into fists, but Sandy-Lynne grabbed his arm. The blood on her fingers seeped through his shirt.

"Come on, Sandy-Lynne." Mickey twisted his fingers into her ponytail. "Time for you to come home where you belong."

Adam lurched again, but Sandy-Lynne's grip on his arm tightened.

"Tend to your dad," she said, her eyes brimming with tears. "Press your hand here."

Adam gathered more of the material and placed both of his hands over Sandy-Lynne's. She slid her hand from beneath his and stood.

"I need to wash up," she said to Mickey.

"Hurry up about it." He gave her hair another twist before letting her go.

The cowboy came around the porch. "Got the horse in the trailer. I need the truck key."

"I'll get it," Sandy-Lynne said before she went inside the house.

"We need to get Dad on that chopper." Adam glared at Mickey. "It's the fastest way to get him to the hospital."

"That chopper's long gone," Mickey drawled. Adam glanced at the sky. Sure enough, the helicopter had left. "Even if it wasn't, do you think I'd let you borrow it out of the goodness of my heart?" He chuckled. "There isn't any goodness in my heart, son."

"You can't leave us here."

"Passed a fancy Charger on our way in. I assume that's how you got here. You can leave the same way."

Sandy-Lynne returned and handed the key to the cowboy. "I'll make sure you get the truck back," she said to Adam. "Please tell your dad how sorry I am."

"You've got to help us," Adam pleaded, not sure whether he was addressing Mickey or Sandy-Lynne. Both? Either? He glared at Sandy-Lynne as tears welled in his eyes. "How can you leave?"

"Do you think she has a choice?" Mickey chuckled again. "Come on, Sandy-Lynne."

Instead of complying, she stared at Adam. "You should never have come here. He wouldn't have found us if not for you."

"Don't blame the young man." Mickey's feigned concern galled Adam's spirit, but Sandy-Lynne was right. This was his fault. He should have waited for his dad to contact him.

"Fletcher found out where you were," Mickey continued.

"Fletcher Wilkes?" Sandy-Lynne narrowed her eyes. "There's no way."

"You always underestimate Fletcher." Mickey tucked Sandy-Lynne's arm into his. She tried to jerk away but he held her too tight. "He hired some girl to break into the doc's house."

"What girl?"

"I didn't meet her. Cute little brunette, according to Fletcher. She tried to play it cagey. Told Fletcher she wanted to be sure she was right before she gave him the address. So I had one of my guys track her phone. Turns out she's staying with this young fella." Mickey pointed at Adam. "We slapped a GPS tracker on his fancy sports car and, voila! Here we all are."

Sandy-Lynne shot Adam a *told you so* look as Mickey pulled her toward the SUV. Adam lowered his head and replayed Mickey's words.

Girl? Cute little brunette?

Adam didn't want to go where his mind was leading him. He focused on his dad's wound, praying the bleeding would stop. Once again Tucker's eyelids fluttered but then he receded into unconsciousness. Probably the best place for him, a haven from the pain.

The SUV's engine roared to life. Adam stared as the driver did a three-point turn and spun mud as he sped away. Sandy-Lynne's image was barely visible through the tinted window.

The cowboy drove the truck and trailer slowly along the

lane. He didn't even glance Adam's way as he maneuvered past the worst of the ruts on his way to the main road.

A moment later, Chaney pushed open the screen door clutching a pan of lukewarm water and a cloth.

"Is it bad?" She knelt beside Tucker and placed the wet cloth on his forehead.

Adam pushed away his questions, the suspicions he couldn't face, and nodded. "I can't believe they left us here."

"I'll go get the car." She rested her hand on his shoulder. The gesture, he supposed, was meant to comfort. But instead her fingers burned.

"I'll be back as soon as I can." She scampered across the porch and ran along the lane, weaving from one side to the other as she dodged mudholes.

Would she come back for them? Or would she take off, too? Obviously, she couldn't be trusted. Why had he ever thought it was a good idea to invite her into his life? Into his home? She'd shown her true colors when she broke in. Everything since then must have been an act.

Tucker moaned, and Adam focused again on his dad.

"We're going to get you to a doctor," he said, his voice catching. "You can't die on me. Not out here. Not like this."

CHAPTER 30

*S*aturday

Chaney rarely prayed. She didn't know how God worked, but she refused to make any bargains or promises. What had she ever done for Him that He should listen to her now? As Adam sped toward civilization, however, her heart cried for God's help. Thankfully, the bullet had gone through Tucker's shoulder and out again—they'd found it when they moved him—but he'd lost too much blood and needed medical attention as soon as possible.

Tension tightened her body. Showing up at a hospital with a gunshot victim was asking for trouble.

"Where are you taking him?" Chaney tried to catch Adam's eye in the rearview mirror. But his attention was focused on the road in front of him.

"We're closer to St. Cloud than Kissimmee." His voice was gruff as if it took all his energy to speak.

"The hospital staff will call the police."

"So what? My dad didn't shoot anybody, and I don't care if that Sandy-Lynne gets arrested." Adam's jaw clenched and he pressed his lips together.

They drove a few more miles, neither of them saying a word. Then Adam passed his phone over the seat to Chaney.

"Find Melody Perez in my contacts." His voice came out in ragged breaths. "Tell her—only her—that Dad got shot. No more than that. Tell her we're on our way to her vet clinic."

Chaney found the number and made the call. After the second ring, a feminine voice answered. "Adam, hello? Have you heard from your dad?"

"Is this Dr. Perez?" Chaney asked.

The person on the other side hesitated then asked, "Who is this?"

"I'm a ... a friend of Adam's."

Adam's eyes jerked to the rearview mirror. His cold expression sent chills along Chaney's spine.

"We're, um, we have Dr. Thorne. He's been shot and we're, that is, Adam is driving to your clinic now."

"Excuse me?" The woman's voice registered disbelief. "Tucker's been shot?"

"Yes, ma'am. Please, we need your help."

"Where's Adam?"

"Give me the phone," Adam demanded, holding out his hand while maneuvering a banking curve. For a moment, Chaney feared they were going into the ditch, but he managed to hold the vehicle steady. She handed him the phone.

"Melody? It's me."

Chaney didn't hear Dr. Perez's side of the conversation, but she guessed the doctor was telling Adam to get his dad to the hospital.

"I can't do that. Please. I need you."

A pause.

"I'll explain when I get there."

Another pause.

"Thanks. See you soon."

He tossed the phone on the passenger seat then focused on

his driving. Chaney returned her attention to Dr. Thorne. If he died because she was afraid to go to the hospital, how could she ever live with herself? It was bad enough she was to blame for him getting shot.

"Maybe we should go to an ER," she said quietly.

"Don't make any more suggestions." Adam's voice was eerie in its coldness. Enough so that Chaney shivered.

She blinked away sudden tears. This wasn't the time to fall apart. She leaned close to Dr. Thorne's ear. "Stay with us," she whispered. "Adam needs you to live. And so do I."

CHAPTER 31

*S*aturday

The clinic parking lot was deserted. Adam drove around to the back and braked next to Melody's Subaru. Before he had turned off the ignition, the attractive, forty-something veterinarian exited the clinic and rushed toward them.

Adam jumped out and opened the rear door. Tucker filled most of the seat while Chaney perched on the edge holding towels she'd grabbed from the cabin on his wound.

"I prepped the operating room," Melody said. "But I don't understand why you didn't take him to the ER."

"You were closer." Adam flashed a grin though the pretense of levity sickened him. Especially since what he said wasn't even true, and he knew she knew it.

"Let's get your dad inside. Grab the gurney."

Between the three of them, they managed to get Tucker onto gurney and inside the clinic. Melody grabbed scissors and cut away Tucker's shirt. "I don't have human blood here."

"You can take mine." Adam rolled up his shirt sleeve. "I direct-donated blood for him when he had surgery a few years ago so I know it's the right type."

"That's good. I promise not to bleed you dry." Melody glanced at Chaney. "I'll need an assistant. Think you're up to it?"

Adam started to protest. Now that they were at the clinic, his gut reaction was to keep Chaney as far away from his dad as possible. Maybe even lock her outside the building and let her find her way back to whatever hole she'd crawled out of.

But he couldn't give blood and help Melody at the same time. Chaney's face had paled, and Adam could almost see her digging deep inside of herself for strength. "Can you do it?" he asked.

"I'll do it."

"Wash up in there." Melody pointed to a door. "And hurry."

Adam sat in a chair next to the operating table and pumped his fist. Melody was proficient though worry clouded her expression. She didn't ask any more questions or bother with small talk. She gave orders and Adam obeyed them.

When Chaney returned, Melody gave her scrubs to wear over her clothes. The room was quiet. So quiet that Adam imagined he could hear his heart beating. Melody remained business-like, as if treating gunshot wounds on human patients was an everyday occurrence.

He leaned his head back against the chair and studied Chaney. She focused on Melody, quick to provide any assistance that was needed. But her face was still pale, and fear deadened her eyes.

He'd considered her an enigma since the first time he noticed her at the Dogwood Diner. A thief who returned a sentimental locket to its owner. A thief who tried to return the money he'd given to her.

A breath of fresh air and, as of right now, his worst nightmare.

I don't know her, God. I don't know anything except that my dad's life is hanging by a thread and I couldn't take him to an ER. Be with us all, Lord. See us through this. Help me to understand Your plan for me when everything I thought I knew has been derailed.

"That's it." Melody removed her mask then covered Tucker with a blanket. "How are you feeling, Adam?"

"I'm fine."

She handed him a set of scrubs. "Your turn to clean up."

He went to the bathroom and stared into the mirror. He hardly recognized himself. His eyes appeared bloodshot and dried blood streaked his hair and face. He scrubbed his hands and washed himself the best he could in the sink.

Of all the blows he'd been dealt over the past few weeks, this was definitely the worst. Surely God would not be so cruel as to take his dad away from him.

When he returned to the operating room, Chaney was sitting in the chair next to the bed, her hand resting on Tucker's arm. She started to rise when Adam entered, but he motioned for her to stay seated. She appeared absolutely exhausted, and the frightened look in her eyes hadn't gone away.

He'd been so angry with her earlier, when he'd heard what Mickey Nolan said to Sandy-Lynne. But now he was too tired to be angry. Too scared.

She needed to explain herself—he would insist on that—but he was more willing to listen now than he had been before. And the explanation could wait.

Melody had gone to the restroom when Adam came out, patting him on the shoulder as she passed him, an encouraging smile on her lips. She'd want an explanation, too. What was he going to tell her? How could he ever explain what had happened or why they'd involved her in this nightmare instead of taking Dad to the hospital? He still wasn't sure why they'd made that decision. Or who had made it.

He guessed he had, since he'd been the one driving.

But why?

Because it had seemed the right thing to do. As if God had whispered in his heart to make the turns that led him to the clinic instead of the hospital.

Adam placed his hand on his dad's arm, the contact connecting them in the only way he knew how.

The only sound in the room was Tucker's soft breathing and the occasional beeping of the heart monitor.

A few minutes later, Melody returned.

"Both of you need to rest. There's a couch in my office for one of you. I already put a blanket and pillow in there."

"Go ahead, Chaney," Adam said. "I want to stay here."

At the mention of her name, she met his gaze for the first time since they'd arrived at the clinic. Her eyes were red and tear-stained. At first, he thought she was going to refuse, but then she nodded.

Melody pointed the way then returned to the table and checked Tucker's pulse. Adam lowered himself to the chair. "I can't thank you enough for this. I didn't know what else to do."

"Just don't tell me what happened, okay? If I don't know ..." She made a notation on a chart."

"No doctor-patient confidentiality?" Adam tried for a light tone, but he utterly failed.

"Dogs and cats don't tell me their secrets."

"He wasn't doing anything illegal."

"And yet this wasn't a hunting accident." She smoothed Tucker's blanket then flashed a weak smile at Adam. "Why don't you camp out in the waiting room? I'll stay here."

"I can't leave him."

"He's not going anywhere. I'll wake you if anything changes."

He nodded and reluctantly left the room. As he passed Melody's open office door, he glanced inside. Enough light came through the curtained window for him to see Chaney curled in a tight ball on the couch, her forehead resting on her knees. Her shoulders shook as if she was crying silent tears.

A lump formed in his throat, and he ran his fingers along his unshaven jaw. Without a word, he left her alone.

CHAPTER 32

Saturday Evening

Chaney busied herself in the kitchen of Adam's home while he kept watch over his dad in the master bedroom. She put on a kettle of water to boil then rummaged through the cupboard above the coffeemaker for teabags and mugs.

Tucker had regained consciousness while she'd been fitfully napping in Melody's office. He hadn't wanted to stay at the clinic, but both Melody and Adam insisted on monitoring him for another hour before bringing him home. After they did, Melody stayed until Tucker fell asleep.

Chaney had felt sick to her stomach since she'd first seen Tucker's shoulder covered in blood. But now that they were home again—okay, they were in Adam's home again—the adrenaline that had kept her body revved up was draining away. She was exhausted, and she was sure Adam felt the same.

Not surprisingly, she was also hungry. Adam must be starving, too, even if he didn't realize it. Neither of them had eaten since breakfast, and that had been hours ago.

Chaney found a container of deli meats and cheeses in the

refrigerator and Kaiser rolls in the pantry. By the time Adam entered the kitchen, she'd created a "fixin's plate" with sliced onions, sliced tomatoes, and lettuce leaves.

He leaned against the door frame, seeming to pay little attention to her, as she took condiments from the refrigerator and placed them on the table.

"The teakettle is hot," she said. "Would you like a cup? I found chamomile and Earl Grey."

"Earl Grey." He took his seat at the table. "This looks nice, but I'm not sure I feel like eating."

She sensed he'd sat down more from deeply ingrained politeness than because he wanted to be in the same room with her. She wasn't sure she wanted to be with him either. Maybe she should have hightailed it out of the house while he was busy with his father.

If she'd had a place to go and the means to get there, she might have.

Though lack of transportation wasn't her primary reason for staying. After all, it wasn't that far to the bus stop. Only a few blocks.

Something happened at the hunting cabin that changed Adam's perception of her. She'd seen an expression akin to hatred in his eyes when she'd taken the tub of water to the porch. A cold hatred that had frozen her soul.

Naturally, he'd been upset about his dad's injury. Upset and frightened and scared.

But the look in his eyes had gone beyond all of that. As much as she wanted to get as far away from that hatred as possible, something else—something she didn't understand—compelled her to stay. To face his coldness. To know why he'd changed before she severed all ties between them.

"Try to eat anyway." She sat across from him, taking the chair that she'd become accustomed to thinking of as her seat.

Funny how people so quickly got into certain habits, certain routines. In the kitchen, they each had their seat at the table. In the living room, he preferred the recliner while she'd claimed the couch. A temporary claim, she'd known that from the get-go. But now that her time here was ending, her heart was heavier than she'd ever expected it to be.

Her only consolation was that Fletcher Wilkes would file the motion for another hearing on Marshall's bail. By this time next week, she and her cousin might be clear across the country, able to watch sunsets on the Pacific rather than sunrises over the Atlantic. Or perhaps they'd go to the northernmost corner of Maine. Sneak into Canada. Learn to endure heavy snowfalls and frigid temperatures.

She unconsciously shivered.

"Are you cold?" Adam picked up a bun and split it apart. "I can get you a sweatshirt."

His tone was as flat as his expression. The fine lines around his eyes seemed to have deepened in the past few hours, and his unshaven whiskers gave him a haggard appearance.

"I was thinking of snow."

"Why?"

His tone made it sound like that was the craziest thing he'd ever heard of. Maybe it was.

"I was eleven, twelve years old before I saw snow," he continued before she answered him. Just as well, because she couldn't tell him the mental trail that she'd taken to reach snow. She couldn't let him know her plans. Better if she simply disappeared.

"Mom and Dad took me out of school for a surprise trip to New York." Adam layered slices of beef, ham, and turkey on his bun then added smoky cheddar cheese. His tone remained flat though a corner of his lip turned up. The memory was a happy one for him. Probably most of his childhood memories were pleasant. No hardships in his life. No doing without. Just a normal kid in a normal family doing normal things.

"Dad had some kind of conference, so while he went to meetings, Mom and I took the ferry to the Statue of Liberty. Ice-skated in Central Park. All the typical tourist stuff. The first morning, Mom called me to the window. These huge snowflakes were falling from the sky. It was amazing. I was at that age where it wasn't cool to be impressed by something as ordinary as snow. But the truth was, I was so excited to go outside I couldn't even wait to eat breakfast. Our hotel had this little courtyard and Mom asked room service to bring our order to one of those tables. They brought our tray and a couple of blankets. We ate eggs and bacon with snow falling all around us. It was ... magical."

Chaney squirted spicy brown mustard in the shape of a smiley face on her sandwich. But her imagination saw a small boy, a miniature Adam wrapped in a hotel blanket, lifting his face to the falling snow as it landed on his cheeks, on his lips, in his hair. Eating eggs dampened with snowflakes but not caring how the moisture affected the taste. He probably wouldn't have even noticed a difference.

If she ever had a child, she'd want to do exactly what Adam's mother had done—turn an ordinary snow day into a magical experience. To give that child a gift no one could ever take away from him, the gift of a memory. One that would bring him comfort when his world was topsy-turvy with fear and remorse.

Not that Adam had any cause to blame himself. Nothing that happened at the cabin was his fault. It was all her own. In her world, Adam and his dad were marks—no more than that. To be used and discarded and abandoned.

Except that wasn't true at all.

"Have you ever been to New York?" Adam asked.

"No." The lie slipped from her tongue before she'd given it a thought, the *no* a natural response to any question that might reveal her past. But for one of the first times in her life, the lie struck her conscience like a poisoned arrow. "That is, I was born there. But we moved when I was young."

A half-lie. She'd returned to the city several times since then.

"I've always wanted to go back." He retrieved a jar of banana peppers from the fridge and a fork from a drawer near the sink. "Planned to go with Piper for the second week of our honeymoon."

He added a few of the pale green peppers to his monstrosity of a sandwich then held out the jar. "Want some?"

"No, thanks. I'm fine." Her own sandwich was only about half the height of his. Guess he was hungrier than he thought.

They ate the rest of their meal in silence, neither of them seeming to know what to say to break the somber mood that hung over and around them. For her part, Chaney feared saying the wrong thing. Adam's gloom appeared to encompass more than his dad's injury and the earlier fear of having bullets flying around him. That was enough to scare anybody and shake them up for hours afterward.

She should know. She shuddered then pushed that particular childhood memory from her mind by focusing her thoughts on Adam.

When he'd talked about the trip to New York City with his mom, his voice had lifted. But when he mentioned Piper and the canceled honeymoon, the gloom-and-doom descended again.

Chaney wanted to ask if he still loved his ex-fiancée. But the question seemed inappropriate. And perhaps unnecessary. He might have been willing to give up her engagement ring, or perhaps he never expected Chaney to return for it when he made the offer. But that had happened before he saw Piper at the community center.

That encounter had affected him. If his heart had been healing, her presence tore off the scabs, leaving him bleeding again from her loss. The woman was beautiful, Chaney had to admit. But Piper was a fool if she thought she'd ever find anyone as fine as Adam. He was the most decent, honest, upstanding man Chaney had ever met.

Though, truth be told, her bar for such men was a low one.

She finished her sandwich and wrapped her hands around the mug. The chamomile fragrance wafted toward her as she raised the mug to her lips.

"Yuck," she said. "That's only lukewarm."

Adam reached across the table while scooting back his chair. "Give it here. I'll nuke it for you."

"I can do it."

"I'm closer."

Adam set her mug and his in the microwave and tapped the buttons. Chaney gathered the condiments and returned them to the refrigerator. He joined her in clearing the table while waiting for the microwave to ding. The clean-up took less than a minute. She put the final dish in the dishwasher while he removed the mugs from the microwave.

"Let's take these to the living room." He started to hand her the mug then pulled back. "Careful, it's hot." For a moment, he was once again the Adam she'd first met. The solicitous, looking-out-for-the-other-person Adam. The Adam she wanted him to be all the time instead of the cold and distant Adam he'd become since the shooting.

She wrapped a folded dishcloth around the mug and the handle. "I've got it."

"I'll join you in a minute. I want to check on Dad." He disappeared down the hallway.

This was her chance. She could sneak out, leave him to care for his dad. Go to Fletcher Wilkes and make sure he kept his word about filing that motion for Marshall.

But like before, her feet wouldn't do what she wanted them

to do. Instead, they took her to the living room, and she curled up in her corner of the couch. As if she belonged there when she absolutely did not.

So why couldn't she leave?

CHAPTER 33

Saturday Night
Adam anxiously watched the rise and fall of his father's chest as he slept. The pain that had earlier drawn Tucker's face into planes of agony must have lessened considerably for him to sleep so deeply now. Though the drive from the clinic to home must have exhausted him. Not to mention the uproar when they got here. When Adam tried to take him to the master bedroom, Tucker put his feet on the floor to stop the wheelchair they'd borrowed from Melody.

"Not going to kick you out of your bed, son," he'd grouched. "The guest room is fine enough for me."

When Adam explained Chaney was staying in the guest room, Tucker stared at him as if he had two heads, glared at Chaney, then exchanged glances with Melody. Chaney immediately volunteered to sleep on the couch and then so had Tucker while Melody volunteered her guest room if they needed it. With all of them talking at once, Adam had let out a long whistle, said thanks but no thanks to Melody, told Chaney she wasn't going anywhere, and wheeled Tucker to his room.

Now that Tucker slept and Chaney rested in the living room

—unless she'd snuck out—all of the day's *what ifs* pounded against Adam's temples.

What if Tucker's wound got infected? What if Nolan came back to finish the job? What if Adam and Chaney had stayed home today instead of going to the cabin?

Chaney.

The words Nolan had said as he dragged Sandy-Lynne away reverberated through Adam's mind once again.

Hired some girl to break into the doc's house. Cute little brunette.

The image of the brunette emerging from the restroom at Lake Eola flashed through his mind.

He sank into the bedside chair and held his head in his hands.

Had Chaney actually taken money from Nolan to find Tucker and Sandy-Lynne? Why would she do that? And how did he reconcile that devious Chaney with the girl he'd been with the past few days? The Chaney who'd returned a woman's locket, who'd returned his money, whom he'd invited into his home?

What do I say to her, Father? How do I learn the truth of who she is?

He ran his hand down his face, intent on hearing an answer. But none came, not at that moment.

I can wait, God. I can wait till You're ready to show me what to do. But what I want to do is call Special Agent Grant. Tell him I was wrong. She is a thief. Worse than a thief.

He clasped his hands and raised his eyes to the ceiling. God was beside him when Piper broke their engagement, providing solace for Adam's hurting heart in a myriad of ways. Like when he jogged through the neighborhood the morning after their break-up and the sun poked holes in the cloud cover. Another time, he'd sat on the bank of the stream that ran through the park as a mama duck paddled among the rushes with her babies.

In those moments, he'd been enveloped in a peace that could only come from God.

But this situation with Chaney pressed against his chest like a boulder, and he was finding no relief. Her seemingly sweet nature upset him more than Pete's arrogance. The board member had pulled the rug out from under Adam, slamming him to his back. He'd lost his job, but not his faith that God cared about him.

After all, he and Pete were never best buds. Adam tried, especially in the early months of the ministry, to get along with the guy. They'd played golf a few times, gone to some of the same charity functions, but they'd never clicked. Three months after he was hired Adam learned Pete had lobbied hard for another ministerial candidate. Apparently, he'd never gotten over his resentment that the board selected Adam instead.

Since then, Adam had taken all of Pete's subtle put-downs, his resistance to Adam's ideas, and his lack of support for the programs that Adam cared about most—those at the community center and homeless shelter—with a grain of salt. But in recent weeks, Pete seemed to step up his game. He'd been especially peeved a month ago when Adam suggested the church help plan a local event showcasing Orlando's social services and nonprofit organizations. A couple of the other board members were also lukewarm to the proposal, but Adam figured, given time, he could win them over.

But Pete had already sown the seeds of discord, and the rumors that Tucker disappeared with a married woman allowed those seeds to become weeds. Pete finally achieved his longtime goal to toss Adam out of the pulpit.

Pete might think he'd brought about Adam's disgrace and ruin. But the lowest moment of Adam's life happened earlier that day when a shot rang out and his father dropped to his knees.

Sensing another presence in the room, Adam lifted his head. Chaney peered around the doorframe, tentative and shy.

Or was that hesitancy an act?

He frowned, not wanting to be that person—suspicious and bitter. Yet even Jesus warned His apostles to be wise as serpents.

And gentle as doves.

The phrase whispered in his soul.

"Is he okay?" Chaney avoided Adam's gaze, focusing on his dad instead.

"Seems to be." Adam rose from the chair and gestured for Chaney to precede him down the hall.

When they reached the living room, she grabbed her half-empty mug from the coffee table and curled up in her corner of the couch. He hesitated a moment before sitting beside her. She glanced at him, eyes widening, then stared into her mug as she seemed to shrink deeper, impossibly, into the upholstery.

To get away from him?

Maybe.

He leaned forward, elbows on his knees, and rested his chin against his folded hands. He desperately wanted to exude calm. To share the light that lived in him with this troubled soul.

But instead the anger he'd been suppressing rose inside him. His heart pounded and his face warmed.

How could he let her stay under his roof if what Nolan had said was true?

How could he send her away when she had nowhere to go?

There but for the grace of God.

He hmphed at the thought. In the mood he was in, the aphorism meant nothing. He didn't have the mental strength to put himself in the shoes of a transient thief.

"Just say it." Chaney's voice quivered, but he hardened himself against his natural tendency toward compassion instead of judgment.

He shifted and glared at her. She still stared into her mug as if it held all the secrets of the universe instead of warmed-over tea.

She was maybe five or six years younger than him and definitely someone with street smarts. And yet she exuded a façade of innocence. He released a heavy sigh and she met his gaze.

"Is there something you should tell me?" he asked, his voice flat.

"I don't know how Nolan knew where we were. I promise I didn't tell him."

"He said he hired you." It wasn't quite the truth. But what other girl who owned a brunette wig had broken into Tucker's house? Only Chaney.

Her hands shook. Adam steadied the mug then placed it on the table.

"He actually said that?"

The dam holding back Adam's emotional torrent broke. "I thought you wanted to help *me*. Instead you were helping him? That ... Neanderthal?" Adam clenched his jaw and fisted his hands. "He actually pulled Sandy-Lynne by the hair. Who does that?"

Chaney wrapped her arms around her knees as tears glistened in her eyes. "I wanted to tell you. But I couldn't."

"Why not?"

"Because I didn't want this to happen. I didn't want you to hate me."

"How much did he pay you to find my dad?" His words cut deep, but he needed an answer.

"I didn't do it for money."

"Then why?" What else could Nolan have offered her?

She turned her head, hiding the pain in her eyes.

He wanted to shake an answer out of her. Instead, he took a deep breath to regain control of his temper and leaned back. Maybe the body language techniques he'd learned in a basic counseling class at seminary would help. If he appeared open and non-threatening, perhaps she'd confide in him.

He waited, allowing the silence between them to do its work.

She glanced his way. "I know what you're doing."

"I'm waiting for you to tell me about Nolan." Adam shifted to face her and rested his arm on the back of the sofa "You owe me that much. You owe my dad."

Chaney gurgled then choked as uncontrollable sobs broke through her defenses. Her shoulders shook as the tears flowed.

Adam again tried to harden his heart, reminding himself that his dad had been shot because of her.

And because of him.

He let another moment pass then wrapped his arm around her shoulder. She fell against him, still curled into her own little ball. Despite his efforts to stoke his anger, he'd slipped from aggrieved victim to protective big brother. Or the dupe in one of her cons.

Her sobs gradually faded, and she swiped at her cheeks.

"Want my sleeve?" he asked.

She stifled a nervous laugh.

"Hold on a second." After retrieving a box of tissues from the bathroom, he perched on the coffee table in front of Chaney. "Here you go."

"Thank you." She bent her head while she blew her nose.

"Feel better?"

"Yes. No." She took a second tissue and wadded the two together. "I never wanted anything like this to happen. If only —" She pressed her lips together.

"I'd listened to you? I wish I had."

She finally met his gaze, and for a moment he was afraid the waterworks were going to gush again. But she sniffed a couple of times and regained control.

"I never talked to Nolan."

"Chaney, don't lie to me."

"It was his attorney. Fletcher Wilkes. My cousin is in jail."

"I know. Remember? Grant told me."

She's a grifter, the detective had said. *From a family of grifters.* But despite the warning, Adam had welcomed her into his life. Why had he done that?

"Wilkes said he'd file a motion for a new bail hearing," she explained, "if I found Sandy-Lynne."

"Why didn't you tell me that?"

"I wanted to. But Marshall is the only family I have left." She grabbed another tissue and twisted it between her fingers. "If I could change what happened, I would."

Wise as serpents, gentle as doves.

"I believe you."

Or he was just plain stupid. Only God knew which.

CHAPTER 34

Sunday Morning

Marshall swam in Adam's pool, which deepened and swirled until he was trapped in an eddy. Chaney threw him a rope, but he couldn't quite grasp it. She started to jump in after him, but he shouted at her to stop. To back away. To let him go.

She couldn't do that. She wouldn't do that.

She lifted her arms over her head, ready to dive, when someone grabbed her from behind. Pulled her from the edge of the pool. She stumbled. Fell. Struggled to stand.

A man's face hovered above her.

Adam.

She pushed him away. Shouted *I have to save Marshall* as loudly as she could.

"You're too late." Adam faded away as his final words echoed around her.

Chaney huddled in the backseat of The Sting, all her belongings crowded around her. The pile grew, pushing against her. She grabbed the door handle, but the door wouldn't open. She pulled on the lock and tried again. The handle broke off in her hand. She slammed it against the window. A thin crack splintered the glass.

She hit the window again and the pile grew and pushed and rose around her and the glass splintered but wouldn't break. Trapped. Helpless. Alone.

A scream surrounded her. Her scream.

Sometime during the long night, the horrid dreams subsided. She slept until sunlight filtered through the closed blinds and into her consciousness. With a groan, she opened her eyes and reached for her phone to check the time.

10:17.

She wanted to pull the comforter over her head, to hide beneath its blue-and-gray-checked thickness the rest of the morning. The rest of the day. The rest of her life.

Instead she called Wilkes, but he didn't answer. Then she took a long shower, grateful for the heat of the water against her skin, and tried not to relive yesterday's horrible events.

After she dressed, she tried calling Wilkes again. Still no answer. There was only one thing left to do.

With quiet, cautious steps, she headed for the living room. A pillow rested on top of a folded blanket on the couch, but the room was empty. Adam must be with his dad. This was her chance.

Her shoes were tucked beneath the end table by the sofa, where she'd left them yesterday. All she needed to do was grab them and escape.

Chaney retrieved the shoes and opened the front door wide enough to slip through.

"Where are you going?"

She jumped and clutched at her chest.

Adam perched on the wide railing that surrounded the front porch, his back against a stucco column. He held the sports section of *The Orlando Sentinel* in his hands.

"What are you doing out here?" she demanded.

"Asked you first." He folded the paper. "Seems like you're always either sneaking in or out of here."

"I didn't want to disturb anyone."

"That's not really an answer. Where are you going?"

"None of your business."

"If you're meeting Nolan or his attorney or anyone else associated with him, then it's definitely my business."

"It's not like I have an appointment."

Adam hopped from the railing and gathered the other sections of the paper scattered on the floral cushions of a wicker loveseat. "I'm going with you."

"Oh, no, you're not."

"Oh, yes, I am."

"You can't leave your dad."

"Melody's with him."

"She's here?"

"Since about seven."

Chaney plopped into one of the chairs. She hadn't heard anyone coming to the door, hadn't heard voices.

"He's okay? Your dad?"

"He's sore and grouchy. But, yeah, he's okay. You should look in on him before we go."

"You're not going with me."

"I've got the car key."

"I'm not getting in your car." Chaney shivered at the memory of Tucker's blood seeping into the back seat, staining the upholstery.

"Good point," Adam said. "We'll take Melody's."

"*I'll* take the bus."

"Really? That's your best comeback?" He stood between her and the porch steps, the newspaper clasped in front of him. "Dad asked about you. Wants to be sure you're okay."

"Tell him I'm fine." She couldn't face him. Not when she'd ruined his and Sandy-Lynne's plan for keeping Mischief safe.

Why did it have to cost so many people so much pain for her to help Marshall?

"Tell him yourself."

"Does he know what I did?"

"I told him what you told me. He understands going the extra mile for family." He tapped her arm with the paper. "Come back in. I'll fix breakfast while you talk to Dad."

"Why won't you stop being nice to me?"

"Apparently I can't help myself." He shooed her toward the door. "Face the dragon, Chaney. I promise he doesn't breathe smoke and fire."

"Only if you go with me."

He reached around her and opened the door. "I'm right behind you."

CHAPTER 35

Sunday Morning

"How is he?" Adam asked Melody, who was sitting in the bedside chair. Chaney lingered in the hallway.

Melody closed her magazine and gave him an encouraging smile. "Grumpy."

"I am not." Tucker growled. "Come here, son, and help me out of this bed." Tucker tried to fling back the covers, but his attempt at a dramatic gesture lost its oomph when the blankets barely moved.

"Stay where you are, Dad." Adam adjusted the pillows behind Tucker's back. "You're still groggy from the meds Melody poured into you yesterday."

"Not too groggy to know my own mind."

"Stop fussing, Tucker," Melody said. "We'll get you up in a little bit."

"You keep saying that," Tucker replied. "How long is a 'little bit' in your estimation, Doctor?"

"As long as I want it to be and getting longer every time you grouse."

Tucker mumbled something under his breath before shifting

his attention to the doorway. "Come on in here," he said, waving his good arm. "No need to lurk in the hallway like you've got something to hide."

"Go easy on her, Dad," Adam warned. "She was headed for the bus stop when I found her."

"Running away from us, were you?"

Chaney halted at the foot of the bed. "I think I've caused you enough trouble."

"And then some. But it seems to me that you were the one saying we needed to *vamoose,* and I was the one who insisted on fixing us all a bite to eat. I hope you'll accept my apology for thinking I knew best when I was so clearly wrong."

"You can't apologize," Chaney said. "This is all my fault."

"Why don't we say there's enough blame to go around and let it go at that?"

"I'm not sure I can."

"Neither am I, but let's give it a try." He rested his head on the pillows and released a heavy sigh. "All this talking has done worn me out. Guess maybe I'll take a little nap if no one has any objection."

"I'll put on my chef's hat," Adam said. "Seems strange to be home on a Sunday morning."

"I'm sure the congregation misses you, son. If not, then they're all fools."

"Spoken like a proud father," Melody said with a laugh. "Though I happen to agree with him."

"There's a first." Tucker focused his gaze on Chaney. "You mind staying with me a minute longer? Something I want to talk over with you."

Adam reluctantly followed Melody from the room as Chaney took his place by Tucker's side. He wanted to eavesdrop, but Melody grabbed his arm.

"No, you don't," she whispered.

He let her drag him down the hallway and into the kitchen.

"What do you think he has to say to her that he couldn't say in front of us?" he asked. "Aren't you curious?"

"I'm more curious about who she is and what she's doing here."

"It's a crazy story." He'd told her bits and pieces over cups of coffee when she arrived that morning. "All I know is that she's like a lost lamb."

"And you're her shepherd?"

"Not me." He pointed toward the ceiling. "Him."

"Don't get cute with me, Adam Thorne. And don't let her pull any wool over your eyes with her 'woe is me' act."

"Is that what you see when you look at her?"

"No, not really. But she does seem vulnerable, and you're in a vulnerable place yourself. It hasn't been that long since Piper—"

"I'm not rebounding. And if I were, I'd find someone closer to my own age. One who knows the story of Esther."

"What?"

"Never mind." He pulled a box from the cupboard. "Pancakes or waffles?"

"I'll go with pancakes. What can I do to help?"

Adam was pouring the first scoopful of pancake batter on the sizzling griddle when Chaney joined them. She hoisted herself onto one of the stools on the other side of the counter from him with a bemused smile on her face.

"What did he have to say?" Adam asked. "Or is it a secret?"

"No secret. Just ... surprising."

"Tell us," Melody urged.

"He wants me to pull a con. On Mickey Nolan."

CHAPTER 36

Sunday Morning
Chaney had told Tucker that she'd never been the mastermind behind a con before. But he'd dismissed her objection. Mischief couldn't run in Saturday's upcoming race without exacerbating his injuries. Sandy-Lynne needed their help. She had no one else. He was even more adamant they needed to act after she told him of Mickey's plan to kill Mischief for the insurance money.

"Tucker is serious," Chaney said to Adam and Melody. "He wants to steal Mischief."

"That's crazy." Adam let too much batter pour onto the griddle. It spread to the grooved edge, and he halted the flow with his spatula. "He's not going to have any more to do with that horse or the Nolans." He pointed the spatula at Chaney. "Neither are you."

She jutted out her chin. "That's my decision, not yours."

"Okay, you two." Melody gestured for a time-out. "I don't know what you're all involved in, but 'pulling a con' on anyone sounds dangerous. Wait a minute." Her eyes widened and she grabbed Adam's arm. "Did Mickey Nolan shoot Tucker?"

"Do you know him?" Adam asked.

"Not personally, no. But I know he's not likely to be named Good Samaritan of the Year. He's bad news."

"See?" Adam glared at Chaney. "I'm not the only one who thinks it's a terrible idea."

"Your dad doesn't think so."

"He's been watching too many cop shows." Adam flipped the pancakes, but the bottoms were burnt. He tossed them in the trash and started over.

"He also came up with the plan to steal Mischief," Chaney said. "He bought that old trailer, figured out where they could hide. It was all his idea."

"I don't believe that."

"He told me, Adam. He wasn't lying."

Melody groaned and buried her face in her hands. "I changed my mind. Tell me everything."

Between them, Chaney and Adam told her about Mischief's disappearance, what had happened at the camp, and why they'd called her instead of taking Tucker to the hospital.

"After all that," Melody said, shaking her head in disbelief, "Tucker wants to take the horse away from Nolan again? That's impossible."

"It'd be difficult," Chaney said, "but not imposs—"

"Forget it." Adam slid pancakes onto their plates. "There won't be a con or a horse theft. Not only is it dangerous, it's ... dishonest. As it is, Dad will be lucky if Nolan doesn't press charges against him."

"He won't," Chaney assured him. "Not when his own wife was involved."

"He could blame it all on Dad."

"I think Nolan would prefer the whole mess to go away." Chaney poured maple syrup over her stack.

"Just to be clear," Melody interjected, "you did tell Tucker no?"

"I told him I'm not a mastermind. That's not my role."

"Con artists have roles?" Skepticism laced Adam's tone.

"Sure, they do," Melody answered. "Haven't you ever seen any of the great heist movies? Everyone on the crew has a job."

"The 'crew'?" Adam rolled his eyes. "And I always thought of you as an upstanding stay-out-of-jail citizen."

"I am," Melody protested. "That doesn't mean I'm not entertained by movies about bad guys taking down even badder—I mean worse—guys." She waved her hands as if to chase away the flusters. "What *is* your role, Chaney?"

"It depends." Chaney considered the best way to answer Melody's question. She liked the doctor, and she wanted the doctor to like her. Maybe this was one of those times when honesty was the best policy. "Usually, I'm what you might call the distraction."

"She can also pick pockets and open locks without a key," Adam added. "I told you about that locket."

He'd told her? Thanks a lot, buddy.

Though she should have guessed. How else would Melody have known to ask Chaney about her role in a crew?

"That was a very kind thing you did," Melody said. "Poor woman. She must have been extremely grateful to you."

"It was no big deal."

"To her it was," Adam said. "You did a good deed, and she'll never forget it."

Their praise warmed Chaney's cheeks. She focused on her pancakes, unsure how to feel about people who didn't pigeonhole her into a criminal stereotype. Adam might still be miffed with her, but he didn't let his irritation negate the one admirable thing she'd done. Grandpa would urge her to exploit that weakness. But what if that so-called weakness—to see the best in someone else, to give the benefit of the doubt—was a strength?

"We're getting off-track again." Melody snagged another

pancake from the griddle. "Chaney, how are you 'the distraction'?"

"I think she's referring to flaunting her feminine charms," Adam teased.

"Sometimes," Chaney reluctantly admitted. "Flirting is a tried and true technique."

"Not only used by grifters." Adam waggled his eyebrows. He seemed more relaxed now that they were talking about cons in general instead of his dad's plan to run one on Nolan.

"A smile," Chaney continued, "flashed at the right time, can preoccupy someone."

"You mean, preoccupy a man," Melody stated with a laugh.

"Who isn't charmed by a lovely smile?" Adam asked playfully. "I'm just relieved you told Dad no. I don't want anything else to do with those people."

Chaney swirled the last bite of pancake through her remaining syrup. What if Wilkes changed his mind about filing the motion for Marshall after what happened at the cabin? In that case, she needed a Plan B. Which might mean saying yes to Tucker.

Sandy-Lynne wanted Mischief out of Saturday's race, and Tucker feared for her safety if she tried to interfere with her husband's plan. Chaney doubted Sandy-Lynne could protect her horse. Nolan probably had one of his goons guarding Mischief. And another watching Sandy-Lynne.

After breakfast, Melody checked on Tucker while Chaney and Adam cleaned up the kitchen. As Chaney closed the dishwasher, her phone rang. She glanced at the caller ID and headed outside so she could talk in private.

"Hello, Mr. Wilkes," she said cheerfully. "It's great to hear from you."

"Thank you, Ms. Rose." Wilkes's voice had that attorney professionalism she loathed. "What is so important on a Sunday morning that I have multiple missed calls from you?"

"You know what's important. I found Mischief. Now it's time to get Marshall out of jail."

"Nothing can be done for your cousin today."

"But you will file that motion? First thing in the morning?"

"Motion?" Wilkes sounded confused. "I'm afraid I don't know what you're talking about."

Chaney's stomach lurched. He couldn't back out on her. Not now. "The motion for another bail hearing. You told me you'd draft it."

"Oh, that." Wilkes feigned an amused chuckle. "I'm sorry, Ms. Rose, but no judge will grant your cousin bail. He'd flee the state as soon as he left the jail. You know it. I know it. The judge knows it."

"You promised you'd help him," Chaney insisted.

"Both you and your cousin have been compensated more than adequately for the meager information you provided." Wilkes' friendly tone disappeared. "If Mr. Nolan hadn't tracked Dr. Thorne's son, we'd still be looking for his horse."

"But—"

"Our business is complete, Ms. Rose. Please do not call this number again."

Before she could respond, he ended the call.

Chaney sank onto the edge of a chair, her heart beating rapidly as her mind struggled to process the phone call.

She'd convinced herself that all was going to be okay—that the ends had justified the means. She hated that Dr. Thorne was injured, but he would survive. She hated that Mischief was back with Nolan. But Marshall would be set free—that was all that mattered—and they could put this entire situation behind them.

But now? All that had happened was meaningless if Wilkes didn't help Marshall. How could she get him to change his mind?

Think, Chaney, think.

Only one solution made sense. It wouldn't help Marshall

with his legal problems. But perhaps she could still save Mischief. And ruin Mickey Nolan in the process.

She hurried back into the house.

"Who was that?" Adam asked.

She didn't answer but rushed to the master bedroom, Adam close behind her. Tucker and Melody stared at her.

"I'll do it," she said. "I'll run a con on Nolan. But I'll need your help."

CHAPTER 37

Monday Afternoon

Adam glanced at the other patrons in the brew pub before sliding into the booth beside Chaney. He'd done his best to talk her out of this crazy scheme, but his dad—surprise, surprise!—had encouraged her nonsense. All Adam could do was insist on going with her. And pray she knew what she was doing.

"Stop acting like a nervous Nellie," Chaney whispered. "We're here to talk, that's all."

"To the guy who stole your car. Bruised your chin." He picked up the menu but didn't read it. "Or did you forget that?"

She touched her jaw as she frowned. Maybe he shouldn't have mentioned the bruise. At least she'd finally told him what had happened to her. But it galled him that anyone dared to hurt her.

"I haven't forgotten. But we need him."

"So you've said." He shook his head in resignation. They needed a plan and her cousin couldn't give her one. Not when his visits were monitored. "I wish there was another alternative."

"But there's not." She unwrapped her napkin from the tableware. "What are you getting?"

"I'm not hungry."

"How about splitting the ultimate nachos?"

"Sure."

"Do you think you could say that with a little bit more enthusiasm?"

He feigned a huge smile. "Sure!"

"Everything is going to be okay, Adam," she reassured him. "I promise."

Hopefully, it was a promise that she could keep.

Ever since Chaney got the brush-off from Nolan's low-life attorney, she'd been gung-ho to go after him. Tucker had told them what he knew about the world of horse-racing and Mickey's business enterprises, most of which he had learned from Sandy-Lynne while they were hiding out at the hunting cabin. Then Chaney dropped the news-bomb she'd already told Tucker—Mickey's plan to kill Mischief for the insurance money.

Adam had encouraged Melody to leave so she wouldn't be involved in any illegal activity that might come from the conversation. But she'd said she was already involved and, besides, it was kind of exciting.

Adam was loath to admit she was right. He could have left the room, pretended his father wasn't encouraging Chaney's sticky-finger proclivities, but he'd been glued to his seat.

Now here he was, sitting with Chaney inside this brew pub on an ordinary day waiting for a not so ordinary potential accomplice to devise a plan to save a horse.

"Your friend is late," he said.

"I'm sure he's already here."

Adam scanned the room, noting the other diners. "Where?"

"I told you to stop looking so nervous." Chaney heaved a deep sigh. "I should have brought your dad."

"My dad? The man with a gunshot wound in his shoulder? Oh, yes, that would have been perfect."

"At least he wouldn't be so obviously amateur."

"How do you know? He's never done anything like this before either." Adam was still waiting for his dad to explain why he'd risked his reputation to run off with Sandy-Lynne. So far, Tucker had refused to answer Adam's questions about that. He didn't deflect them or change the subject. He simply said, *now's not the time*, and that was the end of that. So frustrating.

"Maybe he hasn't," Chaney said. "But he strikes me as someone with a steady nerve."

"And I don't?"

"Not so far."

"Okay then. If your 'friend' is already here, where is he? I thought we came early so we could scope out the room before he arrived."

"True. But he knew we'd come early so he probably came even earlier. And you need to calm down or you'll scare him away."

The waiter arrived with their drinks and a promise that the nachos would be out momentarily. A few seconds after he turned to wait on another table, a stranger slid into the booth opposite them. His sudden appearance startled Adam, but Chaney seemed unfazed.

"Nice of you to join us, Calvin." She sipped her drink as if this meeting was normal.

This isn't normal, Adam wanted to shout at both of them.

"I was intrigued by your call." Calvin tilted his head toward Adam. "Who's this?"

"His dad was involved with that missing racehorse."

"I heard something about that." Calvin seemed to eye Adam with something akin to respect. As if being the son of a horse thief gave him street cred. Not something he'd ever wanted. At least not since he decided to go to seminary.

"Do you know where the horse is?" Calvin asked.

"Back where he belongs," Chaney answered. "That's the problem."

The conversation halted while the waiter appeared with a huge platter of nachos covered with cheese, chili, jalapeños, onions, and tomatoes. Adam gestured for the waiter to give the plates to Chaney and Calvin then waited for the conversation to resume. Instead, Chaney and Calvin munched on the chips as they talked about a blockbuster movie opening the next weekend.

When the waiter returned with a third plate and Calvin's drink, Adam realized why they'd both taken on the personas of old friends lounging together. As soon as the waiter left, those personas disappeared.

Chaney told Calvin about her phone call with Fletcher Wilkes. That had been the turning point for her—as if she had been the mark in a con set by the unethical attorney. In a way, Adam mused, she was. Though it could be argued that Chaney hadn't totally fulfilled her side of the bargain, the attorney and his client had gotten what they wanted because of her. Then they'd reneged on their promise.

Calvin must have seen it that way, too. His demeanor changed as Chaney reached the punch line. "He's not going to do anything for Marshall," she said.

"You want me to come up with a plan to get Marshall out of jail?" Calvin asked. "Or to get back at Wilkes?"

Chaney exchanged a glance with Adam then shook her head. "We need to get Nolan. He's pulling Wilkes's strings. And we need to save Mischief for Sandy-Lynne."

"Go back to the beginning," Calvin said. "Tell me everything."

To Adam's relief, she didn't tell Calvin everything. She didn't tell him about breaking into Adam's home or about him getting fired from his job. She focused on her search for Mischief on Nolan's behalf, her hunch about where Tucker and Sandy-

THE MISCHIEF THIEF

Lynne were hiding out, and what had happened when Nolan showed up.

Calvin scooped chili with a chip. "Bottom line, you want to keep Mischief out of Saturday's race. Don't suppose there's any chance of stealing him again?"

"We could try. But I imagine the security has been strengthened."

"We'd need to check that out. What do you know about racing horses?" Calvin listened closely as Chaney shared the details that Tucker had given her. Then he sat back in his seat, seemingly lost in thought.

"I may have an idea," he said after a few minutes. "I need to think about it some more, plug a few holes." He stared at Adam as if sizing him up. "Can I count on your help?"

"Adam has never done anything like this before," Chaney protested before Adam could reply. "Besides, Nolan saw him at the cabin."

"But he didn't see you, right?"

"No."

"What about Wilkes?"

"He knows me as a brunette."

"I want to help," Adam spoke up. For most of the conversation, he'd felt like a third wheel who had little to contribute, though he'd been impressed by Chaney's clarity as she explained the situation. She never fumbled her words or needed to backtrack to explain a minor point. He didn't want to break the law, but maybe it would be okay to bend it a little. Especially when Mischief's life was at stake. And maybe even Sandy-Lynne's. Not that he believed Mickey would kill her, too. But he could make her life miserable.

Adam was dipping his toes in turbulent waters—questions of situational ethics, even the sanctity of marriage as far as Nolan and his wife were concerned. He shouldn't interfere in their relationship. And he wouldn't.

But could he stand by and let a horse be killed out of his fear of possible repercussions?

"There has to be something I can do."

Chaney appeared skeptical, but something besides skepticism clouded her eyes. Maybe protectiveness? Did she think he couldn't handle whatever Calvin expected of him?

"What about money?" Calvin asked.

Chaney held Calvin's gaze. "There isn't any. The plan needs to be something I can do by myself. With support from Adam." She seemed reluctant to say that, but at least she'd admitted she needed him. "As simple as you can make it."

"I want in." Calvin tapped the table with his index fingers as if he were playing the piano.

"I told you, there's no money."

"But there's something almost as good."

"What's that?" Chaney asked.

"You'll owe me twice."

"No," Adam said firmly, surprising himself as much as he surprised them with his adamant tone. "She owes you nothing."

"You've got yourself a pet there, don't you, Chaney?"

"He's not a pet." Chaney patted Adam on the head. "Are you, buddy?"

"Ha ha." Adam turned to Calvin. "I've got money. Not a lot, but—"

"You're not financing this." Chaney's mood quickly changed from teasing to no-nonsense stubbornness.

Calvin's eyes sparkled. "Every little bit helps. The plan will be to turn that little bit into a whole lot more."

"The plan is to save Mischief and, if at all possible, ruin Mickey," Chaney said, her eyes blazing. "If that's not your focus, then I'll find someone else."

"There is no one else. But I promise you, I won't let the dollar signs influence me. Too much."

"I have your word?"

"You have my word."

"Can we trust your word?" Adam glared at Calvin but spoke to Chaney. "This guy stole your car." He bit his tongue before he blurted out any more accusations. Calvin returned the glare, a stony expression on his face as if he feared showing any emotion.

"I trust him," Chaney said firmly. She rested her hand on Adam's arm. To his surprise, her calming touch stemmed his growing anger. "We'll work out our other differences later."

"Here's what I'm thinking." For the next several minutes, Calvin outlined the rough edges of his plan.

"It's so simple," Chaney enthused when he'd finished.

Who was she kidding? The so-called plan seemed an elaborate web of what ifs and lucky breaks to Adam.

"Let's meet in the morning at Zach's Bar on Colonial," Calvin suggested. "The back door will be open."

"I'll be there," Chaney said.

"*We'll* be there," Adam responded.

"Great." Calvin slid out of the booth then handed Chaney a key. "Your ride is around the corner."

"You brought my car?" She studied the key as if to make sure it was hers. "What's the catch?"

"No catch." Calvin lowered his gaze, looking almost apologetic. But Adam figured there'd be ice-skating in the nether regions of the spirit world before Calvin ever uttered the words, *I'm sorry*.

"Looks like someone broke into it, though," he continued. "A thief with an extra key."

"Maybe." Chaney shrugged, all Miss Innocent.

"Maybe I'm nicer than you think." Calvin winked at her.

Before she could respond, he left them.

Adam was glad to see him go. Too bad they ever had to see him again.

CHAPTER 38

*F*riday Chaney wasn't taking any chances. She'd dyed her hair a vibrant copper similar to Sandy-Lynne's and added extensions. She even dyed her eyebrows. Apparently, Mickey Nolan had a thing for redheads, and Chaney needed every advantage she could get to hook the guy.

She, Adam, and Calvin had spent the past few days at Zach's Bar, which was no longer open for business, going through the plan step by step, practicing lines, making contingencies, and taking care of arrangements. At times, Tucker and Melody joined them, acting as a sounding board and adding their suggestions.

Everyone was on board for Part A of Operation: Mischief—saving the racehorse from Mickey's diabolical plan. All but Chaney and Calvin seemed to have reservations about Part B—somehow tricking Mickey into committing a crime. Or at least confessing to one.

Actually, Chaney was secretly concerned about Part B, too. But their options and resources were limited. They were taking a big risk. Hopefully, they'd be rewarded with Mickey's downfall.

Though if the plan failed, Mickey could take them all to court.

Tucker had talked to Sandy-Lynne, who'd been in touch with an attorney. She had signed a pre-nup limiting her financial settlement in the event of a divorce. But the agreement also stated that any gifts were hers alone. Her attorney believed they had enough evidence to prove Mischief was originally a gift from Mickey to his wife. But Mickey reneged on the gift by not naming Sandy-Lynne as the horse's owner. Even if their plan failed, the court might find in Sandy-Lynne's favor.

But not in time to prevent Mischief from racing on Saturday. And maybe not in time to keep Mickey from killing him.

In her wanderings around the racetrack on this sunshiny Friday, Chaney was sure she'd already caught Mickey's eye a couple of times. As far as he knew, though, she'd yet to notice him. She'd also been to Mischief's stall. The security guard stationed nearby didn't seem to see her as a threat. But why would he when she showed such interest in his opinions on which horses were likely to win their races? Flattery worked wonders to alleviate suspicion.

Besides, Chaney had no plans to lead the horse to a trailer in the middle of the night and drive away. Her plan was more sophisticated and ready to put in motion now that she had received Adam's text.

Buyer dropped out. Seeking new investor.

The text was code. Mickey Nolan had arrived at the stables to see Mischief and the other two horses he owned.

Chaney stood a few stalls away from the one holding Mischief. The security guard smiled and started to head her way, but she held up a finger and pointed at her phone. She called Adam, talking quietly, pacing furtively, a red-headed damsel in distress.

As Nolan came toward her, he slowed, eyeing her appreciatively. She flashed him a small smile while holding onto her persona of someone listening to disturbing news.

"What about Holden?" she said loud enough for Mickey to hear as he passed by. The name was intentional. Matt Holden was Nolan's primary rival at the track. "I'm sure he'd jump at this opportunity." She paused, her back turned to Mickey, as Adam recited the lines that Calvin had written for him and her voice brightened. "I'll go see him now. He'll be a much better partner anyway. He's not the skinflint that—" She pivoted and came face-to-face with Nolan.

He stood in front of her, a pleasant smile pasted on his hog-jowled face and his hands folded in front of him.

"I'll call you after," she said into the phone. "Okay. Later."

She ended the call, nodded, and started to walk past Nolan, but he maneuvered in front of her.

"I'm Mickey Nolan," he said. "And you are?"

"Charlotte Rhinehart." She held out her hand and allowed him to hold it a moment longer than necessary. "You own Mischief," she exclaimed. "I saw the trainer exercising him this morning. Such a lovely horse. It's sad really. But I must be going. So nice to meet you."

She walked away, but Nolan matched her pace.

"Pardon me, Ms. Rhinehart, did you say?"

"That's right. Charlotte Rhinehart."

"What did you mean by that?"

"By what?" She glanced at the diamond watch that Melody had lent her as if she were in a hurry.

"You said, 'it's sad really.' What's sad?" He chuckled as he said it, as if they were old friends. This was a very different Nolan than the one at the hunting cabin. This one wanted to make a good impression on the non-existent Charlotte Rhinehart.

"Did I say that?" She looked horrified then hid her embarrassment at her verbal faux pas behind a laugh. "I shouldn't have. Please forget it. Now I must be on my way."

He blocked her path and she allowed her expression to harden enough to let him know she was displeased and unaccustomed to such behavior.

"May I call you Charlotte?"

She shifted her gaze to look beyond him, feigning a world-weary boredom. "If you like."

"Charlotte, please understand. That horse means a great deal to me. If you know something regretful about him, then I would ask you, as a friend, to tell me what it is."

"I misspoke, Mr. Nolan. That's all."

"Racetrack gossip can be the worst," Nolan said. "Someone starts a rumor and then people think it's fact. If it's something like that, I need to stop it before it makes the rounds."

"I pay no attention to gossip nor do I spread it." Chaney-as-Charlotte crossed her arms and stiffened her jaw.

He stepped closer, forcing her to step back. Her eyes widened as her spine pressed against the boarded space between two stalls. His voice lost its earlier friendliness. "Tell me."

"Okay," she said, letting anger seep into her tone. "You don't need to take that tone."

She took a card from her purse and handed it to him. It was high quality crisp white stock with the name of her alias embossed in gold below a stylized logo of a horse and the letters OEC. A phone number with a New York City area code was discreetly printed in one corner.

"What's this?"

"You don't know?"

He eyed her with skepticism. "You're with the Oriental Equine Club? That's ridiculous."

"If you say so. After all, why would Asian millionaires come to a second-rate track like this one seeking investment opportunities?"

"They wouldn't."

"Exactly. So, if you'll excuse me."

He blocked her escape again. "Then why are you here?"

She hesitated a moment, eying him as if to size him up. "To find potential Triple Crown winners where no one else is looking. The OEC makes selective purchases, paying top dollar for prospective winners. If you must know, your Mischief was on my short list of thoroughbreds."

"And now he's not?"

"True or false: Mrs. Nolan doesn't want the horse to race tomorrow."

"What Sandy-Lynne does or doesn't want doesn't matter. He's a racehorse, and he's going to race."

"She won't want to sell to us." She stepped past him. "Now I really must go."

He stayed beside her. "Is one of Holden's horses on your short list?"

Chaney appeared flustered. "Why would you ask that?"

"You mentioned his name in your phone call."

Chaney quickened her steps until she was walking as fast as her high heels would let her. "No, no. Not at all. Goodbye, Mr. Nolan. It was a pleasure meeting you."

She scurried down the aisle, turned the corner, hurriedly removed the heels, and ran out of the building as fast as she could.

The hook had been baited. Now they needed Mickey to bite.

CHAPTER 39

Friday

The next step was easy. At least, that's what Chaney had assured Adam, but he couldn't see how any of this was *easy*. Crazy was more like it. Not that Calvin, the so-called mastermind, had given him anything hard to do. In fact, Adam doubted that watching Chaney through binoculars as she flirted with Matt Holden was necessary. Especially since Calvin was doing the same thing.

They stood at a strategic spot near the track, their binoculars supposedly trained on the starting gate for a race in which both Holden and Nolan had horses entered. Nolan's thoroughbred was a chestnut with a respectable though not stellar record. That's apparently why Nolan had bought Mischief. He wanted a winner.

Adam tilted his binoculars enough to shift from the starting gate to the spectator boxes. Beside him, Calvin kept an eye on Nolan who, in his turn, appeared to be trailing Chaney as she accidentally-on-purpose entered Holden's box. She wore a light green dress with cut-out shoulders and a matching hat over her dyed hair. The extensions were done up in a complicated braid.

Though Holden was old enough to be her father, he gave her an appreciative leer as she smiled and, according to the script, apologized for her mistake. He gestured for her to take a seat and served her a drink.

Adam shifted the binoculars to Nolan, who was more interested in what was happening in Holden's box than the race. Then he turned back to Chaney. She stayed with Holden till the race was over, enthusiastically cheering with him and frowning when his horse didn't win.

Before she left, she handed him her card, touched his arm, touched her hair, smiled, and laughed.

"Nolan hasn't taken his eyes off her," Calvin said with a chuckle. "He missed the entire race."

Nolan, too, seemed to be unwittingly following their script. From his perspective, Chaney was an invited guest to his rival's box where she was making Holden an offer that she'd refused to make to Nolan. An offer he now wanted.

"How did his horse do?" Adam asked.

"Don't know, don't care." Calvin pocketed his binoculars and straightened his tie. "Time for me to make an appearance."

"What if something goes wrong?" It wasn't the first time Adam had asked that question, but so far, no one had given him a satisfactory answer.

"We improvise," Calvin said, his tone flippant.

"You've said that before. It's not reassuring."

"I get it. You don't trust me."

"You've got that right."

Calvin stared at his feet for a moment then met Adam's gaze. "I got carried away the other night at the parking garage. My temper … sometimes it can be a monster. But we're on a job now. If something goes wrong, I'm responsible for making it right. And I will."

He flashed a smile and the flippant tone returned. "Now

that's settled, I need to keep my date with the charming Charlotte Rhinehart."

Nothing's settled. Not yet.

But when the job was over—however it ended—Adam intended to have a sit-down with Calvin Brady. Maybe he'd unleash a monster of his own.

* * *

AFTER LEAVING HOLDEN'S BOX, Chaney stopped in the ladies' room to take a couple of deep breaths and gather her thoughts. She'd made a positive impression on the old gentleman, which was her only intention. Holden couldn't tell Nolan about any offers because she hadn't made any. But Nolan wouldn't believe that. Simple psychology had hooked Nolan. Now to reel him in.

Chaney took the stairs to the lounge overlooking the track. Calvin sat at a table near the balcony railing. When she arrived, he stood and kissed her on the cheek for the benefit of any onlookers. She did her best not to shudder at his touch. They hadn't talked about his behavior in the parking garage or about Nero's rib-crushing hold. Maybe they never would.

"I got a text from Adam," Calvin said as he sat beside her and took her hand in his. "Nolan has been following you. He'll be here soon."

"I'm ready for him."

"Should we order champagne?" He caught the attention of a nearby waiter.

"Not while we're on the job."

"We need to keep up appearances. Besides, I can hold my liquor."

"White wine, then." She gazed past the balcony railing to the track where the horses for the next race were being led to the starting gate. *My name is Charlotte Rhinehart*, she repeated to herself. *I'm a buyer for the Oriental Equine Club. I'm sophisticated. Elegant. Independent. In control.*

All the things she had to be for Operation: Mischief to end in success.

When Nolan arrived a few minutes later, he pretended surprise at seeing Chaney.

"Ms. Rhinehart," he said, reaching for her hand. "Charlotte. How lovely to see you again."

"Thank you, Mr. Nolan." She smiled as if delighted when he kissed her fingers though her stomach roiled at his touch.

"Please, it's Mickey." He tightened his hold when she tried to withdraw her hand from his, his gaze suggestive, then he let her go. "No need for all that Mister formality."

"May I introduce you to my associate, Cameron Bradford." She turned to Calvin. "Mickey owns Mischief, the horse I told you about yesterday."

"Oh, yes, the ... hm, yes." Calvin shook Nolan's hand. "Won't you join us? I've had a bit of success today, so Charlotte and I are celebrating."

"I'd love to." Mickey took a seat next to Chaney.

The waiter arrived with their drinks. "I'll take a scotch on the rocks," Mickey said. "And put all this on my tab."

"That's very kind of you," Chaney said. "But not necessary."

"I insist." He folded his hands on the table. "I hope you'll come again tomorrow for the Derby's qualifying race. You want a sure thing, bet on Mischief. He's guaranteed to win."

"One thing I've learned," Calvin said, "there's no sure thing in racing."

"That's true enough." A mysterious grin crossed Mickey's face, as if he had a secret. "Except when it isn't."

Calvin and Chaney exchanged barely disguised glances, as if they had a secret of their own.

"I'm sure you're right," Calvin said lightly. "We saw him exercise this morning. He's a fine horse."

"Then you know he's a winner. The perfect investment for the OEC."

Calvin's eyes narrowed. "What does that mean?" Before Nolan could answer, Calvin glared at Chaney.

She darted a helpless glance at Nolan then placed her hand on Calvin's arm. "I can explain. Mickey was at Mischief's stall when I stopped there earlier today. He heard me talking—"

Calvin leaned closer and lowered his voice. "You didn't tell him about the other thing."

"Of course not," Chaney protested. She touched Nolan's shoulder and softened her gaze. "I simply explained our concern about Mischief's ownership."

"Like I said," Nolan replied. "That's not an issue."

"Maybe yes, maybe no." Calvin sipped his drink. "But the only way the OEC will consider investing in Mischief is if someone owns him besides you. They've heard all about your wife's efforts to keep him from racing. I'm sorry, Mickey, but that's the way it is."

"He's a contender for the Florida Derby, and you know it." The edge in Nolan's voice betrayed his agitation. "He's exactly the horse those high-and-mighty Asians want to back."

That's it, Mickey. Come into our trap.

Chaney disguised her elation by gazing around the lounge. Large monitors displayed close-up views of the track during the races. Right now, during a lull, videos of past highlights were being shown.

Nolan's irritation meant he was primed to take action. A man like him hated being told no, and he especially hated the idea of someone else—even worse, a rival like Holden—cashing in on an opportunity denied to him. *Simple psychology.*

"I understand you," Calvin said agreeably. "But like I said, they know Mischief 'disappeared.'" He made air quotes, his mocking expression making it clear he found the incident absurd. "He already missed the Golden Citrus Race. Scuttlebutt around the track is that Mrs. Nolan may have another trick up her sleeve."

"There's nothing else she—" Mickey said before Calvin cut him off.

"Bottom line, Mischief was on the short list. Now he's not." Calvin raised his hands in a *what are you going to do* gesture.

"So you're considering Holden's nag?" Mickey hmphed. His tone was petulant. "Guess you don't want a winner after all."

"Mr. Nolan." Chaney offered her most engaging smile and patted his hand. "Mickey. Forget about Mr. Holden, please. We're not buying his horse. We thought of approaching him with a different offer, but after meeting with him we changed our minds."

"Why is that?" Mickey asked.

"Let's just say," Calvin hesitated, as if choosing his words carefully, "Mr. Holden tends to see the world in black and white. Charlotte and I prefer varying shades of gray." He exchanged a furtive glance with Chaney.

"You know," Mickey said, "if you two are planning something shady, I could talk to the race steward. Put a quick end to your game."

"Nothing shady at all," Calvin replied. "We're interested in a certain horse running in one of tomorrow's claiming races. But we don't have the needed funds to deposit with the Horsemen's Account."

Persuading Nolan to volunteer to fund the claiming race was the next step in their plan. Tucker had explained that all the horses in a claiming race were up for grabs—as long as the potential buyer had funds in a special account and filed a claim ticket at least fifteen minutes prior to the race.

"You considered asking Holden for the money?" Mickey snorted. "That pompous blowhard? Why don't you get that OEC bunch to finance you?"

"Because we plan to sell them the horse," Chaney said. "For much more than we invest in the claiming race."

"Why would they do that?" Mickey asked.

"You wouldn't believe me," Chaney said. "The story is too incredible."

"Try me."

"I think we should go. Come, Charlotte." Calvin pulled out his phone and frowned. "Excuse me. I need to take this call." He stepped away from the table.

Chaney shifted in her seat. Calvin's pretend phone call was part of their script, an excuse to leave her alone with Mickey.

As expected, as soon as Calvin was out of earshot, Mickey turned on the charm. "You were right to forget about Holden. That was *your* decision, right?"

"I have an instinct for people." Chaney swirled her glass. She'd only taken a couple of sips, enough to keep up appearances. But she'd never acquired a taste for alcohol, much to her grandfather's disappointment.

"What do your instincts tell you about me?" Mickey gave her a flirtatious smile.

Chaney responded with an enticing smile of her own. "You know what you want. And you'll risk anything to get it."

"What about you?"

"What about me?"

"Do you call the shots? Or does he?" Mickey tilted his head in Calvin's direction.

"We're equal partners."

Mickey laughed. "There's no such thing, sweetheart."

"You want to know the story." It wasn't a question, but the warmth of her voice invited him to say yes.

"Sure, I do. And if I like it, perhaps I'll put money in the Horsemen's Account." He took her hand. "As long as there's something in it for me."

"You'll need to hurry." Chaney turned toward Calvin who

gave her a thumb's up. "He's talking to a potential partner right now."

Mickey's thumb caressed her palm and her wrist. He leaned closer and whispered, "Then *you* better hurry."

"Remember. This is only a story." She followed the script as she'd practiced it. "What if, despite taking all the normal precautions, a certain mare got bred the old-fashioned way? Only no one knew it except the groom who found her. Everyone thinks her colt comes from one line when he really comes from another."

"The owner doesn't know?" Mickey's tone was doubtful. "Unbelievable."

"So one would think. In this case, however, the owner is a moron and so is his trainer. But once the truth comes out..."

"Sounds like a fairy tale to me." Mickey smirked. "Holden might have believed whatever lies come out of your pretty little mouth, but I'm no fool."

"Believe me or not." Chaney shrugged. "That's your choice."

"Even if all you said was true, how is it you know about this mysterious conception and the owner doesn't?"

"Because I was the groom." Calvin appeared at the table, obviously annoyed. "Let's go, Charlotte. You talk too much."

"I was only telling a story." Chaney scooted back her chair then tapped Mickey's hand. "Do you still have my card?"

He removed it from his pocket. "Here it is."

"Let me give you my direct line. In case you want to talk again sometime." She took the card and, in a sleight of hand movement that would have made her grandfather proud, exchanged it for a different card without a name embossed on the front. Mickey would no longer have proof that anyone named Charlotte Rhinehart existed. She wrote the number to a burner phone on the back and returned it to him. As she expected, he glanced at the handwritten number and stuck the card in his pocket.

THE MISCHIEF THIEF

"It was nice to meet you, Mickey." She took Calvin's arm. "Good luck in Saturday's race."

They sauntered toward the exit, but Mickey joined them before they'd left the lobby.

"After you claim this horse," he said, "you plan to tell the world who his daddy is? Sell him to the OEC?"

"To the highest bidder." A smug smile crossed Calvin's face while Chaney softened her gaze.

"I thought you didn't believe in fairy tales," she said, her voice low.

"Stranger things have happened." Mickey pursed his pudgy lips. "How much do you need to put a claim on the horse?"

"This is a big-time investment, my friend." Calvin said dismissively.

"None of the claims are for more than fifty thousand dollars," Mickey pulled a slender cigar case from his pocket. "I can cover that for, let's say, an eighty/twenty split of the eventual sales price."

"I already have a serious offer," Calvin said. "Sixty-five for the investor, thirty-five for Charlotte and me. Sorry, Mick. You're too late."

"I'll do sixty-forty. And," Mickey pointed the cigar case at Chaney, "you make me a member of the OEC."

"You can't be serious." She gave a sympathetic laugh. "New memberships require a buy-in of at least three million dollars."

"Three mill?" Mickey practically choked. "That's the minimum?"

"Technically, no," Chaney said, hesitating as if reluctant to tell him more. In fishing terms, she and Calvin were standing on the shore while their fish swam toward them of his own free will, totally unaware of the hook and line attaching him to them.

"What is the minimum then?" He fumbled with the latch on

the cigar case, muttered something under his breath, and shoved it in his pocket.

"I'm authorized to nominate a few likely candidates at lower tiers," Chaney explained. "But, Mickey, you must understand. Even those require at least half a million. And naturally I'm very selective with my slots." Her tone made it clear that she didn't believe Mickey could afford the buy-in, even at the lower tier. He'd want to prove otherwise.

"Five hundred thousand." Mickey glanced away from them. "It might take me some time to pull that much together."

"Time is something we don't have." Calvin gripped Chaney's elbow to steer her away, but Mickey stopped them again.

"I'll get you the claim money," he announced, as if he was doing them a favor. "I'll even stable this mystery horse until it's sold. But I want one of those tiers you were talking about."

"I can only promise an introduction," Chaney said. "But you'll need the half million upfront."

"I'll tell you what I'll do," Mickey said. "You put Mischief back on your short list—"

"Not as long as you're the owner, Mickey." Calvin held up his hands. "We've been through this. The head honchos at the OEC think you can't control your wife. Makes them wonder what else you can't control."

"What if you were the owner?" Mickey practically spat. "Would they buy him then?"

"Mickey, darling," Chaney cooed. "Now you're clutching at straws."

"Though it's an interesting idea." Calvin laughed and glanced at his watch. "Charlotte, we're going to be late. See you around, Mickey."

"Hold on there a minute. We haven't finished our business."

"What business?" Calvin asked.

"How about I sell Mischief to you?" Mickey's defiant tone revealed his frustration. Their plan pushed all the right buttons

—pride, greed, ambition. Chaney's gaze was filled with a pity she did not feel but sensed would rattle him even more. She and Calvin had held out the shiny dream of socializing with elite owners and gamblers then snatched it away. Mickey's desperation made him foolish.

"If I had the money to buy Mischief," Calvin said, sounding exasperated, "I wouldn't need a partner for the claiming race."

"Here's my deal." Mickey motioned them to join him in a quiet corner of the lobby.

"I'll sell Mischief to you for next to nothing. You sell him to the OEC." Mickey gave a hearty chuckle as if he'd come up with a brilliant plan. "I get the proceeds minus what you paid me for him plus you can have an additional ten percent as a broker's fee."

His self-satisfied smile made Chaney want to retch, but her expression remained impassive. This was exactly where they had hoped to lead him.

"I don't know." Calvin rubbed his chin. "Seems like a lot could go wrong with a plan like that."

"A lot could go wrong with your claiming race plan, too," Mickey shot back. "You know it probably wouldn't be too hard for me to figure out which horse you're talking about. Place a claim of my own and cut you out entirely."

"You see," Calvin said to Chaney, his voice harsh. "This is why you don't tell strangers our business. He's an amateur. The OEC doesn't want amateurs."

"Call me that again, son, and see what happens to that nose of yours."

"You going to hit me, old man? You can try."

"Gentlemen, please." Chaney intervened. "Look, we all want the same thing. Maybe we can work this out. But," she turned to Mickey, "if we do this, the transactions need to happen immediately. I'm not the only buyer seeking a prospective winner for the OEC."

"What are we waiting for?" Mickey checked his watch. "The steward's office should still be open. They have all the necessary forms."

"You want to do this now?" Calvin gave a deprecating chuckle. "Perhaps I underestimated you. In my experience, the decisive man is the successful man."

"How do you think I made my money?" Mickey's eyes hardened. "Sure wasn't handed to me on a silver platter. I trust my instincts and do what they tell me."

"I respect that." Calvin tilted his head as though considering their plan. "First, you'll need to sign the form giving Charlotte the authority to act as your agent in the claim race and transfer fifty thousand to the Horsemen's Account. Then, if we can work out the arrangements, we'll transfer ownership of Mischief."

"Let's do it." Mickey headed for the lobby doors. Calvin gave Chaney a thumb's up sign behind his back.

Chaney tucked her hand in Calvin's arm as they approached the elevator. She lowered her gaze and took a deep breath. She avoided elevators whenever possible but taking the stairs would mean giving Mickey too much time to reconsider. They needed to get him to the steward's office and the papers signed for both these strange transactions as soon as possible.

The door slid open and they stepped inside. Chaney's grip on Calvin's arm tightened, and he darted a sidelong glance her way. She gave him a weak smile but didn't lessen her grip. This was a mistake, letting him know about her fear of enclosed spaces.

Too late now. Maybe he'd think she was nervous about the con.

Calvin rested his hand on hers, a strangely comforting gesture coming from him.

"What's your next-to-nothing price for Mischief?" he asked Mickey.

"Thirty-five thousand."

Calvin hmphed. "Fifteen thousand."

"He's worth twenty times that to me dead," Mickey retorted.

"And we'll be selling him for at least forty times that. So why quibble?"

"You're the one who wants to play with the big boys," Charlotte reminded Mickey. "I can make that happen, but I understand if you're having second thoughts."

"Not me. Because if you even think about double-crossing me ..." Mickey left the threat hanging. "How about twenty thousand?"

Calvin pretended to hesitate then reluctantly agreed.

When they reached the ground floor, Chaney heaved a silent sigh of relief, but she didn't let go of Calvin's arm until they were out of the elevator.

"I need to call my bank about the transfer." She stepped out-of-earshot of the two men and called Adam. "We did it."

"I don't believe it." He paused a moment and she could picture his tension easing away. "How much?"

"Twenty thousand for Mischief," she said. "Mickey wanted thirty-five, but Calvin talked him down."

"That's good, since we have less than thirty thousand in our account."

Earlier in the week, Adam, his dad, Melody, and Chaney had formed a private consortium. Chaney had limited authority to make transactions on their behalf while the other three financed the partnership.

"I never expected to own a racehorse," Adam continued. "Though my share is probably only enough to cover the hindquarters."

"He's not ours yet. Mickey could still change his mind."

"Is that likely?"

"We're on our way to the steward's office now. Wish me luck."

"I'd rather pray for you. That God will keep you safe through all this."

She ended the call without replying. Why was Adam praying about a con? She'd spent most of the day pretending to be someone she wasn't. What did God think about that? Then it hit her—Adam hadn't said he was praying for their success but for her safety. She wasn't sure God cared about that either, but Adam's concern, his sincerity, touched her.

Grandpa had discouraged friendships with anyone outside of the family. Adam wouldn't have been an exception.

Yet he had stood up for her, stopped her from getting arrested, given her a place to stay and food to eat. He'd even helped her retrieve her belongings from The Sting. All of this and more despite losing his job, the recent break-up with his fiancée, and worrying about his dad.

He treated her, a stranger, like a friend.

Maybe it was time for her to make an exception. Even if it meant breaking her grandfather's code.

CHAPTER 40

Friday
Chaney's nerves were on edge as they entered the steward's office to take care of the transactions. Mickey put fifty thousand dollars in the Horsemen's Account and signed the form naming Charlotte Rhinehart as his agent for the claiming races. Then they completed the bill of sale transferring ownership of Mischief to the consortium Adam had created.

Mickey signed the bill of sale as soon as the purchase amount transferred to his account. Then he handed it to Chaney for her signature.

"Remember," he warned. "This is a formality. Mischief stays in my stable until he's sold to the OEC and I have my money."

"Absolutely," Chaney soothed as she brushed imaginary lint from his shoulder and tried to ignore the tension knotting her stomach. This was a pitfall moment. She needed to sign her real name on the bill of sale, or the transfer wouldn't be legal.

Calvin distracted Mickey by talking to him about the photos of Florida Derby winners showcased on one wall. Chaney tuned out the conversation as she signed the bill of sale, the capital *C* and *R* prominent and flowing while the remaining letters were an indecipherable scrawl. A signature she'd perfected over the years. She showed her genuine driver's license to the steward's assistant in charge of notarizing the signatures.

When the process was completed, Chaney put her copy in her bag along with the claiming race form Mickey had signed. She folded Mickey's copy, placed it in an envelope along with his receipt for the funds deposited in the Horsemen's Account, and handed it to him.

"We're all set," she said. "Tomorrow will be a grand and prosperous day."

"As long as no one else puts in a claim on your mystery horse," Mickey said. "We could lose him if there's a draw." When more than one person claimed a horse, the steward selected the new owner by lot.

"Not going to happen." Calvin chuckled. "We've made sure of that. The horse will be ours as soon the race is over."

Mickey's eyes narrowed. "How did you do that?"

"We can't tell you all our secrets." Chaney handed her phone to Calvin. "Take a picture of Mickey and me. It'll be our special memento."

Calvin immediately took charge, posing them next to a potted palm and snapping several photos. Between his instructions and Chaney insisting on reviewing the photos then flirtatiously begging Mickey for a couple more, they gave him no opportunity for second thoughts.

When the impromptu photo session ended, Calvin shook Mickey's hand. "We're late for another engagement, but we'll see you tomorrow."

"What time?"

"Oh, Mickey." Chaney injected as much warmth and humor as possible in her smile. "Are you trying to find out which claiming race we're interested in?"

"I think you could tell me." Mickey's voice turned petulant. "Now that we're partners and all the papers are signed."

"Only Calvin and I know which claiming race. Only Calvin and I know which horse." She touched Mickey's arm and lowered her voice. "Tomorrow we will celebrate."

"I reserved a box for the day," Mickey said. "Join me there."

"Perhaps for Mischief's race," Calvin answered. "We really must be going."

Chaney gave Mickey a lingering glance as Calvin led her from the office. The corners of Mickey's mouth turned up, and his eyes were hooded. She maintained her façade, but her insides quaked. Mickey hadn't yet done anything illegal. She wanted to ruin him, but maybe saving Mischief was enough.

"You okay?" Calvin asked once they were outside though they stayed in character as they strolled toward the parking lot.

"He gives me the creeps."

"Make sure you're never alone with him."

"Interesting advice coming from you." She touched her jaw, an involuntary gesture, and Calvin seemed to flinch. The bruising had faded, but the spot was still tender.

"About that," Calvin said, his gaze directed at anything but her. "I was angry. The crew was angry. If I didn't do something to get back at Marshall, I'd have lost their respect. You know how it is."

She looked away from him, her voice quiet and resigned. "I know how it is."

Grifters were rarely violent, but Marshall had broken the code when he interfered with Calvin's heist. Even Grandpa might have served Marshall's head on a silver platter to Calvin's crew. Once punishment was rendered, all was forgiven. Though never forgotten.

Trust between rivals renewed. Though never fully restored.

They reached their vehicle, a metallic red Acura that Calvin had rented. Calvin opened Chaney's door, the perfect gentleman for the benefit of anyone who might be watching. For all they knew, one of Mickey's goons had them in his sights.

"Are you ready for tomorrow?" Calvin asked as he drove away from the racetrack.

"Everything is set." Chaney pulled out her copy of the bill of sale, elated yet hesitant to celebrate their success, and stared at the notary stamp and signatures. Mischief belonged to them now, and once Sandy-Lynne was free of Mickey, he would be hers again.

One more step of the plan remained. After that, Mischief would never race again. He wouldn't face the risk of stumbling because of his injuries or the threat of being euthanized. Mickey couldn't kill him then fraudulently collect the insurance money.

Mischief would be safe, but not Marshall. Nothing in this convoluted plan helped him get out of jail.

CHAPTER 41

*F*riday

"We did it. Mischief belongs to us." Chaney placed the bill of sale in front of Tucker and Melody. They were seated at a table in the back room at Zach's Bar.

Tucker scanned the document, then read it again more slowly. "I never had any doubts." He nodded approvingly at Chaney and Calvin. "I only wish Sandy-Lynne could be here to see this."

"Have you talked to her?" Chaney asked.

"Not today. Mickey has someone watching her almost all the time." Tucker chuckled then grimaced in pain. His shirt bulged where it covered his bandages. "Not that it's going to do him any good. As soon as Mischief is safe, she'll implement her exit strategy."

"Which is?" Calvin asked. Despite his nonchalant tone, Chaney's nerves tingled. He knew better than to ask a none-of-your-business question like that. So why had he?

"I don't know, and I don't want to know." Tucker slid a thick envelope across the table toward Calvin. "Sandy-Lynne thanks you for your help. We couldn't have done this without you."

255

"That's true," Chaney said. "You were great."

"I knew someone would come through with money for this job." Calvin opened the envelope and skimmed his thumb across the wad of bills. "This is generous. Thank her for me."

"I'll do that." Tucker extended his hand.

After the handshake, Chaney scooted back her chair. "Adam will be waiting for us, so we should go," she said to Tucker and Melody.

"Are you sure you don't want me to meet you at the track in the morning?" Calvin asked.

"Thanks, but we can handle it," Chaney assured him as they followed the veterinarians out the back door. After saying their goodbyes to Calvin, Melody opened the passenger door of her Subaru for Tucker.

"I'll be right with you," Chaney called then turned back to Calvin. "All that's left to do is go to the steward's office, show proof of ownership, and pull Mischief from the race."

"Are you taking care of that?"

"Me? No."

"Got it." He grinned. "What about Charlotte?"

"She'll keep Mickey away from the steward's office." Chaney poked Calvin's shoulder. "And she doesn't need you being the third wheel."

"Not me," he teased. "You mean Cameron."

"Cameron or Calvin," she said. "I meant what I said earlier. You were terrific today."

He held up the cash. "This makes us even. No hard feelings?" He stuffed the envelope in a pocket and extended his fist for a friendly bump.

She feigned uncertainty, eyeing him for a moment, then tapped her fist against his. "We're even."

"You'll explain everything to Marshall? I don't want to be looking over my shoulder when he gets out."

"He'll be glad to know you stepped up." Though he'd never

forgive Calvin or Nero for harming her. For Marshall's own sake, she might never tell him about that incident.

"See you around, Chaney. Take care of yourself."

Suddenly she clasped his hands then pulled him into a hug. He stiffened, then relaxed as he put his arms around her. A moment later she stepped back.

"Goodbye, Calvin."

"Goodbye, Chaney." He opened the door of his rental then turned back and held out his hand. "My watch."

She dangled it by the strap. "Couldn't resist."

He grabbed it from her, hesitated, then handed it back. "Something to remember me by."

"I can't take your watch."

"I insist."

Before she could protest any further, he hopped into the Acura and waved as he sped out of the parking lot.

He thought he was so smart, giving her the watch in case she'd tampered with it in any way. But the watch had only been a distraction. She'd deftly placed a tiny tracker in his wallet earlier in the day. If he returned to the track or went to Mickey's office, she'd know it.

She slid into the back seat of Melody's vehicle.

"What now?" Tucker asked.

"We take you home," Melody said. "You need to rest."

"I don't need to go home," Tucker grumbled. Melody ignored him as she drove away from the bar.

"She's right," Chaney said. "It's been a long few days."

"That's true," Tucker admitted. "Doesn't mean I have to like being treated as an invalid. Or this next plan of yours."

"It's going to work, Tucker." It had to work if they were going to save Mischief.

On the drive to Adam's house, she told them everything that had happened that day.

"Mickey wasn't suspicious?" Melody caught Chaney's eye in

the rearview mirror. "It seems almost unbelievable anyone could have fallen for that story."

"We gave him two transactions to consider which made it hard for him to focus on only one," Chaney said. "Then there was the power of the trifecta. Greed. Pride. Rivalry. Add a dollop of FOMO, and he couldn't resist."

Or Mickey was on to their game and planned a double-cross. A good possibility if Calvin had betrayed them. A possibility she couldn't ignore.

"What in blazes is FOMO?" Tucker tried to turn around then grasped his shoulder.

"Fear of missing out," Chaney and Melody said together, laughing.

"You need to stay up with the times, old man," Melody teased as she pulled into the driveway behind Adam's Charger.

"Who are you calling an old man?" Tucker softened his retort with a grin. "If not for this bum arm, we'd see who lasted the longest on the dance floor."

Melody's cheeks pinkened. "It wouldn't be you."

Chaney slid from the car, leaving them to their flirtatious bickering. She didn't know what their relationship had been before this week, but they'd definitely grown comfortable with one another in the past few days. Had Adam noticed?

Probably not with everything else he had on his mind. If love was in the air, would he be happy for his dad? Or would Tucker's potential romance cause Adam more pain?

CHAPTER 42

Friday Evening
Adam waited for Chaney and Melody near the tack room at one end of a short corridor of stalls at the racetrack stables. The duffle bag at his feet contained the items he needed to hide Mischief in plain sight, like the missing racehorse in "The Adventure of Silver Blaze." Adam puffed out his chest, proud that his familiarity with Sherlock Holmes had inspired this final step in Chaney's con.

The two women rounded the corner. Chaney had changed into skinny jeans, ankle-high cowboy boots with lace insets, and a lilac top adorned with chunky jewelry. She still wore the red hair extensions, styled now into a long ponytail. Melody, dressed more conservatively in capris and a pale blue pullover, carried a medical bag.

"You're sure Mickey is gone?" Chaney asked.

"You asked me that when I called," Adam reminded her. "I watched him leave. He seemed very pleased with himself."

"That's good." She pressed her hand against her stomach and took a deep breath. "Are you both ready?"

"I think so." Melody's giggle sounded nervous. "I keep

reminding myself that I'm not pretending to be a veterinarian. I *am* a veterinarian."

"That's right." Chaney gave her an encouraging smile. "This situation is real for you. Just be yourself." She glanced at Adam. "What about you?"

"I'm glad to be doing something besides lurking in the background and spying on people through binoculars." He couldn't tell her how envious he'd been of the role Calvin had played. Envy was a sin.

A serious sin.

One of the seven deadly sins.

Adam had tried praying for the guy, but his heart hadn't been in those prayers.

Maybe Pete was right. Maybe he wasn't cut out for the ministry. But if not the ministry, then what? God wasn't opening any doors. Or any windows or any cracks in the walls. Though what could Adam expect? It had been less than two weeks since Pete handed him the termination paperwork. Adam hadn't knocked on any doors, tried to open any windows.

He'd been too busy doing something he never could have done if he'd still had a job.

Is saving Mischief the reason? Part of a bigger plan?

"Earth to Adam?" Chaney bumped his arm.

"Huh?" He glanced from Chaney to Melody and back again. Both stared at him as though wondering what was wrong with him. "Sorry. Got lost in my thoughts."

"We can do this ourselves," Chaney said. "You can wait at the other stall."

"You're not sidelining me. I want to help." No way was he going to miss out on this next phase. He pulled a lead rope from his duffle bag. "I'm ready."

Chaney led them to Mischief's stall, her demeanor subtly changing from carefree girl to sophisticated woman along the way. Her walk changed, the way she carried herself changed, even her voice changed to a deeper register.

Mickey's hired guard, a guy built like an NFL linebacker, sat in a camp chair near the stall door. He stood, a broad smile on his face, as Chaney approached him.

"You're back," he said, somehow making the two words sound like an indecent invitation while giving her a blatant once-over.

"And with very good news," Chaney said brightly as she brandished the bill-of-sale. "I bought Mischief. Isn't it terrific? You can't imagine how excited I am."

"Wait a minute." The guard frowned and his gaze hardened. "You did what?"

Chaney laughed. "I just fell in love with him. And Mickey, he's such a dear. We signed the papers this afternoon. Anyway, this is my veterinarian and my groom. We're going to take Mischief for a little walk, give him a once-over, and, you know, get better acquainted."

Her flirty smile focused on the guard as she gestured for Adam, who stood dumbstruck at her ability to gush without taking a breath, to enter the stall. He lifted the latch, and the guard held up his hand.

"Hold on, now. Mr. Nolan didn't tell me nothing about this sale or taking Mischief for a walk."

"Why would he?" Chaney brushed the guard's arm with her fingertips and held out the bill of sale. "He's not the owner anymore. I just told you that."

She tilted her head as she narrowed her eyes. "I'm not sure why you're even still here."

"Because I'm doing my job. And I'm going to keep on doing my job until I hear something different from Mr. Nolan. In fact," he pulled out his cell, "I think I'll give him a call right now."

"Not before I do." Chaney's tone turned petulant as she

tapped her phone's screen. "I never dreamed I'd be treated this way. And I'm sure Mickey won't be happy about this either."

"Wait a minute now." The guard held up both hands in surrender. Adam didn't blame him. Spoiled-Chaney was scary.

"Too late," she pouted. A muted voice came through her phone. "Mickey, honey," she enthused, "I'm here at Mischief's stall with Dr. Perez, but your guy is being mean. He doesn't care that Mischief is mine now. Why didn't you send him away?"

"Let me talk to him," the voice said, loud enough for all of them to hear. Adam bent his head to hide a smile. Tucker's imitation of Mickey was spot-on.

"Not necessary," the guard said through clenched teeth.

Chaney pointed her phone at him but didn't let go of the device. The name "Mickey, Honey" appeared on the screen along with one of the photos Calvin had taken at the steward's office.

"Hey, boss." The guard feigned cheerfulness. "Congrats on selling Mischief."

"Are you giving my girl there a hard time?"

"No, sir. Not at all, sir."

"Glad to hear it. Listen, you don't need to stay there. I'm not paying you to guard someone else's property. Got it?"

"Whatever you say, sir."

Chaney flashed a victorious smile then walked away with the phone to her ear. "When will I see you again, Mickey?"

The guard stared after her then folded his camp chair and stormed off. Adam entered the stall and held out his hand to the thoroughbred. "Hey there, Mischief," he said softly. "You ready to get out of here?"

Melody and Chaney joined Adam in the stall. The sophistication, the entitled attitude, disappeared as Chaney stroked the horse's neck. "He's beautiful, isn't he?"

"Sure is." Adam glanced at her out of the corner of his eye. So was she in her own adorable way.

"He's magnificent." Melody leaned against the frame of the stall door. "And you, Chaney—that was quite the performance. You're amazing."

"I'm Charlotte." Chaney grinned and flipped her ponytail.

"I don't know how you do it, *Charlotte*." Melody laughed. "I'm still nervous and I didn't have to do a thing."

"Your presence made a difference," Chaney assured her. "Three of us against one of him. He hid his nerves but that 'hold on now' was a sad, vain attempt to gain control of the situation."

"He didn't stand a chance." Adam hooked the lead rope on Mischief's halter. "Ready, ladies?"

They took Mischief to a vacant stall in a different corridor where Melody listened to his heart and lungs. Adam retrieved a bottle of temporary dye and a pack of makeup sponges from his duffle. He dabbed the dye on Mischief's blaze while Chaney removed her extensions.

"Say good-bye to Charlotte." She finger-fluffed her hair. "That gal no longer exists."

"Mickey will be so disappointed." Melody unwrapped the bandages from Mischief's legs. After she finished her examination, Adam and Chaney darkened the horse's white stockings.

"How is he?" Adam asked.

"The swelling isn't bad, but I wouldn't clear him for a race. I'm surprised anyone would."

"Apparently Mickey found the veterinarian who's the exception." Adam tossed a used sponge in a plastic bag before standing back to admire his work. "Not that it did him any good since Mischief has been taken away from him. Twice now."

"Don't celebrate yet," Chaney cautioned. "We still have to get through tomorrow."

"What are you worried about?"

"Nothing in particular." She avoided his gaze as she stroked Mischief's long neck. Which meant she was being less than truthful.

Would she never trust him?

Adam gave her a sidelong glance as he tied up the bag of used sponges. Mischief nuzzled her shoulder as she told him what a handsome boy he was.

Though perhaps Adam's ability to sense her lack of candor was, in a strange roundabout way, evidence of trust. She hesitated to confide in him, but she didn't mask her concerns behind a confident, *no-worries-here* persona. Maybe, in her own way, she trusted him after all. At least enough that she could be herself instead of playing a role.

He wouldn't insist she answer his question. Trust went both ways.

CHAPTER 43

Friday Night

The dreams, vivid and fantastical, shook Chaney awake, leaving her breathless and cold. The images faded as she rubbed sleep from her eyes and calmed her racing pulse. She scratched at her dry throat then padded toward the kitchen. As she rounded the corner, a shadow moved at the table in the dining nook, stopping her heart. She clutched at her chest while stifling a scream.

"It's me," Adam said while she caught her breath. "Sorry I scared you. Couldn't you sleep either?"

"Too much on my mind, I guess." She walked past him into the kitchen where the light over the sink provided a small pool of illumination.

"The kettle is hot if you want tea."

"This is fine." She poured water from the pitcher in the refrigerator then joined him at the table.

"You worried about Mischief?"

"I wish we could have stayed with him." They'd considered spending the night in the stall. But if they were caught, the racetrack's security might check the stall listings and discover the one holding Mischief was supposed to be empty. They'd scan his microchip to identify him and put him back where he belonged. The ownership papers might be questioned, Mickey might be contacted—that scenario would be a nightmare.

"He'll be okay." Adam spoke with quiet assurance. "Mickey isn't getting him back."

"I hope you're right." Chaney drew her knee to her chin, propping her foot on the chair seat. "So much could still go wrong."

"Could. But won't."

She wished she had his confidence. Of course, he didn't know of her doubts about Calvin's trustworthiness.

"Want me to read you a Sherlock Holmes story?" Adam pushed a large book toward her. Even in the dim lighting, she recognized it as the volume of stories she'd seen on his desk the night she broke into his home.

"In the dark?"

He chuckled. "I stayed up and read 'The Adventure of Silver Blaze' again after you went to bed. No matter how hard the puzzle, Holmes always figures out the answer. But Mickey Nolan is no Sherlock. He'll never think to look in the other stalls."

"Hiding in plain sight."

"That's right."

"I'd have preferred a magic spell." Chaney wielded an imaginary wand. "If only we could have turned Mischief into a donkey or a mule. Or Mickey into a toad."

"Sounds like something from the Brothers Grimm."

"You're a fan of detective stories. I prefer fairy tales."

"Illusion instead of deduction?" Adam nodded. "Makes sense for a grifter."

"I suppose. Especially when you realize that fairy tales are a kind of reverse grift." She'd mulled over that idea since she was a child, but she'd rarely talked to anyone about it. Not even Marshall, though he probably would have agreed with her.

Adam's mouth quirked. "How so?"

"Think about it." Chaney leaned forward and clasped her hands on the table. "In a grift, the gold is fool's gold. The too-good-to-be-true opportunity is a sham. But in fairy tale world, the frog is really a prince. The scullery maid is the prince's true love. Again and again, what seems to be ugly and common is actually beautiful and ... extraordinary."

Adam's gaze was steady, his facial expression open and inviting. She dropped her eyes as her cheeks warmed. The whole notion was a childish whimsy she'd held onto for too long.

"I never thought of it like that," Adam said. "But you're right. Not only for fairy tales, but in real life, too. Sometimes the most unlikely person is the hero."

She met his gaze, not sure what she expected to see in his eyes. They shone with a warmth and kindness that overwhelmed her.

"Like you," he said softly. "The thief who saved a horse. The pickpocket who is really a princess."

"I'm no princess."

"Close enough." His teasing smile lightened the moment.

Though not the weight of her thoughts. He imagined her a princess, a heroine, someone noble and virtuous. She could fool him and his dad and Melody for a time. But eventually they'd see the truth—she was and always would be a crone in disguise.

CHAPTER 44

Saturday
Adam waited with his dad and Chaney in the racetrack parking lot while Melody, the only one of them Mickey hadn't seen, checked on Mischief. Chaney, dressed in cargo pants and a light pullover, wore large glasses and a brunette wig over her dyed hair. The disguise helped from a distance, but not close up.

Tucker's phone beeped and he read the text out loud.

Our boy fine. MN caused uproar over missing horse.

"He's already here?" Adam didn't know why he was surprised. Mickey believed this was his big day. In his mind, before the track closed, he'd own the mystery horse from the claiming race and, assuming Mischief raced well, in a week or so he'd be flush with cash from the supposed quick sale to the OEC. Naturally, the man would want to relish his expected successes.

The phone beeped again.

MN left stable.

"We better go to the steward's office," Chaney said. "I'll go in first to see if Mickey is there. If he's not, then you two can go in and withdraw Mischief from the race."

"I've got a better plan," Adam said. "I'll go in first and you stay with Dad. Mickey didn't pay that much attention to me at the cabin. We could be face to face and he might not even recognize me."

"Or he might," Chaney replied.

"He'll definitely recognize you."

"He won't even see me. I'm going in the back door."

"I can go in the back door."

"Give it up, son," Tucker said. "Chaney hasn't failed us yet, so let's stick to her plan."

"Thank you, Tucker." Chaney shot a victorious smile at Adam. He held up his hands in surrender, though admitting defeat galled him. He shouldn't have been surprised his dad took Chaney's side. He seemed to think of her as the daughter he'd never had.

"Do your best to stay out of sight until I give you the thumbs up," she warned them.

"You've got it," Tucker said.

Chaney sprinted toward the racetrack administration building without looking back.

"Everything's going to be okay." Tucker clasped Adam's shoulder. "You'll see."

Maybe Dad and Chaney were right. But Adam couldn't shake the foreboding that surrounded him. He'd prayed about their plans, prayed for guidance, prayed for wisdom. But events seemed to be sweeping him along without time for pause.

Maybe he should have read Scripture instead of Sherlock last night. He used to spend an uninterrupted hour every morning in his church office in Bible-reading, prayer, and meditation. He needed to get into a similar routine now that he was out of work.

He also needed to find a job. Figure out the path God meant

for him to take. It all seemed too daunting. And right now, in the middle of saving Mischief, it didn't seem to even matter that much.

Was that because he was already on the right path?

"We haven't had much of a chance to talk about what happened at the church," Tucker said as they followed the sidewalk to the front of the administration building. "Seems like that Pete Davis has had it in for you for quite a while."

"That's what I think." Adam wasn't in the mood to talk about the board member right now. Or the past.

"Too bad you didn't go to vet school." Tucker adjusted his sling. "You could take over my practice."

Adam shouldn't be surprised by his dad's futile wish, given the cutback in the clinic's hours and staffing in recent months. But this was the first time Tucker had intimated giving up the practice. "You ready to call it quits?"

"Just about."

"I thought you wanted to stay around a few more years for your long-time patients." They veered off the sidewalk to detour between two buildings—all part of Chaney's stay-out-of-sight plan.

"I thought so, too. Now I'm not so sure." Tucker chuckled. "We're supposed to be talking about your future, son, not mine. You could still go to vet school, you know."

"Not happening, Dad. That's not my calling."

"What is?"

"Only God knows. And He's keeping that to Himself right now."

They walked behind the building adjacent to the administration offices. As they rounded the corner, one of the men who'd been at the cabin with Mickey came toward them. Adam grabbed his dad's arm to turn around, but another man, the one who'd shot Tucker, was behind them.

"Mr. Nolan wants to talk to you." He pointed his revolver at them.

"Tell him to make an appointment," Tucker retorted.

"Dad, don't." Adam faced the shooter. "Where is Mr. Nolan?"

"I'll take you to him."

"You can bring him to us," Tucker said. "We'll wait."

"It doesn't work like that."

"We're not going anywhere with you," Adam said. "Now, if you'll excuse us, we have business to attend to."

"You're the preacher, aren't you?" The shooter smirked. "Always thought the Good Book was against stealing."

"I didn't steal anything."

"Mr. Nolan has something to say about that." He waved the gun. "Let's go."

Adam exchanged a glance with his dad. None of their contingencies had involved this scenario. He doubted the man would shoot them, not here anyway. But who knew what he'd do once he got them out of earshot of the jockeys and trainers and spectators?

"I think we'll stay here." Adam stuck his hands in his pockets and, feigning an off-handed confidence he didn't feel, leaned against the building. At least his voice didn't shake.

"Fine," said the shooter. "Though that will make it harder on the girl."

"What girl?" *Not Chaney.* Adam's pounding heart ramped up to a whole new level.

"That redhead."

"You mean Sandy-Lynne?" Tucker sounded doubtful. "Nolan's wife?"

"Not her. The redhead who tricked the boss into selling his horse."

If they had Chaney, they'd know she was now a brunette. Unless she'd removed her wig. Or they removed it. A vision of that donkey butt yanking off Chaney's wig flashed through Adam's mind. He clenched his fists.

"Sounds to me like Mickey wants to renege on a deal," Tucker drawled. "We'll go with you, but I'm warning you. No one better lay a finger on that girl."

"At least you admitted knowing her." The shooter lowered the gun as the other man, who wore his dirty blond hair pulled back in a ponytail, escorted them around the back of the administration building to the far side of the track. They crossed the field to a shed that backed up to the ten-foot board fence stretching across that section of the property.

Ponytail opened the door and the shooter ushered them inside. A bar of sunlight filtered through a grimy side window. On the opposite wall, a couple of board shelves held dusty cans of paint, containers of fertilizer and weed killer, and a dented bucket. Cracked harnesses and frayed lead ropes hung on nails jutting from the studs. A weed-whacker was propped between the handles of a push mower while assorted plastic totes and cardboard boxes were stacked willy-nilly on top of one another.

But no Mickey. And no Chaney.

Adam faced the men. "Where is she?"

"I lied." The shooter's mouth twisted into a grin. "Appreciate your cooperation. Now give me your phones and sit down." He pointed to a large tack box sitting in front of a pile of dust-covered flip-top totes.

"I don't feel like sitting," Tucker said. "And I don't like being lied to."

The shooter shoved the gun into Tucker's ribs. "Mr. Nolan don't like being lied to either. Now sit down like I told you. The girl will be here soon enough, and neither of you gents should even dream of being a hero. Understand me?"

"Do what he says, Dad." They handed over their phones then sat on the broad box. Ponytail wrapped duct tape around Adam's wrists.

"What should I do about him?" He pointed to Tucker's sling.

"Duct tape his free hand to the mower there."

"Not happening," Tucker said.

"Dad, please. Everything's going to be okay."

"Listen to your preacher boy," the shooter said. "Maybe I won't put a bullet in that other shoulder. Or your heart."

Tucker released an exasperated sigh before resting his wrist against the mower's handle. Ponytail secured the duct tape then tossed the roll onto a shelf. Both men stepped outside but left the door open.

"What are we going to do?" Adam whispered. "We've got to get out of here. Warn Chaney."

"May be too late for that," Tucker muttered. "We'll just keep our eyes open. God is with us, son."

"I know that," Adam retorted then bit his lip. Getting snappy with his dad wouldn't get them out of this mess. A breeze wafted through the door, its jasmine fragrance intermittently masking the shed's dusty, chemical odor. Adam inhaled deeply, wanting to believe—choosing to believe—the fragrance came from God. A gentle reminder of His presence. No matter what happened.

CHAPTER 45

*S*aturday Chaney waltzed through the back door as if she belonged in the squat administration building. Thanks to Tucker, who had been in it before, she had a basic idea of the layout. She followed the hallway to the front where the steward's office suite was located and peered through the glass door. The receptionist who'd given her the claiming race form yesterday sat at her desk, her focus on a computer monitor. Two men, possibly trainers, judging by their clothes, huddled near the coffee station. Another man sat, posture perfect, browsing through a magazine.

Fletcher Wilkes. How interesting.

Chaney pressed her back against the wall so she could take additional peeks without Fletcher seeing her. She opened the tracker app on her phone. She'd been monitoring Calvin's movements since she woke up that morning. Though the tracker wasn't sophisticated enough to give an exact location, the blue dot indicated he was now at the racetrack.

As friend or foe?

She peeked through the window again. Fletcher rose and

greeted a young woman who shook his hand then ushered him through a door to the inner offices. He was probably here on Mickey's behalf to protest the legality of Mischief's bill of sale. It didn't matter if the sale was overturned—only that the process was delayed long enough to keep Mischief out of today's race.

Tucker and Adam needed to complete the race withdrawal form while Wilkes was in the back offices. And before the steward contacted his own attorney.

Chaney sent the thumbs up emoji to Adam then made her way outside. She paced the exterior length of the building waiting for him to reply or show up. "Where are you?" she muttered. If he and Tucker weren't in the office in two minutes, she'd pull Mischief from the race herself.

"They aren't coming."

Chaney whirled to face Calvin.

She masked her surprise with boredom, though not fast enough. He'd caught her off guard. Worse, he knew it.

"Who's not coming?"

"Adam and his old man." Calvin stepped closer. Too close. She didn't budge or flinch, though her worst nightmare was coming true. "It's over, Chaney. Mickey wants his horse. Where is he?"

"Where are Adam and Tucker?" Her insides were jelly, but at least her voice didn't quake. She'd hoped for Calvin's loyalty but prepared for his betrayal.

"Hidden away till after the race. They'll be fine as long as you cooperate." Calvin pocketed her phone before gripping her elbow, his fingers pinching her skin. She could stomp on his foot, knee him, and run. But she needed him to take her to Adam.

"Mischief is in a stall."

"You're lying."

"How much is Mickey paying you?" She filled her voice with scorn.

"More than his wife did." He pulled her to a secluded spot near a trio of sago palms. "But this isn't about money. Marshall burned me. Now I've burned you."

"I thought all was forgiven."

"Never." The coldness of his eyes turned her blood to ice. "But after Mischief finishes the race, we'll be even."

"That won't happen."

"Sure, it will." He tightened his hold on her arm. "You see, the guy who shot the old man at the cabin is holding a gun on him and Adam right now. One of them will talk to protect the other. Not that it'll matter."

"Murder?" She choked on the word. "You couldn't."

"Not me. I deliver you and I'm gone." He pulled her alongside him as he took long strides away from the administration building. "What happens after that is none of my concern."

Chaney stumbled to keep up with him as her mind flipped through the contingencies she had in place, the possible scenarios, the potential—horrible—outcome if she made a mistake. She'd never forgive herself if anything happened to Adam or Tucker. Yet she was too afraid of death to greet it with open arms. Could she, if confronted with the choice, find the courage to sacrifice herself?

Don't make me face that test, she pleaded. Hopefully God would hear her. For Adam's sake if not her own.

The stadium speakers crackled, and a voice announced the first race of the day. People milled near the track—spectators, race officials, trainers, and grooms. If she screamed and yelled and fought, they'd hear her. Save her.

She could slip away. Disappear.

And hate herself for the rest of her life.

Be brave, be brave. She took a deep breath as Calvin hurried her along to an isolated shed located near the back fence. Two men stood outside the open door, the two men who'd been at the cabin with Mickey.

"This the girl who stole Mischief?" one of them asked as they drew near. "Thought she was a redhead."

Calvin pulled the brunette wig from Chaney's head, revealing her dyed hair. "Mickey's prize, as promised."

"Finally." The man pulled out his phone. "I'll text the boss. He'll want a word with her."

The other man, the one who'd shot Mickey, turned to Calvin. "Did she tell you where they hid the horse?"

"No, but she will. You get the box?"

"It's inside."

Box?

Calvin pushed her into the shed. She stumbled and Adam, hands bound together, stood in a clumsy attempt to catch her. She fell against him and steadied herself.

"Are you okay?" they both asked at the same time. Worry darkened Adam's eyes, and she smiled at him, hoping to reassure him that they'd get out of this mess. She knelt before Tucker, who was seated on the tack box with one hand duct-taped to the lawn mower, and clutched the fingers of his other hand.

"I'm so sorry," she said. "This wasn't supposed to happen."

"Never you mind." His gaze, warm and tender, bathed her in affection. "I'm here with two of my favorite people. Life doesn't get any better than that."

Tears sprang to Chaney's eyes and she kissed his cheek.

"We don't need none of that." Calvin pulled Chaney to her feet. "Last chance. Where's Mischief?"

The pounding of her heart echoed in her ears. "In a stall."

"Where's Melody?"

"With Mischief."

He gave an exaggerated sigh, grabbed her by both shoulders, and glared at her. "You're lying."

"I'm not."

Calvin frowned and turned to Tucker and Adam. "Get away from the box."

"What?" Tucker exchanged glances with Adam, who shrugged.

"You heard him," said the shooter as he gestured with his gun. "Move away."

Chaney's breath caught and she turned to run, but Calvin grabbed her. She fought, kicked, screamed, her senses failing her as Calvin picked her up. Other voices, scuffling, Adam's shouting abruptly silenced. Calvin dropped her into the box, shoving her arms and her legs inside, and shutting the lid as hot tears burned her cheeks.

Darkness.

She kicked the sides and pushed against the lid, whimpering and sobbing, her breath ragged.

"Chaney?" Adam's voice, soothing, soft. But in pain. What had they done to him? She screamed again then curled into a tight ball, her arms covering her head, her eyes closed as she fought to breathe.

"You monster!" Tucker's voice boomed. "What have you done to her?"

"She's claustrophobic," Calvin said, his voice calm and cool. "Didn't you know?"

How did Calvin? Then she remembered. She'd clutched his arm in the elevator. A slight touch, but all he'd needed.

"Worse than I expected," he said. "But we'll let her out as soon as Mischief's race is over. As long as he runs in that race."

"He's in the stables," Adam said. "In the—"

"Noooo," Chaney wailed. They weren't beaten yet. Not yet.

"Chaney." Adam's voice was close. She imagined him sitting beside the box, on the other side of the wood. So close she imagined she could hear him breathing, and she focused on matching her breaths to his. In and out. In and out. Slow, deep inhales. Slow, long exhales.

She placed a hand against the wood, imagined his hand on the other side, only the wall of the box separating his fingers from hers.

"We have to tell them," he said. "It's over."

She sniffed and wiped her nose on her sleeve. "Not"—deep breath—"yet."

Fear is afraid of itself, she heard Marshall whisper as he'd done so many times before, helping her overcome her crippling terror. *Pat it together.* Like the pat-a-cake nursery rhyme. *Mark it with a C. Throw it far, far away. And be free. Be free.*

She softly recited the made-up poem, breathing through the words, her voice barely a whisper as her hands went through the childish motions. Pat. Make the C in her palm. A C for Chaney. A C for courage. Then throw. *With all your might, Chaney. Like a baseball.* Spread her arms out, wide as she could, and smile. *Be free.*

"Chaney?" Adam tapped the box.

She needed to focus, Implement Plan G. G for Grant.

Her stomach clenched as she forced herself to open her eyes. *Fear is afraid of itself.* The box was dark with only a sliver of light coming through the cracks around the lid.

"Pat it together," she said, her voice gaining strength. "Mark it with a C." Tears flowing, she unsnapped the side pocket on her cargo pants and pulled out the burner phone she'd hidden there. As she recited the made-up poem, her voice masking any other sounds, she texted Melody.

Up 2 U 2 remove M from race. Proceed as planned.

Wiping fresh tears from her eyes, she recited her poem as she sent another text—the last resort but their best hope. Her sacrifice to save those who'd shown her such kindness.

CHAPTER 46

*S*aturday

Adam sat on the shed's wooden floor, his head resting against the tack box. Tucker, still attached to the lawn mower, had ignored Ponytail's order to take a seat. Thankfully, Ponytail didn't insist. To pass the time and, Adam supposed, to keep up their spirits, his dad was telling stories about veterinary life. When Ponytail wasn't looking, Tucker slipped his arm from the sling and picked at the duct tape holding his wrist to the mower. He'd already unwound more than half.

Reciting her poem seemed to have taken all of Chaney's willpower. Except for occasional sniffles, she was quiet, refusing to answer Adam when he asked if she was okay. Or maybe the fear had paralyzed her.

Never before had he witnessed such raw terror. He'd tried to stop Calvin, that rat, from putting her in the box, but Ponytail sucker punched him. His gut still ached. Now Ponytail leaned in the doorframe, his big ears listening to everything they said. But he was obviously miffed at being relegated to babysitter status. Calvin and the shooter were outside, chatting it up and laughing

THE MISCHIEF THIEF

while they waited for Mickey to bring Calvin his thirty pieces of silver.

Adam needed to come up with a plan. Fast. Before he was king, David once acted crazy to get away from the Philistines. Maybe that tactic would work if Adam was by himself. But he also needed to get Chaney out of that box.

"Boss is coming," Ponytail said with a smirk. "That little gal better talk now if she knows what's good for her." He strolled across the grass to meet the group.

As soon as his back was turned, Tucker unwound the rest of the tape, freeing his hand from the lawn mower. "Don't take this off," he said as he cut through the tape binding Adam's wrists with his pocketknife. "Leave it on your skin so it looks like you're still tied up."

"Got it." As soon as he was free, Adam pushed open the lid. Chaney laid on her side, arms and legs tucked close to her body. "Chaney?"

She blinked her eyes. "Marshall?"

"It's me, Adam."

"Hurry, sweetheart," Tucker said. "They'll be back soon."

Adam reached to help her, but she suddenly popped up, her eyes wild as she scrambled out of the box. He grabbed her before she ran out of the shed, holding her close while her body shook.

"You need to hide until we figure out something," Adam said.

Tucker closed the lid on the box. "Behind the door."

Adam led her to the spot then lifted her chin to look into her eyes. The color was returning to her cheeks, though she still seemed dazed. "Hide here. But if you get the chance to run, you run. Understand?"

"I understand." She gave him a shaky smile then glanced at the shelves. Her smile widened as she pulled a can of spray paint from a nearby shelf and shook it. "I'm ready."

"We may be outnumbered, but we'll have surprise on our

side." Tucker rubbed his wounded shoulder before resuming his stance by the lawn mower. His hand rested on the weed whacker. "I wonder if this thing still works."

Adam sat on the box and peered out the door. "Calvin's leaving but the others are coming this way."

"Let 'em come," Tucker said.

"They've got guns, Dad."

"And we've got God. Or did you forget that?"

There was no need to point out that even Christians could be murdered. God might protect them. He might not.

Though He slay me, yet will I trust in Him.

Adam didn't want to die, didn't want any of them to die. But if his life ended now, he knew without a doubt he'd wake up in heaven. So would Dad. But what about Chaney?

He glanced at Tucker. "We can't let anything happen to her, Dad," he said quietly.

"We won't, son."

"Then let 'em come."

CHAPTER 47

*S*aturday

Chaney took the lid off the spray can and gripped it with both hands. She closed her eyes and calmed her breathing. The horror of being shut in the box settled on her shoulders like a dark shadow. But she'd survived. Hopefully, she'd survive this next horror, too. They all would.

Footsteps sounded outside, coming closer, entering the shed. Chaney resisted the temptation to peer around the door. From habit, she reached in her pocket for her phone then remembered Calvin had taken it. The burner ... she'd been so anxious to get out of the box she'd left it behind. After sending that last text, she'd turned on the recording app. Hopefully, it was still running and would record Mickey saying something—anything —to incriminate himself.

"Where is she?" His obnoxious voice boomed, and Chaney wanted to cover her ears. Another deep breath. "Don't tell me she got away from you bozos."

"She's in the box," the shooter said. "Put up quite a fight, but we got her inside."

"Move away from there, Preacher," Mickey ordered. He

knocked on the box lid. "Charlotte, Chaney, whatever your name is. You tell me where you hid my horse so we can get him ready for the race." He spoke in measured tones. "Despite all your foolish playacting, you failed. Mischief belongs to me. He will race and he will win. If not, well, horses die all the time. So do people."

"Mischief doesn't belong to you anymore," Tucker said.

"My attorney is making sure he does. Whatever the cost. To show everyone that no one makes a fool out of Mickey Nolan."

"I think we already did."

"Something you'll regret."

That's right, Tucker. Keep him talking.

"You're not a murderer, Mickey."

"You're right about that, Doctor. Why do you suppose I've got these two on the payroll? I keep my hands clean."

Chaney sighed in relief. The recorded admission might not hold up in court, but it was proof of Mickey's intent. Add that to kidnapping, unlawful imprisonment ... he might be spending a long time behind bars.

Hopefully, she wouldn't be, too.

A whirring sound came closer, growing louder with each passing second. A helicopter?

"That your chopper, Mickey?" Adam asked.

"Go see what that's about," Mickey ordered.

Chaney peered through the crack as one of the men left the shed. A loud roar sounded—the weedwhacker. Time to shake off the vestiges of panic and take action.

Pat the fear. Throw the fear.

She slammed the door shut with a bang. When Mickey whirled around, she sprayed him in the face. He roared as orange paint shot out of the can and into his eyes. Chaney stiffened then erupted with nervous laughter at the irate pumpkinhead.

Meanwhile, Tucker wielded the weedwhacker at Mickey's

ribs like some strange battery-operated medieval weapon, and Adam held the man who had shot his father in a chokehold.

"That's an FDLE helicopter." Tucker grinned at Chaney. "Did you arrange that?"

"Plan G." She took a step closer to Mickey, spray can at the ready, as he wiped the paint from his eyes. "My name is Chaney Delaney Rose. Mischief does not belong to you. He will never race again. And you, Mickey Nolan, despite your threatening theatrics, will rot in—"

"Chaney," Adam interrupted, his tone gently admonishing.

"I was going to say in a hot air balloon headed to the Antarctic."

"Sure you were."

The door slowly opened, and Special Agent Benjamin Grant, followed by two other officers, emerged, guns drawn.

"Looks like we're late to the party." Grant lowered his weapon as his agents handcuffed Mickey and the shooter then took them outside.

"Thanks for accepting my invitation." Chaney exhaled a quivering breath. "Are you arresting me, too?"

"Should I?"

She pointed at the box without looking at it then wrapped her arms around her stomach. "My phone's in there. It's been recording for a while but the last two to three minutes is all you need." Despite that info, she guessed he'd listen to all of it. He'd hear her childish whimpers, learn her weakness. But to ruin Mickey, she had to give Grant the phone.

"In the box?" Grant's eyes narrowed. "Why?"

Chaney lowered her gaze, unable to answer.

"They forced her in there," Adam said quietly. He extended his hand. "Adam Thorne. We met a couple weeks ago."

"I remember you. The minister who gives money to thieves."

"Who gives grace to those in need." Adam introduced Grant to his dad, and the two men shook hands.

After retrieving the phone from the tack box, Grant pointed at Tucker's sling. "What happened to you?"

"If you don't mind, I need to talk to my attorney before answering any questions."

"Afraid of self-incrimination?"

Tucker gave an exaggerated shrug.

Grant turned back to Chaney. "You're looking pale. There's a medical clinic here at the track. Why don't we take you there, get you checked out?"

"I'm fine." A lie. None of them were convinced.

Adam touched her arm. "He's right. You've been through a traumatic experience."

"We all have. Are *you* going to the clinic?"

"Chaney..."

"Don't feel sorry for me."

"I care about you." He suddenly grinned, recalling his earlier thought about her and his dad. "You're like the annoying little sister I never had."

His words surprised her. And unexpectedly warmed her heart. Until now, she'd always believed Marshall was the only family she needed. He still was. But in the past couple of weeks, Adam and Tucker—and even Melody—had invited her into their lives with no reservations. She'd never experienced anything like their generosity and hospitality before.

"I'll go to the clinic with you," Adam said. "Dad, too."

He drew her into a comforting embrace, holding her like Marshall would have if he'd been with her after her ordeal. She rested her head against his chest, inhaled the pleasant aroma of his aftershave, and let his strength flow through her.

This was friendship. Genuine and true.

She craved it.

CHAPTER 48

Saturday Late Afternoon
Operation: Mischief hadn't gone according to plan. Few operations did. But Chaney and her crew accomplished their objectives. In the end, that's all that counted. Mischief didn't compete, and Mickey had been arrested.

After receiving Chaney's text, Melody had rushed to the steward's office and completed the form pulling Mischief from the race. Then she hurried to the stable, dutifully washed the dye from his blaze and stockings, and returned him to his assigned stall. He was there when the FDLE agents, investigating Mickey's accusation that Chaney had stolen the horse, arrived at the stable.

Since Chaney's signature, along with Mickey's, was on the bill of sale, the legality of that transaction was a matter for the civil courts. Sandy-Lynne's attorney planned to file a motion on Monday stating that Mickey didn't have the right to sell Mischief and requesting that the horse be prohibited from racing until the question of ownership was settled. Unless the court ruled in Mickey's favor—a highly unlikely outcome—

Sandy-Lynne would eventually be sole owner of her beloved thoroughbred.

"Mickey says you cheated him out of fifty thousand dollars," Special Agent Grant said. "Something about a claiming race."

They were standing near a paddock at the racetrack where Mischief freely grazed. The slanting sunlight highlighted the red in his glossy bay coat.

"I told Mickey a story," Chaney said. "I told him that I was telling him a story. He deposited the money in the Horsemen's Account. It's still there."

"You didn't claim a horse?"

"He authorized Charlotte Rhinehart to do that. Not me."

Grant hmphed. "He believed *you* were Charlotte Rhinehart."

"He believed what he wanted to believe." Or had Calvin told Mickey the plan before they set it in motion? She didn't believe Mickey was a talented enough actor to maintain such a charade but doubt still gnawed at her. At least, FDLE had caught Calvin, too. They'd arrested him for his part in her abduction before he could leave the track.

"I've got something for you." Grant handed her the phone Calvin had taken from her.

"What about the other one?"

"We need it for evidence." He paused a moment, his eyes focused on Mischief. "I'm sorry."

From his tone, she suspected he wasn't apologizing for keeping the burner. "You listened to the recording. All of it."

"Yeah." He shifted his stance to lean against the whitewashed fence. "Calvin said you were claustrophobic. I think it goes deeper than that."

"I'm not telling you my life story."

"I don't expect you to. But maybe it'd be helpful to talk to someone." He handed her a card. "My sister is a therapist with a local victims' advocacy group. Everything's completely confidential. You can talk badly about me and I'll never know it." He snorted. "If you tell her that I'm overbearing and arrogant, she might even agree with you."

In her heart, Chaney knew he meant well. But talking about her claustrophobic trauma meant talking about her parents, about her family. About a nightmare she couldn't face. She could bend her grandfather's code. She wasn't ready to break it.

"I'll think about it." She pocketed the card, positive she'd never make the call.

In the paddock, Mischief raised his head. His black mane flowed over his arched neck as he flicked his long tail. He seemed to be gazing at the sun, sinking lower in the painted sky as afternoon slid into evening.

Everything Chaney had endured over the past couple of weeks, even the time in the tack box, was worth this spectacular moment.

Operation: Mischief. No other con meant so much.

CHAPTER 49

***A* Few Days Later**
Adam sat at his desk, staring at the photo of him and Piper. She'd called him, her voice quivering with concern, after the news broke that he'd been Mickey Nolan's hostage. He wanted to reach through the phone and take her in his arms, to hold her again, to get lost in the tantalizing fragrance of her perfume.

But when she suggested they get together so she could see for herself that he was unharmed, he put her off. He didn't know why he refused. Maybe his heart needed more time to heal before he could consider her as no more than a friend.

He still loved her, but he couldn't shake the nagging thought that she wanted a role in the story. She didn't deserve his suspicion, and he tried to bury it. But in his mind's eye, he imagined the local media's enchantment with her beauty and poise. Even though he believed her concern for him and for Tucker was genuine, she'd have reveled in the role of frightened fiancée.

If she'd only waited a few more weeks before breaking their engagement, she might have had her fifteen minutes of fame.

Or not.

If he'd still been engaged, would he have invited Chaney into his life the way he had? Perhaps. After all, he needed her to find his dad. But he doubted their *Les Mis*-inspired moment, even if it still happened, would have led to him driving her around the city's junkyards in search of her car or breaking into his dad's clinic after hours. Not with Piper by his side.

Such a time as this, Tucker had said. Maybe he was right, and maybe God had orchestrated the break-up and the firing so Adam could take in the homeless waif who stole his mom's wedding ring set. And maybe God had sent Chaney to help him find his dad and thwart Mickey's despicable plans.

"Knock knock." Tucker appeared in the doorway. "Shouldn't you have left by now?"

"Just finishing up a couple of things." Adam took one last look at the photo then placed it in a box with the other photographs, the kitchen calendar with the crossed-off dates, and a few more keepsakes from his time with Piper. "Are you sure you don't want to go with me?"

"I've got a few things to take care of myself." Tucker sauntered toward the desk as Adam closed the box. "It's not easy, packing up the past. Sometimes it doesn't want to let go. But this"—he tapped the box—"is a step forward. I'm proud of you, son."

The warmth of the words covered Adam like a cozy blanket on a drizzly day. "How about you, Dad? Are you packing up the past, too?"

"All but the good times. Those include every day I had with your mom and with you."

Adam rounded the desk and pulled Tucker into an embrace. The past few months had been harder on his dad than he'd known until a couple of nights ago. After a hefty meal of grilled steaks and baked potatoes, Tucker had confessed to Adam and Melody how he'd racked up gambling debts with Mickey Nolan by betting on the races. Because of the debt, Mickey forced

Tucker to clear his thoroughbreds for racing despite any injuries they might have.

Tucker had sold Adam the house and used over half the proceeds to get out from under Mickey's thumb. But guilt and depression gnawed at him. When the injured colt stumbled during a race and had to be euthanized on the track, Tucker's guilt turned to anger. Though he hadn't cleared that particular colt to run, he still felt responsible. When he overheard the Nolans arguing about Mischief, he resolved to help Sandy-Lynne protect her horse.

After Tucker finished his story, Adam and Melody prayed with him. In the chill of the early evening breeze, the sweet aroma of jasmine had freshened the air.

"Everything's going to be okay, Dad." Adam released Tucker from the embrace.

"Everything's going to be perfect. Do you have it?"

"In my pocket."

They chatted a moment longer then Adam stashed the box of keepsakes in the garage. As he walked to his dad's truck, which Sandy-Lynne had returned as she'd promised, he took a deep breath.

Jasmine again.

A sure sign God was with him.

CHAPTER 50

*T*hat Afternoon
The shadow, in the outline of a tall man with an athletic build, slid across the wrought iron table where Chaney Rose read a thick, well-worn paperback.

"Sorry I'm late," Adam said as he took a seat across from her. "Have you been here long?"

"Long enough to read 'The Goose Girl at the Spring.' And to order you a drink." She closed her copy of *Grimm's Fairy Tales* and pointed at the cup. "Iced tea okay?"

"It's fine, thanks." He unwrapped the straw and stuck it in the lid. "Where have you been staying?"

"Not your concern." She'd left his home early Monday morning, before he or Tucker got up, unwilling to take advantage of their hospitality any longer. She might be a con artist, but she wasn't a freeloader.

"It doesn't matter to me," Adam teased, "but Dad worries about you."

"How's his shoulder?"

"Healing nicely. He stopped wearing the sling, though

Melody told him not to. Maybe you could come back and nag him."

"I'm sure he'd love that." She gazed across the street at the jewelry store, the bank, the hotel. A little over two weeks ago, she'd sat at this very table, as uncertain of her future then as she was now. Yet so much had changed.

"Sandy-Lynne's lawyer is meeting with Marshall later today." Chaney rested her folded hands on her book. "She said he's taking the case *pro bono*, but I think she's paying him."

"She's grateful for what you did for her. For Mischief."

"We did do a good thing, didn't we?"

"Yeah. We did." Adam slid a small silver box across the table. "This is for you."

"A present? Why?"

"Because Dad and I are grateful, too. The man who shot him is behind bars thanks to you."

Along with Mickey and Calvin and the other lowlife who'd held them hostage. Apparently, Fletcher Wilkes, wanting to save his own skin, was singing like the proverbial canary about past transgressions. Mickey wouldn't be getting out for a very long time. If ever.

"Open it," Adam urged.

Embarrassment and excitement flushed Chaney's cheeks as she removed the lid. A ring with a house key and a silver horse charm lay on a square of cotton. Butterflies attacked her stomach and her thoughts whirled as she tried to make sense of the gift. She opened her mouth, but no words came out.

"It's the key to the pool house," Adam said. "Dad and I cleaned it out. Straightened it up. It's yours."

The pool house? Hers? It was too generous. She couldn't, shouldn't accept ... but oh, how much she wanted to.

"You can't mean it." Her voice dropped to a murmur. "A place of my own." In the backyard of the man she trusted most in the world. That is, except for Marshall.

"For as long as you need it," Adam said softly. "Dad and I both want you to say yes."

Chaney held the ring, brushed her finger along the charm, then read the engraving:

For the Mischief Thief

She laughed. "Was this your idea?"

"Maybe." Adam leaned back in the chair and grinned. "So what do you say?"

She gripped the key, holding it close to her heart. "I say yes."

MY LETTER TO YOU

Dear Friend,

You have zillions of books to choose from—I'm honored you chose to read one of mine.

The Mischief Thief began as a *"Les Misérables* meets *Leverage"* idea. I quickly learned that everyone I said this to knew the story of *Les Mis* but hardly anyone had heard of *Leverage*—one of my favorite television shows.

The show's premise is that a former insurance investigator is the mastermind of a team of wanted criminals who help ordinary people get justice from corrupt government officials and business executives.

I've always been intrigued by these kinds of stories, from the classic western *Alias Smith and Jones* about "two pretty good bad guys" to the irrepressible *A-Team* ("I love it when a plan comes together").

Yet it was a little daunting to create a heroine with a skewed moral compass. However, when Chaney meets Adam, who grants her much-needed grace, she takes the first steps on a spiritual journey that will lead to the deepest desires of her heart—and of ours—an eternal home with our Heavenly Father.

MY LETTER TO YOU

As the story developed, I fell in love with my conscientious con artist and ministry-less minister. I hope you love this unlikely duo, too.

If you enjoyed this story, please take a few minutes to leave a review on BookBub, Goodreads, and your favorite online retailer.

You're also invited to subscribe to my newsletter which highlights TWO giveaways each month.

I'd also love for you to join my Facebook group, Johnnie's A-Team.

The A stands for Amazing—that's you! And for Alexander—that's me!

Johnnie

DISCUSSION QUESTIONS

1. How does an honest person trust a thief? How does a thief, who's been raised to trust no one, overcome those childhood lessons? Both Adam and Chaney struggle with trusting each other throughout the story. What scenes stand out to you as examples of their trust increasing and falling apart? How does trusting others teach us to trust God? How does trusting God inspire us to trust others?

2. A compelling though subtle theme in the story is *hiding*. In the first chapter, Chaney and Special Agent Grant hide their eyes—said to be windows into the soul—behind dark sunglasses. Mischief is hidden in plain sight, similar to Silver Blaze in the Sherlock Holmes story. What other moments in the novel strengthen the *hiding* theme? How do we hide our deepest selves from our loved ones? From God?

3. Adam is a Sherlock Holmes fan. Chaney reads fairy tales. What do their preferences reveal about their personalities? Do you think the way they were brought up influences the kinds of stories they like best? What childhood stories resonate with you?

4. Why do you suppose Chaney considers The Sting (her

DISCUSSION QUESTIONS

dented Ford Focus) to be a safe place, even a refuge, when she's terrified of enclosed spaces?

5. At one point in the story, Adam realizes that the "light he'd used to view Piper shifted slightly to illuminate a facet of her personality he hadn't seen before." Have you had a similar experience? What actions might cause you to think differently about someone?

6. Chaney dreams of turning "an ordinary snow day into a magical experience" if she ever has a child. Why is it important to create treasured memories for the ones we love? What is something special you can do for a family member, a friend, or even a stranger to turn an ordinary day into an extraordinary one?

7. Adam reflects that God has provided solace for his "hurting heart in a myriad of ways." How has God provided solace for you or enveloped you in peace during painful times? What do these moments reveal about God's character and His love for us?

8. "Brains over brawn had been the family code for generations." What else do we know about Chaney's family code? How does she embrace the code and how does she resist it? Do all families have a "code"? Does yours?

9. "The past is a heavy chain to drag around." Can Chaney escape the negative influences and harmful experiences from her past? What do you think the future holds for her and for Adam?

10. What were your favorite moments from the story? Do you relate more with Adam, with Chaney, or with one of the other characters? Who is your favorite?

ACKNOWLEDGMENTS

One of the joys of writing is talking to others about the story. My sister, **Hebe Alexander**, came through once again, listening to what ifs and offering ideas. She suggested the claiming race angle of Chaney's con, and I can't thank her enough for that.

My dear friend, romantic suspense novelist **Patricia Bradley**, also chatted about different aspects of the story with me. Her encouragement after reading an early draft gave me a needed boost.

Carol Anne Giaquinto doesn't own a jewelry store in Orlando even though I gave her one in the novel. She is one of my closest friends and biggest fans. We share treasured memories of movies, celebrations, Bible studies, game nights, holiday dinners, and so much more. She read an early draft and provided helpful feedback. We also had a fun conversation about blood types. (LOL!)

Mark Mynheir is a retired Florida Department of Law Enforcement agent, one of the first real-life novelists I met when I attended the Florida Christian Writers Conference for the first time, and an all-around nice guy. He answered my big and little questions about procedural issues, jail visits, Special

Agent Benjamin Grant's wardrobe, and how much trouble Tucker could be in for not reporting his gunshot wound. Such a joy to tap into his expertise.

Dr. Stephen Galloway, veterinarian extraordinaire, assured me that my fictional vet clinic would have the necessary medical equipment to provide anesthesia and a transfusion, treat a gunshot wound, and monitor Tucker's recovery. Here's what he wrote in his email: *Physicians treat one species, vets treat all the rest!*

Kristen Stieffel, speculative fiction novelist, writing coach, and freelance editor, hopped into a Facebook thread where I had asked for suggestions on where to hide a horse. She mentioned Sir Arthur Conan Doyle's story, "The Adventure of Silver Blaze." I already knew Adam Thorne was a Sherlock Holmes fan so her suggestion was perfect.

Renee Osborne was one of my favorite critique partners during the early years of my writing career. I was thrilled when she agreed to edit this manuscript for me. She sprinkles encouragement along with her suggestions, and her comments often make me laugh.

Sara Davison, a new friend and also a Mosaic Collection author, did a tremendous job on the final round of edits. I truly appreciate her "fixes."

I also want to give a shout-out and a hug to:

• Tamela Hancock Murray, my lovely and supportive agent.

• Johnnie's A-Team ~ my tremendous book launch community.

• The Mosaic Collection authors and Camry Crist, our amazing VA.

As always, much love to my family: Bethany & Justin Jett; Jeremy, Jedidiah, and Josiah Jett; Jillian and Jacob Lancour; Kaydi and Presley Lancour; Nate Donley & BreAnna Lees.

ABOUT THE AUTHOR

Johnnie Alexander is a wannabe vagabond with a heart for making memories. She creates characters you want to meet and imagines stories you won't forget.

Her award-winning debut novel, *Where Treasure Hides*, is a CBA bestseller and has been translated into Dutch and Norwegian. She also writes contemporary romances, cozy mysteries, and historical novellas. *The Mischief Thief* is her first suspense novel.

Johnnie is on the executive boards of Serious Writer, Inc. and Mid-South Christian Writers Conference, co-hosts an online show called Writers Chat, and interviews inspirational authors for her Novelists Unwind program. She also teaches at writers conferences and for Serious Writer Academy.

A fan of classic movies, stacks of books, and road trips, Johnnie shares a life of quiet adventure with Griff, her happy-go-lucky collie, and Rugby, her raccoon-treeing papillon.

ALSO BY JOHNNIE ALEXANDER

Where Treasure Hides

"The story is well written and intriguing with all the secrecy, mystery and dangerous plots that don't diminish during the entire book." Amazon 5-Star Review

MISTY WILLOW SERIES

HISTORICAL NOVELLA COLLECTIONS

RESORT TO ROMANCE SERIES

Includes my short story, "The Caretaker's Christmas"

STORIES FOR ANNIE'S FICTION

Victorian Mansion Flower Shop Mysteries

- *Bloomed to Die*
- *Pine and Punishment*

Hearts of Amish Country Series

- *To Choose His Love*

Inn at Magnolia Harbor

- *Love's Surprise*
- *Cherished Legacy*

COMING NEXT FROM THE MOSAIC COLLECTION

TETHERED

by Eleanor Bertin

Perfectionistic librarian Jacqui Penn is ripped up by the roots when she's dumped by her longtime boyfriend. She is drawn two thousand miles west across Canada to the last place she ever thought could offer stability—the old homestead where her father grew up.

Renovating the derelict house soon becomes a personal battle as it stubbornly resists her efforts. While Jacqui struggles to renovate the home, she spends time with the family Pops bitterly resented. Her hunger for roots grows stronger as she fights to discover the long-buried reasons her father fled the house as a beleaguered teen. But will she ever find the belonging she craves?

ABOUT ELEANOR BERTIN

Surrounded by the rhythms of ranching country in central Alberta, Canada, Eleanor Bertin is inspired by its welcoming people and beautiful, but challenging environment.

Prior to thirty years of raising and home-educating a family of seven children, Eleanor worked in agriculture journalism. She holds a college diploma in Communications and later returned to writing, first with a novel, *Lifelines* followed by a memoir, *Pall of Silence* about her late 18-year-old son Paul.

She blogs about contentment at Jewels of Contentment.

TETHERED

Chapter 1

Jacqui slammed the hatchback against the bulging contents of her car. The thud and click muttered goodbye. Or more like good riddance.

In deciding which of her belongings were essential, she'd done a lot of paring down punctuated by moments of painful nostalgia. But now, twenty-two years of adult life were jammed into a few cubic meters of her mid-size, fuel-efficient vehicle. Well, not jammed exactly. Despite her hurry, like a game of Tetris, she'd wedged every cubbyhole and centimeter full of her belongings, keeping what she'd need on the trip near the front for easy access.

Dread of confrontation had compelled her to act now, during Geoff's five days away. What, after all, could she possibly say to him? His new love-interest left her aghast and he thought she would be pleased for him? She'd settled for a note of a few terse lines.

To fend off the unspeakable, she'd worked at fever-pitch to pack and now leave before his return. In arranging storage for the bulk of her belongings, she'd been scrupulous about taking only what she had paid for herself plus half of what she and Geoff had purchased together. He would not return to a condo stripped bare. She was determined to take the high ground, which was more than could be said of him. Or was it? Who was to say he wasn't right?

She slid behind the steering wheel and shut the car door, resisting the urge to look back, to long for what had been and to mourn for what was lost.

Arriving at her own piece of the earth the day of her fortieth birthday would be perfect. *Bury that day in oblivion.* Not a soul knew her there in central Alberta, so she could have no expectations and no disappointment. Jacqui calculated it would take precisely thirty-four hours to cross the Canadian Shield and most of the Prairies, which, allowing for stops for food, sleep, and breaks, would put her at her new place about the middle of the first week of July. Of course, she was entirely free to prolong the trip as long as she wished. And unlike the precise travel plans she and Geoff had always made when they travelled, she had no return date. This was to be an adventure, after all. But the long habit of deadlines and goal setting didn't die easily. *Go west, young—er—middle-aged woman!*

And so, she drove north from Hamilton heading for the TransCanada highway, a more circuitous yet more scenic route than going through the U.S. Who knew, after all, what American Customs might have done with her—no job, no permanent address, no certain destination?

Scanning the view through her windshield, she was astounded at the vast wilderness. It truly was beautiful country. Why had they never camped up here? *Oh right.* They never camped anywhere, Geoff favouring luxury hotels and night life. She pushed that line of thought firmly behind her. The thick forest encroaching on the highway recalled the 19th-century

Canadian classic, *Roughing it in the Bush*. At the thought of the tooth-jarring, bone-jolting travel over the corduroy roads of Susannah Moodie's day, Jacqui gave the steering wheel of her faithful steed a grateful pat.

Farther on, sporadic radio and Internet signals tested her endurance. *Ah, a road sign ahead.* She was famished for the written word. That brought to mind her precious collection of classic books left behind in storage for the sake of downsizing and space limitations. The thought of being forced out of her spacious home brought a fresh wave of resentment. *Focus, Jacqui!*

Waubamik, the sign read. *Waubamik-mik-mik-mik.* It had a certain rhythm. Farther on, another town: Shawanaga. She sang the musical names together keeping time with her thumbs on the steering wheel. Geoff would have sung variations—a calypso beat, an Italian oratorio, a jazz rendition. But no more Geoff, came the stern reminder.

Hours later, a road sign pointed north to Kapuskasing. For a few kilometers, mispronouncing and redefining the unfamiliar town name provided entertainment. Kapus*k*asing—a drapery technique for enclosing a curtain rod. *Enough with the home decor allusions, already.* Alternatively, Ka*pus*kasing—the sudden emergence of bodily fluid from an infected sliver. *Obtained while helping your mate with renovations. For nineteen years. Boo hoo.* Or possibly, Ka*poos*kasing—a northern Ontario karaoke event celebrating outhouses. *Oh yeah, that's more like it, Jacqui!* The smile she cracked felt foreign to her unaccustomed cheeks. How long had it been since anything made her laugh?

But really, what was with all the trees? And rocks. And rocks and trees, interrupted only by an occasional deer-crossing sign.

To keep from being lulled to sleep by the repetitive scenery she had to pull over every so often, get out and walk around breathing in great gulps of the pine-scented summer air, and a few black flies too, if the truth were told.

And yet, what was the rush? Why make a mad drive across the country for the false deadline of her birthday? It wasn't like she had anyone waiting for her there. Just like she had no one waiting for her to return. She was under no obligations, completely independent, set free.

Then why does it feel so much like I've been cut loose? Adrift was exactly how Jacqui had felt at eight years old when her mother had stuffed her and a couple of suitcases into the car to leave her father—rootless, tossed about by the erratic winds of her mother's whims.

Today as nothing and no one to tie her down, no partner, no dependents, no family. Well, except Pops. But as infrequently as she saw him, even living in the same city, the distance would make little difference, as long as she called once in a while. She quelled a pang of guilt at not making the time to see him once more before she left.

Maybe she should take it easy, drive at a leisurely pace, stop at all the points of interest along the way. *Who decides what makes a point interesting, anyway?* The trip could be a sort of personal Discover Canada odyssey. *Yeah, that ought to be a real You-tube winner. Inept photographer searches motherland to find herself. And then what?*

No, Jacqui couldn't imagine dragging the trip on any longer than necessary. At least covering the distance felt like some kind of progress. So, she drove on, north, then west, skirting Georgian Bay off Lake Huron. More trees, more rocks, more road curves flew by, and fewer and fewer towns appeared as she topped Lake Superior. The shadows lengthened as evening drew on. Her headlights groped through heavy fog that crept in menacing wisps across the road. She'd had grand intentions of reaching Thunder Bay the first night, but after all these hours, her hands cleaved to the steering wheel.

Is cleaved the past tense? Clove? Cleft? Weird that the word can mean "adhered to" or its exact opposite, "split or broken apart." Like

Geoff and Jacqui, split apart. No, don't go there. Her mind, weakened by weariness, was drifting into the bizarre.

The monotony of highway-hugging forest and endless yellow center line enticed her to slumber. A sudden rumble of her tires on the grooved center line jerked Jacqui alert. She pulled to the right, corrected the steering wheel and was instantly wide awake. Fear of falling asleep driving and her cramped lower back finally forced her to stop short of her destination goal.

A small, vacant picnic site overlooking a tree-crowded ravine became Jacqui's first camping spot, if it could be called that. She pulled her sleeping bag and pillow from behind the driver's seat, flattening the seat to lay out the bedding. Before settling in for the night, she grabbed a towel and her toiletries bag and climbed out of the car intending to use the outhouse. An army of bloodthirsty mosquitoes ambushed her. She fought the attack with flailing arms, dashing to the cobwebby, smelly wooden shack.

The only running water was an outdoor spigot. In a spastic dance of continual bug-swatting, Jacqui wiped down her face and neck with the icy water, brushed her teeth and raced back to her car, slamming the door against the hungry horde. She spent the next few minutes in a bloody massacre of anything that buzzed or fluttered. Finally, she slid down into the sleeping bag. It wasn't an ideal bed, with the seat buckle digging into her hip on one side and the arm rest pressing in on the other. Had it been so uncomfortable when she and her college girlfriend travelled this way? *But I wasn't forty then!* She squirmed for a more comfortable position. *So this is what it's like to be homeless.* No doubt about it, tomorrow night would be a hotel night.

Darkness fell suddenly, with the close-pressing evergreens blotting the light in a blackness deeper than night ever was in the city. On the highway behind her, traffic was reduced to the swelling and fading of the occasional semi-truck, accentuating her aloneness. The quiet was by far the worst part. Thoughts and memories buzzed around her brain like the last persistent mosquitoes that plagued her through the night.

Made in the USA
Coppell, TX
08 September 2024

36971048R00184